# Objective:

# Crimson Empire

Objective: Crimson Empire

Second Edition

Copyright © 2015 KC Riley-Gyer

Please note the author is Australian. Therefore, all spelling, grammar, punctuation and measurements will be Australian based.

This is a work of fiction. While based in a real location, any reference to anything real is a coincidence. All brand names belong to their maker.

National Library of Australia Cataloguing-in-Publication entry

Author: Riley-Gyer, KC, author.
Title: Objective: Crimson Empire / KC Riley-Gyer.
Edition: 2nd edition.
ISBN: 9780992467722 (paperback)
Series: Riley-Gyer, KC Unnaturals of Brisbane; 1.
Subjects: Vampires--Fiction. Fantasy fiction.
Dewey Number: A823.4

Published with the assistance of www.inhousepublishing.com.au

# Objective:

# Crimson Empire

## KC Riley-Gyer

Also by KC Riley-Gyer

*The Unnaturals of Brisbane Series*
Objective: Crimson Empire
Changes in Degrees
Changes in Life

# Acknowledgements

A special thank you to my oldest friend Doug for his time and patience every time I turned to him with a problem.

This story is for my fishie friends from a particular pond that doesn't exist any more (you know who you are =smiles= ). If it wasn't for them, Doug, my Mum and a few others, for encouraging me then this story may never have become a novel.

An extra special thank you goes to the Ladies of the Famous Five (you too know who you are) as they helped me with some of the editing of this edition.

Trivia: By Microsoft Word's calculations, I have been working on this story for well over 800 years (probably over 900 after all the editing this time round). I know I'm old but I didn't realise I was that old =laughs=.

# Part 1
# The Harbinger

# Chapter 1

Well, I'd set myself up for it yet again and shook my head at my own stupidity as I wondered when would I learn. What was that saying about me? 'Fool me once shame on you, fool me twice shame on me', and this *was* the second time.

This time round I'd been left standing on the crowded dance floor of the night club all alone. It wasn't the first time my co-workers – they're called co-workers because work mates don't treat their friends like that – had done such a thing to me. However, it was certainly going to be the last as far as I was concerned.

What a waste of a Friday night, and it was my own fault.

The first time was over a year ago when the nine of them had invited me out to dinner, to even out the numbers they'd said. I'd accepted in the effort of not being so shy and make friends. Back then, before that first outing, they hadn't been so nasty. Between them and I, it had been typical office staff interactions.

We sat in a pleasant café with restaurant-styled service, ate dinner, made useless small talk as they'd never asked any true questions. Whenever I did, they gave nonsense responses back. Once the food had been eaten they then started disappearing in twos and threes only to have left me with an expense of two hundred dollar plus, instead of fifteen to twenty, which would have been my share.

What they'd done to me kept them amused for the following week or more. The second time, and definitely the last, they invited me out to the night club to go dancing with them. At lunch time, they cornered me in the staff room...

"We're all going to the new dance club on Newmarket Road tonight. We've been there before and it has great atmosphere, reasonable drinks, some food and music. Why don't you join us? We'll arrive at ten, dance for a few hours, and have a drink or two. It'll be fun." One co-worker said.

"Yeah, come on. The only expense is the entry fee and one round of drinks each if you have something to eat before coming out and then dancing the night away." Encouraged two others.

"Oh yeah, and don't forget the all the cuties looking for a good time." Piped up a fourth.

"Oh definitely can't forget those. Come on, say yes, you'll enjoy yourself." The rest urged.

Suffice to say I said sure. They had sounded genuine and sincere, that maybe they were truly interested in being friends. Stupid me!

The arrangement was that we would meet at the club. So, I went home and spent the early part of the evening having dinner then finding light-weight filmy clothing where the layers would look good. I didn't have anything in the way of clubbing clothes but I did have some wonderful velvet, gauzy and silky fabrics which were stylish and of colours that went well together.

In the end, I'd decided to go with black velvet tights and a blue with a black floral design long sleeved asymmetrical hem lined shimmery satin top. It was the best I could do, with a couple of other layers underneath on the top half of me. Being winter, I didn't want the top half of me getting too cold to and from the club.

The finishing touches were a vibrant red sheer scarf around my waist, black velvet ten centimetre heeled knee-high pirate boots and a touch of make-up. A quick glance in the mirror and I was done.

After catching a taxi, I arrived at the club at ten that night. Since I barely went anywhere, I had the money to splurge on a taxi to and from the night club. However, it was a good thing that I did because it was pouring rain when I walked out to the footpath. The street lights glittered off every wet surface possible and, while slow, the trip to the club was a light show in of itself.

In reality, I didn't mind the slow trip to the club. Staring out at the neon colours glittering off all the wet surfaces, I was nervous and apprehensive. Deep in my gut I had a feeling the night wouldn't end well. For the umpteenth time I mentally shook my head and willed myself to give them the benefit of doubt. It didn't ease the knot of tension in my stomach.

My co-workers were waiting for me just outside the front doors, like they'd said. Not long after that we'd paid our twenty dollar entry fee and were all dancing near the bar after I'd bought the first round of drinks. My first clue that I didn't pick up on.

The place was full of dark walls and dark décor with the lights down low and occasionally strobing to the loudly pounding music. Because of the low lighting I had no way of working out what colour the décor was.

I didn't know how long we had been dancing for when, as before, they were subtle in their disappearances. Without me realising it, they let the dancing crowd swallow them up and not come back. The second clue I didn't pick up on. By the time I *did* notice, it was too late.

Oh, and my round of drinks had been the first and only round bought, so I was the only one down by almost a hundred dollars. Not including the entrance fee.

Falling for the prank a second time I guess I deserved what I got, but that hadn't stopped it from hurting. God! Am I that desperate to make friends?

In a professional capacity, or whenever the office manager was around, they were polite to me; a receptionist at a consultancy company. Any other time they wouldn't talk to me and I was the butt of their occasional teasing and snide remarks. However, they would never actually say anything to my face but always made sure I was within hearing distance. Their attitudes and behaviour were extremely childish and cruel. It was worse than being at school, and that was almost twenty years ago for me.

Ever since I can remember I've been called a freak, weirdo and any other name along those lines people could think of. Some to my face, others behind my back and others within hearing. At thirty-five years old, one would think I would be used to it. So, why do my co-workers and people in general treat me in such a manner?

Maybe it's my height – I'm 185cm tall of slightly less than medium build. Maybe it's because I'm quiet and shy despite my height. Maybe it's because all anyone ever sees of me – either at work or away from work – are my hands and face as the rest of me is always covered in clothing. I have fair skin because I don't go out into the sun much while the colour of my lips are a fraction darker than normal and that allows me to get away with not wearing lipstick. I mean, I don't think I look that bad or different from anyone else really.

I have an average looking face that's not ugly and not beautiful. My lips aren't too thin or too full and my nose is straight. It's neither too large nor too small. Maybe it's because of my hair, my eyes, or both. I've heard some say I dye my hair and wear coloured contact lens. I do neither. My colouring is all natural.

My hair is straight black with natural dark blue to purple highlights of medium thickness to my shoulders. My eyes are dark blue bordering on black that sometimes seem purple/mauve/lavender or whatever colour you want to call it. They also have flecks of greyish blue and a purple which can look pink or red or a combination of all three at times.

In other words I have no idea why.

Sighing at my thoughts, I stared neutrally at a guy who had bumped into me. He tilted his head back so he could stare down at me with a sneer then melted back into the crowd. The stare down was non-existent since he had to glare up at me. With a shake of my head, I visually searched for my co-workers as realisation of what they had done finally hit home.

To top the evening off, I just so happened to have noticed a rather attractive guy sitting at the bar. He was dressed in black loafers, black jeans and a rather firm fitting dark brown silk looking shirt. It shimmered in the overhead lights with hints of gold whenever he moved which wasn't all that often. Maybe, for the cool factor, but he was also wearing a long black leather coat.

I only saw him from the feet first because I was looking up from the floor when he caught my eye. He also appeared to be the same height and build as me but had what some would term an average looking face. He had short slightly wavy chocolate brown hair, dark eyes I couldn't see the colour of and a rather nice looking mouth. I wondered what it would look like if he smiled.

Actually, everything about him appeared nice. However, his face was totally expressionless whenever he gazed at me, so no interest in me from him.

I sighed when I first noticed his indifference, and even though our eyes met a number of times during my abandonment of the night, I never saw a glimmer of interest in his eyes. In fact every time I glanced at him I'd noted he was looking at me, but still no sign of attraction from him. I didn't even bother hoping for some sort of salvage of the evening by walking out with some guy who would find me fascinating.

A bonus, I guess, was that he regarded me neutrally, while others stared at me like I was a freak.

After I'd realised the last of the co-workers weren't coming back...

"Well fudgerigars!" I snarled to myself even though I couldn't hear myself over the loudly thumping music which had started to give me a headache.

Right then I'd decided that I'd had enough. Enough of the co-workers meanness and enough of making a fool of myself with my want of friends and to find love. Enough of the sideways glances from those so damned judgemental around me and enough of not even a vague hint of interest or attraction from even just one guy. And finally, enough of everything in general. I was sick and tired of it all.

With a decision settling into the foreground of my mind, I worked my way off the dance floor with its blinding – strobing – lights and the mass of tightly packed moving bodies, and headed to the front doors to leave the place. I paused when I caught sight of the doorway.

Standing there were the co-workers watching me and laughing their heads off. One of them pointed to herself with two of her fingers up then pointed at me with her fingers in a zero, indicating they were two up on me. Then, continuing laughing, they disappeared from sight again with little waves in my direction.

I sighed. Standing there because I didn't want to run into them again, I noticed I was more tired than I should have been. I felt run down in a way that had nothing to do with what had just been happening. Sighing again, I started to walk towards the doors once more with a bone deep weariness settling within me. They should be gone now. I so didn't want another confrontation with them.

Barely a few steps towards the door, I was snapped out of my thoughts when a hand gripped my upper arm. Not really painfully but definitely tight enough for me to be unable to shake it off without hurting myself. Then felt the sharp point of a knife pressed against my side and into my flesh slightly as it slid through the layers of my clothing.

Closing my eyes I went still, feeling a tiny trickle of blood as it slid down my skin. Just turning my head, I opened my eyes to see who my assailant was. Had to look up slightly to see all of his face instead of just his nose, lips, chin and not so squarish jaw line.

"Do as you are told and you won't get hurt." Quietly stated the rather nice rich voice of the man I'd noticed at the bar.

It bloody well figures! What?! Do I have this freaking neon target painted somewhere on me where I can't see it?!

He was half a head taller than me and just as good looking up close as he was from a distance. He started walking towards the door leading to the Ladies and Gents toilets and pulled me along with him.

What could I do since he had a knife at – in – my side? I went with him without complaint, a sound or expression of any kind. I didn't even tear up or feel sorry for myself.

The moment I started moving, he withdrew the knife and paced ahead of me. With that grip of his, I was a step or two behind him. Getting a glimpse of him from the rear, I did get to note his hair was longer than I'd thought with it being just past his shoulders and tied back at his nape. Couldn't see much else as his long leather jacket hid the rest of him.

As we arrived at the door leading to the toilets, he looked to our left towards the front doors of the club. I glanced as well and saw two men dressed alike, both wearing sunglasses. At the same time, they indicated towards us with a nod of their heads. I gathered that meant we, or more to the point he, had been spotted.

Oh great! It was like being in an American gangster movie. It took all my effort to not roll my eyes.

My kidnapper opened the door in front of us, only to find the hallway crowded. He pushed his way through towards the emergency exit, dragging me with him. The going seemed slow as if those in the hallway were deliberately blocking our way as they loudly complained about us barging through, until they realised we weren't interested in the toilets. After what seemed like five or more minutes, we finally reached the exit. Opening the door we were confronted by more people outside.

"You guys want in?" He asked them. He had his back to me so I couldn't see his face.

"Shit man! Hell yeah!" Was the enthusiastic chorus with a few other choice words included.

"Then this is your lucky night. Don't abuse the privilege and do me the favour of delaying the two men in sunglasses. However, don't get physical with them as they will hurt you if you do." My kidnapper stated as we stepped out.

They rushed into the corridor passed us with profuse thanks from all of them just as the other two men had entered through the door at the opposite end.

The two men then started shoving their way through the now larger and uncooperative crowd as my kidnapper closed the door on the last of the entry fee-jumpers with us on the outside. In the brief glance I had of the pair chasing my kidnapper before the door closed, they shot a scowl in our direction.

So, why didn't I call for help from all of those people? Because it bloody well didn't occur to me until he had closed that door. I couldn't believe my own stupidity and lack of thought. Instead, I gritted my teeth and allowed myself to be pulled along.

Hell! Maybe I went along with being kidnapped because I was attracted to him and could pretend he was attracted to me. Maybe it was because being kidnapped was an improvement over being abandoned and ignored. Either way, it was more excitement than my life normally gets since I became an adult and lived out in the world on my own.

With long strides he dragged me with him as he headed to the car park at a fast pace – with me stepping in almost every puddle along the way. Great, just bloody well great! At least it wasn't raining at that moment, even if the puddles were rather largish and deep enough to reach the tops of my feet ruining my boots.

He started trying doors on cars until he found a small to medium sized four-door sedan which was unlocked and still with the keys in it. While it was a stupid thing for the owner not to check, I was now the prisoner of an attractive car thieving kidnapper. Perfect, just perfect!

He shoved me into the passenger seat and yanked the seatbelt firmly into place across my body. Next, he rushed around to the other side of the car and glided into the driver's seat then drove off. I'd slid the seat back to accommodate my long legs, laid the back of my seat down a bit so my head didn't brush the roof of the car. Then I slouched down a fraction and stared out the window, and kept quiet the entire time.

With him that close to me, I couldn't help but smell him, and he smelled rather nice. His scent was faint, barely there, like a distant memory. The scent from his neck, from when he leant over to strap me in, reminded me of something warm and spicy on a winter's night. And just like a memory, it was elusive and teasing. I mentally sighed and forced my mind elsewhere. Had to remind myself that I was his prisoner, not his date.

As we drove in silence through the rain soaked streets, I didn't see many cars on the roads which suggested it was sometime after midnight. We didn't speak and there was no music playing, which was just fine by me, as I at least wasn't interested. I just sat there and watched the occasional lightning flash in the distance out the window of the passenger door.

Why the hell hadn't I put up a fight? Was it just the knife in my side that stopped me? Or was it because I allowed his good looks and the fact that he's taller than me to blindside me? Was it just self-preservation or that Mister Hottie Kidnapper chose a weirdo instead of any of the beauties that were readily available? I didn't know the answer. At least, not yet.

At a set of lights – waiting for them to change to green – he reached across, gripped my face and turned it towards him. I didn't know what he had planned but as soon as his hand grabbed at my face, I pressed his hand to my mouth and sunk my teeth in as hard and deep as I could. Right into the fleshy section between finger and thumb, and refused to let go while not daring to look in his direction.

He made no sound as I felt and tasted his blood dribble onto my tongue and down my throat. Also started to gross myself out as I felt my teeth almost close together, but not quite touching. I was only grossing myself out because I was doing the biting.

However, I didn't let go and he still didn't make a sound. I automatically swallowed so I wouldn't choke. Normal people would spit it out but I hate the sight of sprayed blood, hence I swallowed.

It wasn't the first time I'd tasted blood and more than likely wouldn't be the last time. Though, previously, it was mine I would be tasting.

Not getting the chance to do anything else, his other hand gripped my wrist and pressed it firmly enough with sufficient pain to make me let go of his hand. I winced and bit a little deeper as a result, causing my top and bottom teeth to come in contact with each other. While the hand I was biting then dug its fingers into my jaw and forced me to open my mouth. It worked, it hurt.

I pulled my face out of his hand, which hurt along with the other two sets of pain he'd given me. Since I didn't stand a chance of getting out of the car before he would grab me, I sat to the left as far away from him as the car would allow. Not an easy thing when the car was smallish and we're both over 185cm tall and of medium build.

Not saying a word, I didn't cry and kept my expression as neutral as possible as I stared in his direction but not at him. It was enough that I would see him move should he do so. While I knew I wouldn't be able to dodge his blow should he lash out, I tensed and waited.

Long moments passed where neither of us moved. Then I glanced at him, I couldn't help myself, and saw he was staring at me. For the life of me, I couldn't interpret his expression.

We sat like that for a few more moments. I was expecting retribution but, instead, he faced the front again and continued driving since the light was green once more.

While I wasn't going to complain, his inaction confused me. I'd done less in my life which had me punished. I went back to staring out the window. Once I realised he wasn't going to hit me, I set about cleaning his blood from my mouth with my tongue. Again I swallowed because, so far, my clothes were still intact and since I didn't know when I would get the chance to clean them, I didn't want them ruined with permanent blood stains.

We drove for an hour in complete silence and even though I was staring out the window I barely paid any attention to the passing scenery. My senses were on him. I barely even thought of anything. Just because he hasn't hit me yet didn't mean he never would.

Occasionally I recognised the odd area or two as he headed south west through Indooroopilly, before he pulled up on the side of some residential street in front of a house next to a corner shop. He came around to my side of the car and pulled me out, after undoing the seatbelt, because I hadn't moved. I had no intention of moving.

Gripping my arm again, he headed off down the street away from the shop and the house he'd parked in front of, dragging me along with him. When I tripped over the cracked uneven cement it forced him to stop, which just so happened to be under a rather bright street light. He frowned as he glared at me. Probably thinking I was being deliberately clumsy.

"You're bleeding and leaving a trail." I said to him in a quiet tone.

In stumbling, I'd noticed the blood trail and he looked down at it as well in surprise. Then, for some unknown reason – instead of running away when he had let go of me – while we stood there, I pulled my arms through the sleeves of my various tops. I pushed up a cotton camisole around my neck, threaded my arms back through the remaining tops then pulled the camisole off over my head.

Glancing up at him, I caught him raising an eyebrow as he watched me. Ignoring his expression, I proceeded to tear the top into four pieces, tied three of them together and bundled the last piece into a dressing.

"Show me." I stated as I stared at him.

He just stood there for a moment longer staring at me but I

wouldn't meet his eyes. Then he unbuttoned his shirt to reveal a rather deep and long looking knife wound in his left side. It started just below his ribs heading towards his navel with blood still flowing from it, even if it was rather sluggish. His shirt was ruined. Not just by the blood but also the knife slash in it.

While his wound was bad, I'd seen worse and was therefore not totally grossed out by it. What was amazing was the one who'd gotten close enough to slice him like that hadn't finished him off. As I didn't think my kidnapper had done that to himself.

"Too much to expect you did that to yourself?" I said neutrally to him, despite what I'd thought a moment ago, as I placed the padding over the wound. I didn't look at him when he didn't answer.

"Hold it in place please." I muttered as I concentrated on organising the makeshift bandage then bandaging the padding into place once he'd done what I'd asked. I tied it off firmly and he made a slight grunting sound.

"If you tuck your shirt in firmly enough it should help hold the dressing in place." I murmured.

I started to feel confused over saving my kidnapper's life and self-conscious about having been so close to him with my arms around him while I was wrapping the makeshift bandage around his waist.

My face had been firmly against his lower face and upper neck and I couldn't help taking in his scent once more. It smelled as wonderful and intangibly enticing as before. However, that hadn't stopped me from noticing his bare smooth chest, which had felt as hard as a brick wall covered in silk. It had a little tuft of dark hair in the centre of his chest between his nipples.

From under my lashes, I watched him tuck his shirt in. His movements were graceful despite his quick actions. Never had I seen the like before Then he grabbed my hand, instead of my arm, and we headed back to the car.

Becoming more confused than usual just then, all because his grip was gentle compared to his earlier harshness. Also, the air around us didn't feel as oppressive as it had when he first kidnapped me. Once we were in, he drove off again.

As we drove off, luck was with him as it started to rain again. It would wash away the blood he'd dripped on the footpath and where the car had been parked.

After a while he parked the car once more and dragged me out again. Albeit gentler than previously. However, it was still raining and we became soaked. A few minutes of walking down the street after taking a left, right, right and another left, and me losing track, we finally entered an apartment building. He dragged me up three flights, his hand freezing in mine, then down a corridor before stopping at an apartment. He shoved me in after he'd unlocked the door, only to lock it again.

Stumbling a step or two into the darkened room, I found a wall to lean against and stayed there while I dripped on the carpet. I felt him walk passed me so I made my way back to the door. Then a light flicked on.

He suddenly grabbed me and turned me to face him with my back against the wall near the cream coloured door I was trying to get out of. I got a brief glimpse of russet coloured walls as his body pressed against mine as he stared at me. Our faces were so close we could have kissed.

Ohhh... Was he going to kiss me? Holding my breath, my eyes

flicked to his lips before gazing back up at him.

As I looked into his eyes, I realised I could see them clearly. They are dark milk chocolate brown with golden – not just a yellow or a light brown or any other variation thereof, but true metallic-like golden colour – flecks through them. At that point, it occurred to me I shouldn't have been able to see them as clearly as I could in the dim light off to one side of us.

Then, for some reason, I realised he was a vampire.

Despite jumping to conclusions, with the way my night had been going it was perfect in every conceivable way; ironically, sarcastically and idealistically. Strangely, if he was a vampire, I wasn't afraid of him. I didn't understand why I wasn't and my mind didn't give me the time to think upon it as it raced on to other things...

He was injured, had lost a lot of blood and would therefore need to replace that blood. That would explain why his hand was so freezing in mine. Not just the fact that it was winter, wet and windy. Not only that, but I just so happened to be a convenient source of blood. However, he didn't move. He just stared at me and didn't move.

Was he or wasn't he a vampire? Only one way to find out. Since he didn't seem inclined to kiss me, I decided to encourage him in attacking me.

I stomped hard on his foot then elbowed him in the side of his jaw which staggered him slightly and I made for the door again. He grabbed me and slammed me hard into the wall, which hurt, and I watched as his canines lengthened into fangs confirming my assumption about him.

My thoughts raced. The only thing I knew about vampires was

that they were just like any other predator. They could sense fear and that fear excited them, encouraging them to hunt, to feed, to kill. I knew he needed to feed. In fact, I *wanted* him to feed. But I knew for him to do so in the way I wanted him to, he needed to sense my fear.

There was only one thing that would bring that much fear to the surface, so I dug inside myself for that which frightens me most. I let that fear well up within me to sweeten the bait I allowed myself to become. I struggled against his unrelenting grip knowing I was only driving him closer to the feeding we both desperately needed. With his fangs still exposed and the snarl deepening, I'd finally become food. He only had to take three to four litres and it was the perfect way to end the night.

Then, with the speed of a snake, he struck.

With a slight pain he sank his fangs into my neck. With my heart pounding so hard, I pumped my blood into him. I continued to struggle as I thought about my primary fear, while he drank. Until blackness claimed me.

# *Chapter 2*

I awoke. Well... I was sort of awake, but my eyes weren't open, with what felt like a horrendous hangover and I couldn't remember drinking. In fact, I barely drink at all. What the heck had I done last night?

I started to crawl out of bed then had to sit on the edge. I had to wait for the wave of dizziness to pass and the world to settle back from its excessive spinning and swinging. Once cleared, the pounding headache was evident again, stood up groggily and left my room to go to the bathroom.

However, once I'd managed to stumble my way to where my bathroom was, I couldn't find the door to get into it. So I leant against the wall, where the door should have been, and sighed. I tried to think my way through a problem that shouldn't have been too difficult in the first place. To top it off, my energy chose that moment to run out and I slid down the wall to the floor.

"Who's that?" A voice asked.

It took a moment for my brain to kick into gear to think that he shouldn't be in my apartment.

"An innocent." A second voice murmured as he came closer.

An innocent?! I'd never been called innocent before whether I was or wasn't.

"What are you doing out of bed?" Voice two asked gently next to my ear as one of his arms went around me.

"Bathroom." I managed to whisper after finally working out how.

Next thought was: while he sounded familiar, he too shouldn't be in my apartment. Only, I couldn't think clearly enough to tell him, and the other one, to get out. Then I wondered how I was going to make it under my own steam since I couldn't seem to find it. Well... It would have been thought in that manner if my brain had been firing on all cylinders.

"I'll take you." The second voice murmured then I rose into the air, carried for a bit then was set down. "I'll wait outside for you." He said gently.

During a vague thought of how amazed I was that he could carry me since no one had ever been able to carry me during the past twenty years, blackness consumed me again after he had closed the door. I think.


I awoke and slowly looked around a room that wasn't mine. Even the bed was more comfortable than mine. Then, wondered where the hell I was.

The room was dark and I noted the walls were a dark colour of some sort. I couldn't work out details like a wardrobe or any other furniture. Not even light reflecting off a mirror; if there was a mirror. Looking around the room, I saw the door was a much lighter colour and was closed. So I looked towards the room's only window. I found where it was because one of the dark curtains was open slightly and I could see it was dark outside. I wondered what day it was.

Then, with a groan, I remembered everything. I think. From the events at the club, to patching up my kidnapper, to encouraging him to feed and me still being alive. With that information flooding back in, I therefore understood why I felt so horrid.

However, I still didn't know how much time had passed. I didn't get the chance to do anything when, a moment or two later, the door opened. I rolled away from it when I saw him enter. He was dressed similar to the way he had been at the club but his shirt was black this time and minus the coat. He was still attractive and still holding me prisoner.

Behind me, the mattress dipped slightly as I felt him sit on the bed beside me. Then he gently rolled me back towards him and I was too weak to fight against him.

"I'm sorry Enola. I have never lost control like that before." and he truly did sound, and look, sorry.

"No need to be sorry as I understand why you fed from me." I didn't have to try to keep my voice neutral as I didn't have the energy to put any emotion into it anyway. Then I realised he knew my name but still couldn't work up the interest to react to the fact. I didn't even have the energy to worry about why I was feeling the way I was at that moment.

"That's not what I meant. If you hadn't been so afraid..." He started with a slight frown, thinking I had misunderstood him.

"I knew what you meant and you still don't have to be sorry. Besides, I hadn't been afraid..." With the way I was feeling someone could have told me they were going to kill me and I wouldn't have been able to respond emotionally one way or the other, let alone give a damn in the first place.

"You were. I felt it, tasted it..." He insisted, interrupting me.

"Besides, I hadn't been afraid of you..." I interrupted back as I finished what I had tried to say before and started to turn away from him.

With a touch that was both gentle and firm, he grabbed at my face and forced me to look at him. He was frowning. "You *were* afraid Enola. If not of me then what?"

I refused to answer him. Then I felt a force of will wash over me as he glared at me, our eyes locked.

"If not me then what Enola?!"

I had the urge to tell him the truth and I was about to when something deep within me made me realise it was my truth, not for anyone else. Suddenly perspiring, I clenched my teeth, fought the compulsion and the resistance to blink, and didn't tell him. The simple act of blinking allowed me to break his compulsion upon me. It left me weaker than before when I felt it release me.

His eyes widened slightly in surprise as he stared at me. I thought I saw a sparkle in them, but if there was then it was brief when his expression became serious.

"Tell me Enola!" He demanded in a quiet voice.

The compulsion was back and stronger, feeling like it had smashed into me like a physical blow, or maybe I was that much weaker. With a whoosh of breath leaving me, I struggled with immense effort to not blurt out the truth. As a result the first word came out with strenuous difficulty through clenched teeth.

"Iamn... ything... to induce fear within me so my heart pounded and my blood pumped into you. Powerful enough within me, combined with the struggling, so you wouldn't stop feeding." I blurted in a rush of exhaustion.

21

It was a compromise so I wouldn't reveal the full truth but he wouldn't know I hadn't. By the time his compulsion released me, I was drenched with sweat and panting for air. Somehow I knew it wouldn't have been as bad if I hadn't fought it.

"Why?" He sounded confused, shocked.

Not that I understood why he would be. Not that I really cared. I closed my eyes so I wouldn't have to look at him. At his emotions. At his attractiveness.

"Damn it Enola! I have never killed a mortal just to keep myself alive. Now why?" He demanded of me as his hand gripped my face again and a little tighter than before.

"Why not? I didn't have need of it and trading it to help you live was the perfect way." I said weakly. I had no more energy left.

"I wouldn't have known…" He started saying, sounding angry, with me? I didn't know.

"And that really matters?" I whispered.

"To me yes. Don't do that to me again Enola, please." He said, his tone going quiet.

"I'm sorry." I whispered.

Just my luck, I got a hunky car thieving kidnapping vampire with a conscience about killing to feed. Regardless, I was truly sorry for making him feel bad. I let my eyes close as I could no longer keep them open. If he'd said anything more I hadn't heard it as unconsciousness claimed me almost immediately.


When I awoke again, I could see faint daylight outside the window. I also observed I was still dressed in the same clothes from Friday night and still felt so run down with my head feeling thick and heavy. I decided to see if I could get away since my life didn't seem to be in danger from him. Especially now it was daylight.

Slowly, I crawled out of bed and quietly opened the bedroom door. I noticed I'd started feeling nauseated and empty as if something was lost from within me. I tried to ignore both sensations as I peered around the corner. Everything was dark with what looked like thick curtains at the windows. It was quiet within the apartment and I couldn't see where he was. After noting the coast was clear, I crept to the front door.

The two feelings became stronger when I'd made it to the door and it interfered with my concentration as they almost dropped me to the floor in excessive weakness. I reached out to steady myself when another hand leant on the door next to mine.

"Leaving without saying goodbye Enola?" He murmured in my ear. I couldn't help the strange but likeable flutter that ran through me as his breath caressed my skin.

Somehow, I could feel the amusement in his words but I didn't get the chance to think about it. He was standing so close to me that I should have felt heat radiating from his body. Even though his wasn't touching mine, I should have felt something but couldn't.

As fear blossomed within me, I elbowed him somewhere on his torso. He grunted, only for his arm to wrap itself around my waist and hold me tightly against him. His hand came up to my mouth and I bit it hard and deep like I had in the car.

It wasn't until his hand pressed a little tighter into my mouth, cupped my jaw firmly so I couldn't release his hand and tilted my head back against his shoulder that I realised I'd done the wrong thing.

His blood trickled freely down my throat.

In the back of my mind I'd noted his breathing was slow and calm, that my bite didn't seem to be hurting him. At first I started to choke but then I swallowed.

He held me so tightly I couldn't struggle as well as I would have liked. I wasn't used to being restrained by someone larger and stronger than me. In fact, I never have been since I became old enough and tall enough. And to be honest, despite being afraid, his restraint and strength thrilled me.

Then he released my face and I opened my mouth immediately. As soon as he removed his hand…

"What have you done to me?" I whispered, horrified as I finally remembered the fact that he was a vampire. Which I'd forgotten when I'd bitten him.

"Nothing you hadn't already done yourself." He said gently against my ear. His hold and tone had become intimate, and it felt as if our bodies were closer together. If that was even possible. It didn't go unnoticed by me how well our bodies seemed to fit well together.

Oh god, there it was again. It's like I'm full of butterflies swirling en masse. I closed my eyes as it travelled pleasurably through me. I didn't understand what he was doing to me and I didn't know how to deal with what he had said or that intimate tone. So I didn't as I shoved all thoughts to the back of my mind and just dealt with me having bitten a vampire. Again.

"I didn't know what you were then. I'm… not a vampire now?" I whispered as my horror receded as something suggested itself to me that I would be okay.

"And yet, you don't cry your horror Enola. However, no. It has been over two days since I fed from you." He again murmured next to my ear as he continued to hold me tightly against him.

I closed my eyes against the third round of pleasurable sensations.

Not understanding his comment, or my reaction to him since he was my kidnapper, I opened my eyes and resumed struggling as hard as I could. Even though I knew it was pointless due to him being stronger than me, I couldn't not try.

I could scream, be angry, get frustrated, feel horror and sadness, find something amusing and everything else – except happiness – in between, but crying was something I'd stopped doing years ago. I wasn't afraid of what he was but I was becoming afraid of what he would do to me. So I fought and struggled against him.

He turned me to face him as if my struggles meant nothing to him. It showed off his vampire strength rather impressively. His face was so close to mine even with me leaning as far away from him as I could.

"Stop it Enola. It's not doing you any good. You still aren't well enough from the blood loss. Now, come and eat. You have been without food for two and a half days at least."

This time, with his words, I felt his concern. It was the only explanation I could come up with in the briefness of the moment. I didn't understand how I could be experiencing his feelings and didn't get much time to think about it. Part of it was because I was still having a difficult time focusing and concentrating on anything. Taking hold of my hand he headed off to his modern kitchen with me in tow.

"Sit." He told me as he gently pushed me into one of the kitchen chairs. Then he set about making me a roast chicken and salad sandwich, and a cup of tea.

Slowly looking around, I noted his kitchen was done in a black and white theme. Black counter tops and white appliances with white cabinets that had broad decorative black handles. The walls were also white, while the tiles for the splash-back and floor were a co-ordinated black and white decorative design instead of just checker board.

Then my eyes tracked back to him.

Him making food for me surprised me because I didn't think he would have had normal food in his apartment. Mind you, him knowing how to prepare food, even a sandwich, surprised me because I hadn't thought he would know how. For some reason, I had that perception about him because he felt old to me. From a time when men didn't cook or prepare food for themselves.

Then I didn't understand how I could come to such a conclusion. Just by looking at him, I would have thought he was about the same age as me, give or take a few years.

He gazed back at me, his eyes warm and gentle looking as he watched me for a few moments.

"I have a friend who is human and has dinner with me every now and then. Even though I can't eat, he allows me to cook for him as I have always loved cooking and preparing food." He said in a polite conversational tone as if he'd read my mind.

As for his explanation, maybe the surprise of what he was doing was plain on my face. Once done, he handed me the sandwich.

"Eat." He instructed me gently.

He then proceeded to make me a cup of tea once the kettle had finished boiling and handed it to me after he gave it a final stir. When I took that first sip, I was surprised he had made it the way I liked it. How did he know? I wanted to ask but between shyness and struggling to eat, I couldn't. Instead, I sat there like an idiot.

While he sat there watching me, I did as I was told because I didn't have the strength to do otherwise. My energy levels seemed to be quite low and quickly exhaustible. I had started drinking my tea but didn't remember if I finished it or the sandwich.

Something woke me and couldn't work out what it was. I just laid there trying to get back to sleep. Since I didn't remember going back to bed, I could only guess that he carried me back. I still thought that fact was amazing...

My thoughts were interrupted when I heard a whisper of clothing of someone going past the bedroom door. I guess it could have been just my kidnapper.

Looking at the window, I could see it was dark. Whether it was the same night of when I was last awake or not I didn't know. I laid there debating whether to get up or not and, perversely, my curiosity was piqued. I sighed and decided to go check to see if it was just him or not since I wasn't falling back to sleep.

Slowly, I crept to the bedroom door, opened it a little and peeked out. I didn't see anything and was about to go back to bed when I heard the sound of a fist hitting flesh. I knew that sound too well. Pushing invading childhood memories back – as I didn't need *them* right at that moment, I crept out into the hallway. Grabbing a metal statue off a little display table while passing it, I headed towards the kitchen.

Peering around the corner into the kitchen, I saw my kidnapper dodge a knife slash then punched the one with the knife, causing knife-wielder to stagger backwards towards me. I lifted the statue high and brought it down hard on the crown of knife-wielder's head. I jumped back in fright when he turned towards me baring fangs – after crying out with pain – and started to come at me.

Fudgerigars! Vampires fighting each other.

My kidnapper then tackled him before knife-wielder could reach me. They struggled for a fraction longer, trading blows faster than I could barely follow, before my kidnapper ripped the other's head off after landing a successful punch to the jaw. While that was gross, and I did blanch a smidgen, the sight of something like it was nothing new to me.

While I stood there not knowing what to do next, my kidnapper snatched at two items as he passed them then grabbed me by the hand and dragged me out the door at a rather fast pace. And me with no shoes on.

As we left his apartment, he sent a message from his mobile with one hand while pulling me along with his other. I had to move quickly, to keep up with him or tumble head first down the stairs. Everything had happened so fast I hadn't understood what was going on.

He pushed me into a car that was parked out front of the apartment building, a different one to the one he'd originally stolen the night he'd kidnapped me, and drove off. Either he was the luckiest man around or there were a lot of stupid car owners around. Maybe a combination of both.

While I didn't understand what was happening, I thought I could make guesses and be fairly close to the truth. I think. However, as we travelled the damp streets of Moggill Road then onto the Centenary Motorway heading south-west then south, I just sat there staring out the window.

Looking at the light-reflected low hanging clouds as they threatened more rain, the feeling of tension increased. However, his reflection kept checking his mobile phone as if expecting/waiting for a response of some kind. Not knowing how I knew, I realised he needed someplace to lie low and quickly because the sun would be up soon.

Then he growled in frustration as he tossed his phone on the dash. It slid and bounced around for a moment or two before it became wedged in one of the air vents. His reflection in the windscreen scowled as his hands strangled the steering wheel.

"Go to a train station on the Cleveland line and park on the inbound side." I said to him a few minutes later after he still hadn't received a response. Then wondered why I was helping him yet again.

He was staring at me, I could feel it, but he didn't say a word. Even though I saw him take the Seventeen Mile Rock Road turnoff and started heading south east, I still had no idea of where we were going. While I tried to work it out, I was tired and must have dozed off for a few minutes before waking up again.

The only indication I had of him accepting or refusing my suggestion was when he parked in Gillingham Street and we walked the few metres to the Buranda train station. On the city side platform I stopped at a ticket machine.

"Any money or a travel card?" I asked.

He handed me the small bag I had with me Friday night, which I thought I'd lost. I now understood how he knew my name.

It also figured I would have to pay for helping my abductor. I ignored my public transport travel card and dug out some change to buy tickets for both of us to the city. Once done, he then took hold of my hand again. In the back of my mind I liked the feel of him holding my hand. Despite his being cold, it was strong but gentle and while he was holding mine I felt safe, which was kind of weird since he was my kidnapper.

We went over the pedestrian overpass to the outbound platform after I had mentioned we should be on that side.

"Next train is in five minutes." I murmured and noticed him watching any and all movements coming to and passing the train station.

Oh god! What was I doing? With just his voice alone he's made me feel delightful little shivers. For some reason I just can't understand how or why but I'm sensing his feelings and it's like he can read my thoughts. Is it possible? I don't know about what powers a vampire has so, for all I know, all this is because of him.

Not only that but in the space of two car rides I'd come to realise he stole them then ditched them to hide his tracks. I then frowned at myself, while I stared at my hand in his, as I wondered how I could know such a thing. Is it also part of his powers?

My hands – a safer topic and less confusing – aren't lady-like in looks, despite my long manicured nails. However, in his larger, slightly darker skinned hand – with somewhat longer and thicker fingers than mine – mine appeared elegant and pale. It was the first time that any part of me felt lady-like. With him being taller than me that also made me feel a little lady-like. While I've always behaved like a lady, I've never felt like one due to my size. Sitting or standing beside him, for the first time I truly did feel like a lady. Then my thoughts were interrupted by the arrival of the train.

He'd continued his guard duty as soon as we'd boarded the train. Sitting us at the back of the last car, with me next to the window, he watched the few who travelled at that hour of the morning. To look at him one would think he was just people watching, but sitting next to him I could feel the tension within him. Even through our clasped hands, which he never let go of, he never relaxed since leaving his apartment.

Despite him being my kidnapper, privately I admitted to myself that I liked him holding my hand.

Thirty-seven minutes later I was digging my keys out of my bag and unlocking my door after a walk in the rain, with him still holding my hand, from the Lindum train station.

"Your place?" There was a hint of surprise in his voice. It was also the first time he'd spoken to me since I'd last been awake.

I paused before we entered.

"Is it unsuitable?" I asked in concern as I gazed up at him, not having considered that fact before. I knew he needed to be safe but had never thought he might deem my apartment as not safe enough.

He shook his head, sending drops of rain flying from his hair.

"No, it's fine." He murmured as I watched the way his wet hair moved with his action.

Having spent a few waking moments with him, I'd noted his hair was thick and in layers. Longer than usual, it was past his collar, and therefore slightly wavy. Now wet, the waviness became more pronounced and I couldn't help but think how lovely it looked.

Dragging my attention away from his hair, we entered. I glanced towards the living room and saw the light of dawn pressing against the cream coloured floral curtains. I hadn't noticed it when we were outside. I paused slightly before turning towards my bedroom and opened the door.

"This is the only room with dark heavy curtains so you'll be safe in here. I'll sleep in the lounge room." I informed, having no intentions of sleeping in the same bed as him.

Turning to walk away, he grabbed my hand and dragged me in after him. I started to panic. I'd spent so much of my life alone that being with someone in such a private way and without my consent scared the hell out of me.

Plus, I didn't want him to see me like that. If he did, he would react like the others. I'd rather he left because his reasons for keeping me with him no longer existed. That way I could preserve the growing fantasy that we were short time lovers.

"Be calm Enola, nothing will happen. I just want you where I can see you." He said gently but firmly.

"This is my home. Where am I going to go?" I asked through the rising panic as I squished certain thoughts that had started to rise as well.

He raised one eyebrow at me then kicked off his shoes after he had closed the door. With him standing between me and the door, he shucked out of his calf length leather jacket and I noted him looking around my room as he did so. As for me, I watched him. I couldn't help it.

Not my choice of decoration, my bedroom was basic with cream coloured walls, bare wooden floor with the polish worn dull and no rug. A double bed – not mine but belonging to the apartment – that was so uncomfortable that it needed to be replaced, a built-in single door wardrobe, tallboy and no mirrors in the room anywhere.

The only things which were my choice were the dark bottle green curtains to keep the daylight out and the forest green and woody brown bed covers.

After removing his jacket then followed his shirt and pants. Sexy or not, I was most thankful when he left his singlet and boxer briefs on – singlet not tucked into his briefs. Another point in his favour in attractiveness. Then he dragged me to the bed.

"I can't lay down in these wet clothing. Please leave the room so I can change." I stated breathlessly as I tried to get a grip on myself as my heart rate started to beat faster than before.

"And give you the chance to run off? I don't think so Enola." He said calmly with a slight smile.

It was the first time I'd seen him even remotely smile and he did look wonderful. I clamped down on that thought as well. I thought I saw his eyes sparkle, but I wasn't sure. However, it annoyed me that he'd voiced my earlier partially formed thoughts.

"Then turn around and don't look." I whispered as my heart pounded hard within me and tried to gain control of myself.

His smile widened slightly but he complied. With him still

between me and the door. However, his smile wasn't enough to distract me from my growing fear.

While facing his back, I seized the towel I'd left on the end of my bed Friday. Then I stripped and placed the wet clothing in the plastic laundry basket I had on the floor. After drying myself, I re-dressed into dry dark blue long cotton pants and a slightly lighter blue long sleeved cotton top as quickly as I could. It annoyed me that the process took longer than it should have. All because my fingers kept fumbling.

Once done, I just walked over and sat on the door-side of the bed without saying a word or looking at him. He had obviously heard me as he turned around then laid on the other side of me. Dragging me down, he spooned me with his arm firmly around my waist.

It took a while before I fell asleep because of the fear within me. However, that fear was slowly being replaced with the thoughts of how nice he felt against me as he just laid there without moving. Gradually, I relaxed into his embrace to eventually fall asleep.

# Chapter 3

I awoke with a start at the feel of a body alongside mine and an arm draped around my waist. Then I remembered and just laid there. While it wasn't a new experience for me, the peacefulness of it was.

That surprised me. Due to my past, I didn't think I would ever find the experience peaceful. It was also the first time, since I turned seventeen, I'd had someone taller than me beside me. The only thing I didn't enjoy was the lack of warmth from his body against mine.

With a decision that also surprised me, I secretly decided to lay there and enjoy the feel of him along the length of me. In a deep dark corner of my mind, I allowed myself to imagine us as lovers.

While I laid there as the day ticked away, I remembered hearing the phone ring a number of times, but had no way of removing his arm from me so I could go answer it. It was during the first ringing that I realised I hadn't switched on the answering machine before I'd left for the evening on Friday. Not that I'd been expecting calls at any time.

After a while, I tried to gently extract myself from his embrace when his arm tightened around me. Even though my heart started pounding with apprehension and a dash of joy, I went still and barely breathed.

"Evening Enola." He murmured near my ear. Must be his way of letting me know he was awake and I couldn't get away. I did my best to ignore the little flutter that ran through me.

"Evening. Since you're awake you can let go so I can go to the bathroom." I said quietly. He let go and sat up when I had done so.

"What's your name by the way?" I asked as I stared at my hands. Figured I might as well ask since he and I didn't seem to be parting ways any time soon by the look of things.

"Varrik." He stated. His voice was quiet and rich sounding as if he never yelled.

I was surprised that I liked the sound of his voice then I sighed to myself.

"Varrik. Nice." Was all I said as neutrally as possible. Although, I had thought his name was very nice and liked the way it sounded as I repeated it a number of times in my mind. Then I headed to the bathroom.

When I came out he was standing there. Leaning against the wall with his arms crossed over his chest, he looked every bit the sexy stud in two items of clothing which left nothing to the imagination.

Tall, slim but with muscles most clothing would hide without any effort, lent to the subtle strength he displayed. I'd already felt them against me so seeing was more of a pleasure than a surprise. I squashed those thoughts before they got out of hand. Yet again, I had to remind myself that I was his captive.

"Feel free to have a shower if you want." I'd started heading towards the kitchen when he grabbed my hand and dragged me back into the bathroom after him.

"Oh no!" I stated as I tried to resist him.

His grip on my wrist was like a handcuff... solid, loose and unbreakable. Tug as I might, I couldn't release myself from his grasp as he towed me behind him. He headed towards the shower.

"I'm not letting you out of my sight." He informed me with a slight smile as he pushed me into the shower cubicle and started to undress himself.

Rather quickly I turned my back on him so I faced the corner tiles of the shower cubicle. As much as his physique intrigued me, I was too scared to indulge in the eye candy. For the first time he laughed and it was a wonderful laugh. It sent a delightful feeling through me, but it still wasn't enough to make me turn around.

"You might want to strip or you're clothing will become wet." He murmured from directly behind me as his hand brushed my hair away from my face.

Before I could stop it, fear exploded within me but I refused to move.

"Relax Enola. I'm not planning on doing anything to you." His earlier humour was replaced by concern and what sounded like a frown. Yes, frowning can have a tone to it.

"Just have your shower." I whispered fearfully. However, I refused to move from the corner I faced.

There was a silent pause after the shower door closed. A moment later I jumped when the shower came on cold then, gradually, the water warmed up. He proceeded to have a shower while I kept my back to him with my head down staring at the tiles. On the odd occasion I felt a hip, butt or arm brush against me; among other things. Whether it was deliberate or not I didn't know and still I didn't move.

Fortunately or unfortunately – I still can't make up my mind about it, he was between me and the shower door.

For the duration I slowly counted backwards from nine thousand to distract my mind from my fear and any other imaginings. Counting backwards from nine thousand was just too easy. Therefore, I was not overly successful against those imaginings.

Mercifully, his shower was quick.

He chuckled as he brushed my wet hair out of my face.

"I'll leave you to have your shower alone Enola." He said quietly. I could hear the amusement in his voice. Then he stepped out of the cubicle and a few minutes later I heard the bathroom door open then close.

Chancing a glance, I saw I was alone. Sinking down onto the tiled shower floor with my head back, the shower made it look like I was crying. I wanted to but couldn't so I concentrated on calming my fear. A few minutes after managing to compose myself, I stripped out of my saturated clothing and had my shower. I too kept mine quick.

After wringing out my clothing and hanging them over the glass shower partition I'd just finished drying myself and had wrapped a towel, which covered me from my armpits to my mid thighs, around me when the bathroom door opened.

He had some of my clothing in his hands and a smile on his face which disappeared as he paused in mid stride. He regarded me from head to toe and back again.

While it was thoughtful of him to bring me some clothing, it was unfortunate that I couldn't appreciate the gesture right at that moment.

"Get out!" I snarled at him as I hastily seized a second towel to hide more of myself. I backed away from him as fear exploded within me so quickly it consumed me totally. It was like a fire storm and I hadn't stood a chance of preventing it from happening.

"Enola…" He started with concern and confusion in his voice as he took a step towards me. Again, he slowly gazed at me from head to toe and back.

"GET OUT!" I screamed at him as I backed myself into a corner and could go no further.

He frowned with hesitation and distress plain on his face. Then, after placing my clothing on the closed lid of the toilet, he slowly backed out of the bathroom.

The moment he closed the door I sank down to the cold tiles for a second time that evening. For the umpteenth time, I wished I could cry as a form of release while I tried to regain control of myself. Because I didn't understand it, I chose to ignore the fact that I had *felt* his concern. I had to ignore it so I could calm my fear.

I didn't know how long I'd been sitting there before finally calming down enough to dress and leave the bathroom. I did note my hair was mostly dry without me having to touch it with towel or hair dryer.

Walking into the kitchen without looking at him, I tried to move past him as if nothing had happened. He gently grabbed my hand and turned me so I was facing him. However, I wouldn't look at him. I didn't have to, to know what he was feeling. I felt my own sense of confusion now and still had no answers to the mystery.

"You were in there for so long I thought you were crying, but you weren't were you?" His gentle voice hurt almost as much as his grip days ago had.

Ignoring his question, I ripped my hand out of his, only to wince in pain because even though his grip was gentle his hold on my hand was firm. I set about making myself a pot of tea. I didn't know how to answer him. Well, I did but I didn't want to share that answer with him since we weren't even friends. I seemed to be forever reminding myself that he was my kidnapper, nothing more.

"I have no food here for you... except me..." I informed tonelessly as I changed the subject without looking at him.

"No!" He stated so adamantly it was enough to cause me to glance at him before going back to what I was doing.

"You haven't recovered from the last... *donation*. I can arrange delivery. Do you have any problems if I have a friend bring me some supplies?" He asked gently.

"No, I don't have a problem." I said as I organised milk, sugar and a cup, and placed them on the table. Exhausted, I concentrated on those little things so I could stay calm.

'Donation'... a polite word for it I must say. I then peered into the freezer to see what was available to eat while waiting for the kettle to finish boiling. Anything so I wouldn't dwell on what he was more than likely thinking, now he had seen some of the real me.

Once something was chosen I then set about thawing it out in a tub of hot water. A few minutes later I sat down with my pot of tea and started making a cuppa as Varrik ended his call. I hadn't paid any attention to his call at all. Not good to be so out of balance like that. Dangerous even, since I'm a prisoner of a vampire.

"Enola..." He started gently.

"Don't." I cautioned abruptly in a quiet tone.

I didn't know how but somehow I knew what he was going to say and I clamped down on my thoughts and memories. I didn't want to talk about what he had seen in the bathroom. Thankfully, he'd let the subject drop. Then it hit me. My fantasy in regards to him was busted, over and I was more than a little disappointed.

"Wayne, my friend, will be here in roughly an hour." He said quietly instead as he sat down and just watched me.

I nodded, not bothering with the effort of making conversation. Not out of a sense of rudeness but because I didn't know what to say and couldn't think of anything. After I finished the first cuppa I made a second one then set about making tandoori chicken with jasmine rice and a side salad for dinner.

The act of preparing dinner helped ease the residual traces of my fear away because it was an act of normalcy. By the time I'd finished cooking dinner, my pot of tea was empty, the taste of the fear was gone and Wayne had arrived.

Varrik had answered the door. I don't think he trusted I wouldn't run away. He was probably right. Maybe.

"Hi, well, you look better than the last time I saw you." Wayne greeted me cheerfully with a grin. He was shorter than me and stockier than Varrik, had hazel eyes, blonde hair and tanned skin that seemed rather weathered.

That was all I noticed in the quick glance I had given him. My shyness had kicked back in and I found it difficult to look at anyone again.

"Last...?" I started saying but stopped myself when I sort of recognised his voice but couldn't really remember where from.

"I'm just about to serve myself some dinner, would you like some?" I asked quietly, changing the subject with another quick glance at him.

"Hey, thanks. Nice of ya to offer." He said with a smile, after he'd glanced at Varrik then back at me, before turning his attention to his friend.

"Here Varrik. Is three enough for the moment?" He asked as he handed a store-brand shopping bag to Varrik.

I set about serving up dinner for Wayne and myself.

"Thank you Wayne and yes it will be." Varrik said.

Then we sat down and I began eating without waiting to see what the other two would do.

I'd pretty much switched off at about that point while the two men continued to converse during dinner. I tried not to think about anything as I'd had enough of everything in general. Varrik hadn't just kidnapped me, but had invaded my senses and my mind, and I didn't understand how.

I knew of the existence of vampires and were-creatures... what were they calling themselves now? Tha... ther... therians... Yes, therians, and beyond the super basics I knew nothing about either of them so I had no knowledge of their powers. I didn't know what Varrik wanted with me and even in my own home, my refuge, I was still a prisoner.

"Enola!" Varrik called gently as he touched me. I jerked out of my reverie in fright.

"Are you okay? You weren't responding when I spoke to you."

Still I didn't respond. Didn't know how to respond so I remained quiet as I just blinked up at him rather stupidly. I didn't even know if Wayne was still around or not. Didn't know if I cared or not. I glanced nowhere else other than at Varrik once when he spoke to me, then back at my plate.

Varrik's hand gently grabbed my face and made me look at him then frowned at me. He stood, picked me up without giving me the chance to do or say anything and carried me to my bedroom. With my head against his shoulder I couldn't help but be impressed that he could carry me but I didn't get much time to wonder about it when he placed me on the bed.

"Sleep Enola." I felt his compulsion hit me and it was the last thing I remembered.

Something crashing within the apartment awoke me and had me sitting on the edge of my bed without me realising I'd even moved. Despite thinking it was going to be a repeat of what happened in his apartment, I knew I would go out there anyway. My stomach knotted in foreboding as I snatched up the wooden ornament on my bedside table and crept out of my room towards the living room.

All lights were off but the place wasn't in total darkness due to the nearby street light shining into the living room. Shivering slightly because of the coolness of the air, I'd just rounded the corner when a pale haired man suddenly appeared in front of me, with fangs snarling at me.

Frightening the daylights out of me with his unexpected presence, and without thinking about what I was doing, I smashed the piece of wood in my hand into his face as he came towards me. The impact snapped his head back and jarred my arm almost painfully but I followed the action up by slamming my shoulder into his chest to send him flying backwards away from me.

His yowl of pain and anger was cut short as my kidnapper ripped off the intruder's head before he could recover and fight back. Varrik had no shirt on and I could see the knife slash from his right side up along his back.

I shook my head as I stood there.

"What is it with you and knives? You still have food left?" I asked him, my eyes refusing to meet his as I stared at his injury.

"No, the... cretin slashed the last two bags." Sounding like he was going to say something else, Varrik's voice was tight with his anger. He hadn't moved with his hands in fists at his sides.

I went to him.

"Then you have no choice." I said softly as I stood so close to him that a big breath in from either one of us would have had us touching.

I wanted to touch him but I locked that thought down. Hard. I stared at his mouth because I couldn't meet his eyes as it felt intimate due to me being in his personal space. So, I just stood there waiting.

This guy, this vampire, had kidnapped me and I was getting feelings for him. It annoyed and confused me, and I locked those thoughts down as well since I didn't have the time to think too deeply about it all. So, I waited for him to feed from me.

"No." He said again. His expression was tight and seemed angry, and his anger seemed to be directed at me. Not that I understood why.

"Bloody stubborn men." I muttered under my breath, knowing he would hear me, as I went past him into the kitchen and grabbed the first aid kit. I then set about bandaging the wound.

I was disappointed at his rejection. Maybe it and his anger were because of what he had seen when he brought my clothing in to me. I didn't know.

"Bleed to death for all I care." I muttered into his chest, but the problem was I did care even if I didn't understand why. Let alone dared not to admit it out loud.

I wasn't rough but I wasn't as gentle as I had been that first time and he grunted with the pain caused by my movements. In bandaging the new knife wound I'd noticed the first one had healed up completely as there was no sign of it. Well, now I knew one extra thing about vampires, they heal fairly quickly.

As I was putting the first aid kit away he got dressed, sent off a text message then grabbed my arm and hauled me out of my apartment. Fudgerigars! Bloody well fantastic! NOT!

Not only did I no longer have a job because it was now Monday or Tuesday or maybe later without the boss hearing from me, but now I no longer had a habitable apartment. Which at that moment had a dead headless body in it, which meant I would end up being kicked out without getting my bond back. Also, I didn't have my bag so no money or IDs and I had no shoes on again. *And* I was in sleepwear.

Then he started checking the cars at the apartment building

and, yet again, the lucky undead found one unlocked and with the keys in it. After shoving me in we were once again driving around the streets of Brisbane heading south. Only this time I had no suggestions of help for him. Not that I should have been concerned about such a thing as he already had it organised as I was soon to discover.

Being somewhat more aware this time I recognised when we hit Wynnum Road from Lindum to Tingalpa. He followed that until he turned onto the Gateway Motorway and headed south. For some strange reason he got off at Old Cleveland Road exit and headed west towards the city.

Then his route became truly weird and unexplainable as he got on to Creek Road heading south, only to turn north west onto Cavendish Road through Carindale to Mount Gravatt East. After that he turned onto Nursery Road only to turn south onto Logan Road through Upper Mount Gravatt. Continuing along either the Gateway or Creek Road would have gotten him to his final destination sooner.

An hour and a quarter later after the same routine of drive for a while – until we were in the southern end of Upper Mount Gravatt somewhere, ditching the car then walked to an apartment building and being rained upon during that ten to fifteen minute walk, we were finally inside.

With my feet killing me – I think I found every pebble on the footpaths between the car and the latest apartment – my head was feeling heavy and thick. With a headache coming on, I suspected I was suffering from an impending dose of the flu. Sinking to the floor just inside the door, I didn't have the energy to go any further.

Typically, Varrik didn't leave me beside the door as he picked me up. Carrying me to the bedroom, he laid me on the bed. I rolled onto my side and fell asleep.

# *Chapter 4*

Feeling disorientated, from the constant darkness and new locations every time I woke up or so it felt, when I came to – still in my wet clothing – I got up. I'm not normally this pathetic but it's probably my punishment for attempting what I had a... few...? nights earlier.

Certainly not my luck running out or deserting me because I've never had any. Who knew. Because I definitely didn't. I was about to see if there was any food and tea in the place when I heard quiet voices talking just as I started to reach for the doorknob.

"Wayne, I need you to do me a favour. W..." Came Varrik's quiet rich voice.

"Anything Varrik, you know that."

"Thank you my friend. I need you to take this message to Orenda. She needs to see this immediately, except I can't get close enough without getting myself killed by those who are trying to stop me. She knows you so you won't have any problems getting in to see her."

"Are you safe?"

"Even though they've found me three times already I believe so, for the moment at least but that could change at any moment the way things are going. Orenda needs that first part now and I'll be able to deliver the rest myself in a couple of days' time."

I could hear the frown in his voice. He didn't sound happy.

"I'll see that she gets this. Be safe Varrik."

"And you my friend, thank you."

Then I heard a door open and close, and Wayne must have left because it was quiet beyond the bedroom.

I wondered what that had been all about. Was what Varrik had said the reason for all of the attacks? I had no answers and was just more confused than I already was.

I waited a few moments before heading out. I didn't really want to but I was hungry and thirsty and my stomach was nagging at me but not vocally yet. Only, I ended up jumping in fright when I almost bumped into Varrik as he was coming in. It took a lot of effort to just stand there instead of back-peddling as my heart pounded.

Varrik didn't say a word as we stood there for a moment then he grabbed my arm and pulled me into the kitchenette. I could feel he was still angry with me and still I couldn't comprehend why. Why he was still irate with me and why could I feel his anger in the first place?

Why didn't I just ask him? I didn't because I didn't want to provoke him into violence. That was a painful lesson I had learnt years ago. He hadn't really hurt me yet but, whatever's eating at him, his anger towards me might push him past that point.

He sat me down rather firmly at the table and started preparing food for me. I sat there and watched him as he moved around from cupboard to fridge to bench with an economy of abrupt movements then he set the food in front of me and sat down. Still he hadn't said a word to me.

Meanwhile, I just sat there and ate and didn't say a word either, because I couldn't think of anything to say and my shyness was starting to overwhelm me once more. I was lost. Why was he upset with me? I tried to think of what I might have done to upset him but nothing came to mind.

Once I'd finished, I murmured a thank you and was intending to clean my dishes. Unexpectedly, he snatched them from me and started doing them himself. Apart from sensing his anger, his movements proved his animosity towards me. I just stood there a moment or two staring at his back then headed to the bedroom and fell asleep with a heaviness within me.

Groggily, I awoke to the sounds of fighting. The sounds seem to go on for ages. Yet, all I could do this time, was sit there in the dark and stare at the door.

Just as I'd gathered the courage to move towards the door, all went quiet. with my heart threatening to explode out of my chest, I stumbled to the door and threw it open. Despite him being angry with me and me being afraid of what I would see, I still had to know if he was okay or not. I squished the thought of what would I do without him before it could fully form.

Only, I didn't get to see anything when suddenly he grabbed me by my upper arms and slammed me against the wall. Stars burst behind my eyes from the pain of my head connecting hard with the wall.

"Oh, you played your part well; and in your own home furthermore. How much did they pay you?" Varrik snarled in a quiet and menacing tone with his fangs flashing threateningly mere centimetres from my face.

I didn't know what he was talking about so all I could do was just stare at him in pain and total confusion.

With his fingers pressing painfully into my flesh, he pulled me towards him only to slam me into the wall again.

"How much?!" He quietly snarled again as he dragged me towards him once more.

"I don't understand what you are talking about." I whispered.

I fought to stay conscious through the pain, fear of his anger and the heartbreak of him not trusting me after all I'd done for him. Despite me being *his* victim. Once again I wanted to cry but tears didn't even start to well up.

He threw me against the wall one more time and let go as he turned away from me. I slid down into a heap on the floor as waves of anger beat down at me, not far from yet another decapitated body. A few moments later, after a bit of beeping like mobile phone buttons make...

"Orenda, I'm compromised." I heard him say angrily and in a rush. "No, my phone hasn't rung at all. Wayne was to... What do you mean he's just told you I was fine and perfectly safe...? Did he give you the message I gave him...? Fuck sake! I trusted him." He growled then his tone changed to one of concern. "Oh Shit! What have I done? Listen, here's the basics quickly...

"Norton is planning to move against you and yours. He is planning to take control of the city once you are out of the way. His forces have already started arriving in town. Dates may change now because they know I know... Yes, they know who I am... I don't know... However, the original strike was planned for a week from tomorrow because some of his top and powerful allies can't arrive until the day before...

"No, I have more detailed information but I want to give that to you in person because it's too sensitive to trust... No, don't. Let him think you believe him and let him think his life is in danger as well, that... ahhh... oh... you've heard the enemies mention his name in relation to gaining control of me, and therefore he needs to stay with you to keep him safe. He's mine to deal with... I have to go Orenda, I've hurt an innocent... What...?! Shit, I will... Yeah... Okay I will... I will. Bye."

I felt him bundle me to him, "Enola...?" was all I heard as I lost the battle with unconsciousness and darkness claimed me.

I dreamt of Varrik stripping me, whispering gently in a horrified tone.

"What the hell happened to you Mein Unschuldig?"

I hadn't realised he was German, even if I hadn't understood the last word he'd said.

Unexpectedly, memories I kept locked away flooded in and I was a child cringing away from the one person I thought would love me. I couldn't stop screaming as that person reached for me because of the pain that would follow. Then I was me, now, and of course that just made the punishment worse for me, but I couldn't stop screaming as I tried to fight that one off. Then it was Varrik I was seeing before me and I tried to resist him because I hadn't wanted him to hurt me, or see me like that.

However, he continued as if my struggles were nothing to him. I thought I heard soothing words followed by no more screaming as he just held me then my eyes closed. My nightmares were becoming confused.

When I next opened my eyes he was dressing me.

Maybe I hadn't struggled at all and only thought I had. Then I caught glimpses of him changing into different clothing. All the while my eyes kept closing against my will.

The next I knew he was carrying me down some stairs then it felt like we were in a car for some time. Despite not being conscious enough to see where we were going, the seat I was in was laid back so I was almost in a prone position. After that we were walking in the rain – well... he was walking while carrying me, then I was on a bed and he was changing my clothes yet again.

Trouble was I didn't know if what I'd experienced and saw was real or not because I couldn't work out if I was conscious or not.


Surprised, once more, to be alive and awake, I peered around the darkened room. With what I could see, if the décor was anything to go by, I was in a totally different apartment; yet again. I couldn't see colours but the patterns of light and dark were different to the previous apartment.

Then, by the feel of them, I realised I was in clothing that wasn't mine which meant the dream hadn't been a dream. Panic burst through me as I started to move, only to groan in pain. Except, it wasn't just my head. I ached everywhere, from head to toe and all in between.

"Enola?" Varrik called quietly, cautiously, as he entered the room.

Much to my astonishment I burst into tears as soon as he spoke. With everything else he'd done to me, and with all the times I wished I could have cried over the years and couldn't, why did I cry right at that point?

He was suddenly on the bed beside me and cradling me in his arms.

"You didn't believe me." I managed to stammer out amongst my crying.

I cried and I couldn't stop crying and all the while he kept saying he was sorry. That was what I'd been afraid he would do to me. That he would make me feel, care again. If only things had ended the way they should have that first night because I knew nothing would happen between us. Especially since he'd now seen all of me.

During my crying, I felt the flu choose that moment to hit me in full force. I thought it was extremely suckful and inconsiderate timing of it as I eventually lost consciousness.

I awoke coughing and with a pounding headache, while the nausea and that sense of loss, emptiness, were back again. I thought I was going to be sick. I tried to get out of bed so I could be sick in the bathroom but was having difficulty moving. My body just wasn't responding the way I wanted it to.

So, I just laid there on my back panting in exhaustion when I heard the bedroom door open followed by some muted sounds before the bed moved under the weight of someone sitting on it. I didn't have the energy to open my eyes even. Then I felt a hand slip under my head and lift it.

"Drink this Enola." Varrik said gently as he placed a warm cup against my lips.

As a thickish liquid started to fill my mouth, I swallowed and was confused about the weird taste of it. I'd tasted it before but couldn't work out what it was. At first the nausea seriously threatened to rise when I first started drinking. I tried to turn my head away so I wouldn't drink any more.

"The nausea will ease once you finished drinking the rest of this. Please Enola."

It was the please that got me. Eventually I finished and the cup was taken away and, after a moment or two, he was right. The nausea was starting to ease.

"Now drink this Enola."

Another, colder, cup was placed against my lips and I drank a water-like liquid that tasted worse than the first. Not that the first tasted bad, just strange, but the second liquid definitely tasted horrid. I couldn't help pulling a face when I tasted it. It tasted something like aspirin. When the cup was taken away I was laid back down on the bed and fell asleep almost instantly.


Lightning flashed followed almost immediately by a deafening crack of thunder. Sheets of wind driven rain could be heard faintly as it slashed at the windows over and over. I was walking barefooted down a deliberately dimly lit, carpeted corridor of average length with numerous closed doors and I could hear Varrik calling me.

When a brightness from another room slowly crept across my eyelids as a door was slowly opened, I knew then I was awake and not just dreaming. I merely laid there as if I was still asleep. Not really deliberately. Simply a lack of energy as the flu had its way with my systems. I guess I was just waiting to fall back to sleep since I was feeling lethargic enough. Only, I didn't.

Lightning flashed and thunder crashed through the room again rattling the windows fairly hard, along with the sound of heavy wind-blown rain hitting the window. I was confused as to if the earlier round was a dream or not. If not then what had it been about? I didn't get the chance to think on it when...

"This is your innocent?" A man's not Varrik's asked.

The voice which wasn't Varrik's was smooth and deeper, but not as rich sounding. They were close by but not beside the bed. Maybe in the doorway. I was surprised to hear another voice in the apartment as I hadn't thought Varrik would allow anyone else to know where he was after the last three attacks. How did he know he could trust this person if Wayne had betrayed him?

"Yeah." Varrik answered quietly.

"Pretty. Why did you involve her?"

"She is... No one reason and none of them justifiable with what I have put her through for the past five days." I could hear the regret in Varrik's voice. However, I was surprised to hear they both thought I was pretty. No one ever had before.

"Then why didn't you release her?"

"When I first took her she bit me and imbibed my blood and..." Varrik continued in the same quiet voice.

"You bound her?" The second man interrupted incredulously.

"It didn't start out that way as she didn't know what I was."

"But?"

"But, once she had done it I... I took advantage of it the second time." Varrik sounded sort of confused over his words, or action. I didn't know which.

"Damn it Varrik! Due to your current circumstances, what the hell were you thinking?!" The man sounded angry as well as incredulous.

"How I..." Varrik sighed. "I wasn't. Not clearly."

I wondered what he was originally going to say.

"How many times?"

"Three."

"She bit you three times?" Again the other man sounded surprised, but *I* could only remember two bitings.

"No, only the two but I fed her a third because she is ill and did not want her worse than she already is when the effects started to wear off." Varrik stated and I could hear the concern back in his voice. It was strange hearing someone be concerned about me as no one had ever been so before; at least since I was eight.

"I've never seen one become sick after they were bonded." The other man said with curiosity.

"I have twice before but only when they were newly bound and the illness was already within them as well as already having a truly strong hold on them. She must have caught the flu before the bonding." Varrik informed.

The second man sighed.

"You can't come back to the coterie yet as they have all entrances covered. While they are keeping their distance so we can't actively retaliate, they will kill you if you attempt to."

Coterie? The word basically meant a gathering of people with something in common. Could he be referring to a particular group of vampires? Did it have anything to do with that person Varrik had called after slamming me into the wall? At that point in time I had no way of knowing.

"Yeah, I sort of figured that would happen. Damn it! I need to... Darius, what about the private entrance? Do they have that covered as well?" Varrik first sounded frustrated but, after a pause, his question came out slowly as if testing a theory.

"Well shit, didn't think of that one. Hmmm... The last time I saw, no they don't." Darius stated in amazement as if he was surprised he'd forgotten about it in the first place.

"Then that's how I'll get in." Varrik said with determination. It sounded like he was back on track with his mission and I wondered what was going to become of me.

"I will double check it for you and will contact you if it is safe for you to make your way to it. You have to leave here as soon as you can, either to another safe house or to the coterie. If you do not hear from me within the hour then you will know the coterie is not safe. Also, you are going to have to come to a decision as to what to do with her." Darius informed. His voice was becoming quieter as if he was moving away from the door.

"We will leave an hour after you have left and yes, I know I..." Varrik started saying as he too moved away and closed the door at the same time.

I quickly suppressed the panic I'd started to feel at the thought of him leaving me behind because I didn't really think he would. However, I had so many feelings running around within me, where he was concerned, and I didn't even know him. Not really. God! I was so confused.

Then I started going over some of the things I'd heard between the two of them.

Bonded? What did that mean? And what effects was he

referring to? I don't think it was the flu as that would make me feel better as it wears off. Shaking my head, I couldn't work it out. Besides, my thoughts were all over the place at the moment.

I couldn't believe I wanted to go with him, to still be with him but I did and didn't understand why I would. I had no answers so I lay there for a while longer trying to pack away any thoughts and feelings I couldn't do anything about at that point in time.

Then, slowly, I got out of bed so I could change clothing since we seemed to be leaving the current apartment. I had to do it all slowly because I didn't have much energy with the flu attacking me. Searching through the drawers and wardrobe, I found new underwear and outer clothing I could wear. They were all in a variety of sizes as if catering to anyone who might stop in the place.

Sitting the clothes and myself, on the bed I gradually undressed. At least I would be ready when the time came to leave.

It sort of figured that, when I was about to start redressing, the door would open. With fear rising within me, I slid off the side of the bed furthest from the door and hid beside it. Legs bent up around my chest to hide my nudity and myself in general, I huddled in on myself on the floor. I tried to stop the fear but these past few days it had gained a life of its own.

"Enola," Varrik called quietly, gently as he cautiously came round the bed towards me and crouched down in front of me.

He reached out to me but I cringed away from him. Only for him to encircle his arms around me and hold me against him tenderly with the side of his face lightly touching mine.

"What happened to you?" He asked without changing his tone

as he continued to hold me and softly caressed my shoulder.

I couldn't answer for quite a while as I fought to ease my fear and pounding heart. Even my mind when momentarily blank.

"Someone who is now dead and no I didn't kill them." I whispered then thought 'unfortunately'.

"They look old, how old were you?" He murmured against my hair as his thumb continued stroking the same spot.

"I was eight." Again I whispered. I couldn't reveal such details too loudly for my own peace of mind. So I thought them – remembered them – instead, thinking no one could hear me.

*The memory of a photo of an average looking man with a shock of brown hair and a gentle but sad smile floated to the surface. Standing in front of the man, was a little girl with hair darker than her fathers. His hands on her shoulders and she was bare-footed. Beside the man a tall slim blonde woman who was mildly attractive but with an expression that said she thought herself better than those around her.*

*So cruel and unforgiving regardless how small the infraction from either of us. Many times I'd felt the sting of her maliciousness. We both had.*

*"Don't touch me you worthless excuse of a man and take that snot-nosed snivelling brat with you! I don't know why I married you when you couldn't stop yourself from giving me the one thing I never wanted!" The little girl heard and just knew the woman was referring to her.*

*One night she got him drunk, set fire to the house and left me inside as well, all because of her dislike of me – I was just a burden to her. Only she became trapped with us as well. I tried to save him but I was too little and he was too heavy and already on fire.*

*Then the memory of the little girl's clothing catching fire rose during her attempt to save him. She tugged and tugged as she tried to drag him towards the door. There was a loud crash then deep voices and water rained down on her and her father. An arm snaked around her waist, ripping her away from the only person who cared about her.*

*"DADDY!" She shrieked as she struggled to go back to him. Two firemen surrounded him and that was the last she saw as she was carried out of the burning house.*

*"Both her parents are dead. Poor kid." One fireman said to another as she was being bundled into the waiting ambulance. Memories flick by of so many months in hospital with numerous operations and a lengthy healing process. The memories ended with that of the little girl with permanent scars shoved from one foster family to another, over and over, with quick glimpses of a variety of abuses.*

Scars from the fire are in patches on my arms, legs, buttocks and torso, front and back. They aren't too bad, or all over, but enough to suffer the brunt of teasing. That is why I wear clothing that covers all of me.

*I am sorry you suffered so badly, but no more Mein Unschuldig.*

I heard Varrik's comment in my head and I cried, again. I hadn't realised he could hear my thoughts and now he knew everything.

Varrik just held me as tears started to flow.

*This is the second time I have seen you cry. Why now and not at any of the earlier times where they would have been most likely?* He asked gently.

"I'd stopped crying twenty-three years ago during the healing process. I hadn't realised I would, or could, any more." I whispered, as I wiped at my tears, because I couldn't seem to make my voice go louder. Besides, I wasn't used to telepathy. Not only that but it was too intimate and I didn't think we were that close. Then I changed the subject.

"How could you have doubted me? After all the times I helped you, gave you my blood, after you had kidnapped me. Do I honestly look like someone who would use sex to betray anyone?" I whispered wanting to know now that I wasn't crying; which was still a shock to me.

"I saw the way you kept looking at me at the night club Enola. What was I supposed to think?" His voice had no inflection at all so I couldn't tell what he was thinking or feeling.

"Sure I looked, who wouldn't? But you never showed any interest so I didn't pursue you. Not that I would have. Not only that but I was leaving when you chose to drag me away with you. At knife point if I remember correctly." I paused to steady my breathing then I continued, feeling a little sorry for myself as I said it.

"Besides, it had only been wis... with the way I look..." While I could only whisper through my fear, my voice dwindled away to nothing and I couldn't bring myself to complete either part of the last sentence.

"I am sorry Enola. I... I don't know what I was thinking when I took you with me. Is this why you tried to commit suicide?" He referred to my scars but surprisingly hadn't moved away from me. His fingers ran over one of them gently and it felt nice to be there in his arms with him willingly touching me. But, with a mental sigh I pushed that thought away as well.

I didn't answer straight away as I tried to work out what to say. "A part of." was all I managed to whisper.

"Why Enola?" He asked gently.

I shook my head, hiding my face against his neck, as I couldn't answer his question without seeming foolish; and at my age as well. But then, ignoring reasons, I'd discovered age has nothing to do with what drives one to such extremes.

A long moment later and without removing his arms from around me, I felt him turn his head towards the bed.

"How much of the conversation did you hear?" I was pleased he chose to change the subject, with his cheek leaning against the top of my head, but there was no reproach in his tone. It was still gentle.

"From when the door opened." I answered timidly because I was expecting to get into trouble. I always got into trouble even when I wasn't doing anything wrong. I had to try and calm the rising fear of the expectant retribution. Some childhood fears never disappeared.

Only, his anger never came.

"I'm sorry Enola, I realise you must have questions but I can't answer them just yet. I will soon, I promise, but when we are safe. I know you aren't well but we need to go." He paused slightly then said, "I'll leave the room so you can get dressed then once I have changed we will go." He said then started to stand up and move away.

I couldn't help noticing how much colder I felt once he had moved away from me. I mentally sighed over my stupid wishful thinking.

"You may as well stay and change since you've seen me now." I whispered as I tried to regain control of my fear for what felt like the umpteenth time since I'd been in his company. He would be the first to see me this way, so completely, in the past twenty-three years.

Varrik crouched down again and brushed my hair behind my ear. "Then let me help you up." He said in a quiet voice as he held out his hands to me.

I paused then hesitantly placed my hands in his. While deliberately keeping his eyes on mine, he gently helped me stand then sat me on the bed. All without looking at any other part of me. That in of itself helped ease some of my fear.

"What did you call me? It sounded German."

"It is and it means my innocent." He responded quietly with a gentle smile.

I think I blushed, difficult to tell when already heated due to being sick. I didn't know how to respond to his explanation so I nodded and started dressing.

Then he turned away and proceeded to change his own clothing. As much as I would have liked to, I didn't look at him. I couldn't. I was too shy to, so I concentrated on what I was doing instead.

# *Chapter 5*

A cloud of urgency hung around us ever since we changed clothing. After a cup of tea and a quick sandwich for me, Varrik received a text message on a new mobile phone to say the private entrance was clear. It was mid evening. Just a few hours after sunset when we left the apartment.

While Varrik and I were waiting for a bus, of all things, he was sitting there watching everyone. Car and pedestrian alike and everywhere in his range of vision, on total alert. Once again he was holding my hand and, to myself at least, I had to admit I did like that. I liked that so much more than whenever he gripped my upper arm. Other than that, I was left to my own thoughts. If that's what they could be called within my flu clogged brain.

If I'd heard Varrik correctly then it was now Wednesday. Five days! I couldn't believe I'd been with him for that long already, while at the same time it didn't really feel that long at all. Maybe it was because I'd spent so much of that time unconscious – a severe 'blood donation', being slammed against a wall a few times, followed by the flu all contributing to that. Oh, and just for something completely different… it was raining again.

Heh, of all the quotes to pop into my head, it had to be Monty Python.

I was confused as to why I was helping him at every turn when I should have been trying to get away from him.

No, that's not true, not anymore. But right then was not the time to try to think it through. Thinking about such things while sick is never a good idea. So, I would wait another day or so before I dealt with it.

When the bus pulled up we boarded, paid our fares and sat in one of the sideways seats at the front. There weren't many people, maybe five others, on board but that didn't stop Varrik from checking them out and keeping an eye on them during the entire bus ride. It seemed like we got on at the right stop, because the bus then became express all the way to the city. We sat in silence for the entire twenty plus minutes' long trip.

Final stop was the Myer Centre on Queen Street. After we got off and made our way up to street level, I tugged him into some shadows.

"Why are we in the city? It's too visible for you here." I whispered then I broke into a coughing fit. While I understood why I was worried about him, it did surprise me at how quickly I'd become concerned for him. I'd never allowed anyone else become that close to me before.

His arms went around me to keep me upright and support me while I coughed away. When I managed to stop coughing...

"Where I need to go is at the southern end of Edward Street where it connects with Alice Street. We have no choice Enola." Varrik said softly as he took hold of my hand again and gave it a gentle squeeze.

After that we continued on our way. However, the simple act of walking wasn't that simple. While we were in a rush we couldn't walk too fast. We had to stroll along in a leisurely manner so we wouldn't draw attention to ourselves. Hence why he was holding my hand I guess. Not that I was going to complain.

When we hit Albert Street we turned right onto it and continued along it until we reached Charlotte Street and we turned east onto it. Elizabeth Street, in passing it on the way to Charlotte, was almost as crowded as Queen Street. Once we started along Charlotte Street we couldn't help but notice how few the lights were along the street and their numbers didn't get any better the closer we got to our destination.

Charlotte Street had always been a dark looking street for many decades. Too many dark spots for Varrik's liking, let alone mine. We continued along Charlotte only to turn right onto Edward. We had to walk another three blocks before we came to the corner of Alice and Edward Streets. While the distance wasn't really that long it seemed to take ages.

Being winter the breeze was cold and the rain freezing. With all the walking we were once again doing, I was just glad it had stopped raining by the time we'd gotten off the bus and that it still wasn't raining. I'd had enough of being rain soaked for a while. The streets were still damp and water was dripping everywhere. Cars drove along the one way streets but none of them stopped near us unless it was for the traffic lights.

During the entire walk, Varrik was so alert I could feel it battering against me in constant waves as he watched everyone who came anywhere near us only for them to continue past and for his alertness to settle into a semi-gentle rolling of waves. At one point, when a couple of teenagers were fooling around and jumping out of the shadows at each other but really close to us, his alertness spiked so badly it practically knocked me to the ground. I would have fallen if he hadn't caught me.

"Calm down, will you Varrik? I don't know how much more I can take." I whispered breathlessly as I clutched at him while he set me back on my feet.

How could such a thing affect me? Was it the urgency of the situation or part of the bonding I heard him and Darius mention? I had no clue whatsoever, so I just concentrated on regaining my breath. With an arm around me, he gently swept my hair behind my ear.

"I'm sorry. Not much further to go now." He murmured.

However, instead of continuing down the street, Varrik guided me into a nearby darkly shadowed area then gently cupped my face to make me look at him.

"Enola, I..." For the first time I saw him appear uncertain then he continued. "I need you to drink from me again." He said gently as he gazed into my eyes.

Only, there was no compulsion from him. Just an intense kindness and a sense of urgency that I didn't understand.

I looked at him. From my understanding of the conversation between him and Darius, to do so binds me to him and this would be a fourth. Although, I didn't know when the third had happened other than I knew it hadn't been via a bite. Varrik had confirmed that in his discussion with Darius.

Did I want to be bound to him that way? It was a question I couldn't answer because I didn't know what the binding entailed.

"Please Enola. I don't want you worse than you already are, than you will become, and this is the only way I know how to prevent it right now." He said gently as his thumb lightly brushed my cheek bone.

I'm sorry to say that I almost went weak kneed when his thumb brushed against me and the 'please' got to me as well.

I nodded as I gazed into his eyes because I couldn't find my voice to answer him. I wasn't sure what would have come out if I had tried. Varrik then turned me around so my back was to him and his arms went around me. Holding me tightly, but not in a restraining way, he brought his left wrist to my mouth.

"Bite me." He whispered against my ear with amusement in his voice and I could feel a smile lightly touching his lips.

I too couldn't help but smile at the pun then I complied. More willingly than I thought I ever would as my hands gently held his forearm in place. From insult to something erotic and practically sexual, my pulse thudded a little faster as my teeth sank deep. Breaking his skin, he hissed softly when I did but not with pain, his blood flowed into my mouth. I had to concentrate on breathing slowly so I wouldn't choke on the tepid thick liquid as I swallowed.

As soon as his blood hit my tongue I remembered a warm cup with what I had thought was a strange tasting thickish liquid and I understood in that moment when the third binding had happened.

I drank until Varrik gently pulled – with what seemed to be reluctance – his wrist away from me then licked his wrist. Once he had moved his wrist away from his mouth, I watched my teeth marks close and disappear.

During the whole time I drank from him his heart rate sped up and his breathing became harsher as if he was having sex. He held me like a lover and without thought I had relaxed into his embrace throughout. Finally he slowly, and seemingly unwillingly, released me.

I stayed where I was once he'd released me. Because it had felt so intimate, I wasn't sure if my legs would hold me if I tried to move right at that moment. As he moved to the side of me, he took my hand. With a gentle squeeze, we continued down the street to our destination. My legs still felt a little rubbery but I was pleased they were able to propel me forward with him.

Starting to feel better, we were still quite a few metres from our destination when Varrik halted us in partial shadows but we'd been seen. Five men ranged out in front of us blocking our way as they faced us.

Varrik gently pushed me against and down behind a manicured shrub along a slight path that led to an entrance to a building so I would be out of the way of the impending fight. With his movement, the five spread out and came towards us. Despite being night, street lights sparkled off everything wet with rain that it caused the men to appear as dark, un-glistening, shapes against plants, buildings, footpaths, road and vehicles.

I lost sight of them after I'd been pushed down behind the plant so, while they were fighting, I searched the surrounding area for anything to use as a weapon just in case. Only, I didn't find anything other than bark chips used to prevent the growth of weeds around the display plants and small twigs, and both were useless as a weapon. So, I crouched there feeling useless while Varrik had to face them by himself. I couldn't see the fighting but I could hear it with a lot of cursing from the assailants.

Varrik? He was quiet in his attacks.

Suddenly, someone who wasn't Varrik loomed over me. I couldn't see him because the light was behind him. So I hit him between the legs then, with his downward momentum, I pushed him backwards over the shrub away from me.

However, while I was dealing with him I hadn't seen the other one coming up behind me. I didn't even know he was there until something sharp was rammed into my back between my shoulder blades and pain ripped right through me.

*Varrik* was my last thought before I fell to the ground.

I vaguely heard what sounded like a roar of anguish from a man's throat, a bit more fighting then nothing.

# Chapter 6

I awoke in a bed that was extremely comfortable and it was daylight. Bright daylight.

So glaringly bright I squinted against the pain since it had been a week, or so, when I'd last seen it. After my eyes had acclimatised, I took stock of myself... No flu, no pain, no weakness... Then I remembered the fight and something being stabbed into my back. Looking around the room I saw a mirror so I crawled out of the bed.

It was at that point that I realised I had nothing but panties on and the panic which usually rose, didn't. It was there, but it didn't engulf me like it usually does. That surprised me but I didn't understand what had happened that I wouldn't be wracked with my ever present fear. Somewhere in the back of my mind it also astonished me when I didn't pursue the situation and had just let it slide as I proceeded to deal with other things.

Instead, I went over to the mirror and tried to peer at the spot between my shoulder blades. Twisting this way and that, I finally caught a partial glimpse of a round scar bigger than a fifty cent coin. They freaking staked me?! Well, fudgerigars! I sighed. At least it had company I guess.

However, in trying to look at the scar again, I then wondered how long I had been out for because it was mostly healed. At a guess I would say the attack must have happened two or more weeks ago. With no real answer, I opened the wardrobe door and found clothing to wear so I got dressed.

After dressing in a red turtleneck knit jumper and a pair of jeans and simple pair of black ballet flat shoes, I went through a different door and discovered I was in another apartment but there was no evidence of anyone else being in the place. It was the first time I had been truly alone since being kidnapped.

I opened what I thought was a front door and saw a corridor with other doors along it and it reminded me more of a hotel rather than a set of apartments. I closed the door and waited. I wasn't really sure what I was waiting for but I sat on the lounge and waited anyway.

When I was hungry I made myself some food I found in the apartment, poured myself a drink when I needed one, cleaned up after myself then went back to waiting. For the following thirty-six hours I didn't see or hear from anyone at all, and still I sat there and waited. Not that I knew where I was. Not that it occurred to me to check. I inspected the place thoroughly and even dozed off a couple of times, either on the lounge or in the bed but still no one came to see me or called me.

I knew I should have been upset over having been abandoned but for some strange reason I wasn't. In fact, I felt sort of detached from everything. Something like being numb. Eventually, I got up and went to the front door, grabbed at the purse on the little table that stood by the door. I'd noticed it when I went out into the corridor. Then I opened the front door, walked out and closed it behind me.

As I slowly walked down the corridor I recognised it. It was the one from my dream before the conversation between Darius and Varrik. I paused and looked around at both ends and yes it was the same one. Only I didn't hear Varrik calling me.

After another moment's pause I continued. Not long after that I found an elevator so I pressed the button to go down. A few moments later the doors opened and I entered to head to the ground floor.

When I stepped out of the elevator I saw the place was bustling and I recognised the view outside as being Elizabeth Street in the city. So I wandered outside, squinted a little from the brightness of the day.

I also winced from the loud noises of people and traffic. Once acclimatised to them, I turned right and slowly made my way to Riverside Centre and continued towards the river. I didn't really take any notice of where I was going as I just walked and looked around.

After a while I noted I was standing in line for the City Cat ferry and decided to go for a trip down the Brisbane River. I eventually got off at Hawthorne and continued walking. I didn't take any notice of where I was truly going – vague points only, or the time of day. It wasn't until I got on the train at Morningside that I realised I was making my way home.

Instead of heading home, however, I got off at Murarrie and I went to the local park, just sat there and watched people go past. Sitting on the ground under a tree and hugged my knees to my chest, I was feeling sick, lost and as if I was missing something.

At one point, in the late afternoon, I was planning to get back on the train to head home but was feeling too weak and nauseated to try to move. So, I just stayed where I was and closed my eyes.

*Enola*

I opened my eyes to the faint sound of someone calling my name and looked around. Only, I couldn't see anyone then I noticed it was dark and quiet. The park was practically deserted with only the occasional person hurrying home for the evening. I thought about going home but was still feeling too weak and nauseous to try to move so I closed my eyes to rest some more in the hopes of it easing.

*Enola*

Opening my eyes and looking about I still couldn't see who was calling my name. It was still dark so I had no idea if it was the same night or not. The call was a little louder than the first one but still there was no one in visual range who could have been the originator.

I decided to go home, only to fall to my hands and knees when I tried to stand up. Waves of nausea and dizziness washed over me and I was shaking so badly I didn't have the strength to stay on my hands and knees that I collapsed onto my side and just laid there.

I was grateful for not throwing up though as I didn't have the energy to move away from it if I had. The sense of loss and emptiness was worse than earlier as well. Once again I closed my eyes and huddled in on myself.

*Enola!*

While it sounded a little fainter than the second calling, it also sounded urgent. I didn't bother opening my eyes as I knew I wouldn't see anyone. I had come to the conclusion that the calling of my name was part of me feeling so ill.

I knew I was awake because I could smell the earth so close to my nose and hear the traffic going past along with the trains. Time had obviously passed if the traffic sounds were louder. I was also glad the rain had stopped. By the feel of the ground it hadn't rained for about two to three days.

*ENOLA!*

It was fainter than the first time I heard it but it also sounded like it was shouted as well as being desperate. Ignoring it, because I didn't seem to care much about anything by that point, I decided to sleep.

Something was poking into my ribs and hurt like crazy as it forced me awake. It was cold when I awoke and the ground definitely didn't make a great place to sleep. I was sore and stiff. By the feel of the air I would say it was the early hours of the morning, dawn but maybe just shy of sunrise. My hair and clothing felt damp to the touch from lying on the ground all night.

I stood up on shaky legs and made my way to the train station across the road from the park. Buying a new ticket, since the previous one had expired, I caught the next outbound train and received a bunch of weird looks which I ignored since I was used to it. While ignoring those around me I looked at my ticket and frowned.

I grabbed out my other ticket and stared at the two of them.

Almost three days had passed with me sleeping in the park. I couldn't believe it. I didn't think that much time had passed. I'd almost missed my stop as my mind went numb from the realisation.

It wasn't until I arrived at my front door that I realised I might not live in the apartment anymore. Not only that but I didn't have a key to get in as it had been left in the apartment when I'd been dragged out of it. I leant my head against the door with a slight thump as I tried to think about what to do next, but thinking was a tad difficult at that moment. I needed food before I could even attempt to start thinking.

I sighed and walked back down the stairs to head off to the bus stop just down the road to wait another hour or two before deciding anything else. Since no place with decent food nearby was open just yet, waiting was my only option at that point.

Suddenly a hand grabbed my arm and I reacted automatically. I stomped on the foot I could see near mine – the owner grunted from the pain – then went to hit whoever it was in the face with my fist. Only my hand never got there as another hand enclosed over mine.

"Enola."

In disbelief I looked up at the voice's owner and snatched myself out of his grasp and started to turn away to leave. My mind refused to think other than 'no not again'.

"Enola!" He repeated, frowning as he grabbed at my arm again.

I tried to shake him off but in a move too quick to follow he just threw me over his shoulder and stomped up the stairs.

"Put me down you neanderthal fang-face." I snarled at him

and thumped him in the back. I heard him grunt from the impact.

"I'll give you neanderthal fang-face." He growled softly then slapped me hard on the rear end. Leaving his hand resting on my rump, his other held me in place across the back of my thighs.

I let out a squeal of surprise and pain that didn't hurt for long.

"Quiet or you'll wake the neighbours, Enola." Varrik ordered in that quiet rich voice of his. His hand was still resting on my backside.

"Well, fudgerigars." I muttered and gave him one last hit in the middle of his back. I couldn't believe he was treating me in such a manner; even if I was granted a fantastic view of his snugly clad rear end.

He snorted with what sounded like amusement at my comment and he slapped my butt again as he walked into my apartment.

I'd let out another little yelp and was thankful none of the neighbours had come out by that stage. It would have just been too embarrassing if anyone saw me like that. I watched as his foot hooked the edge of the front door and gently kicked it closed.

Still carrying me over his shoulder with my hands fisted in his shirt, he made his way into my bedroom then threw me onto the bed. I let out another little squeal only to be hit with a wave of dizziness and nausea. My squeal turned into a groan and I had to clutch at the covers to prevent myself from falling off the bed – or so it had felt that way. I had the vague notion that I'd ripped his shirt when he threw me.

"Enola." He sounded concerned as he came to me and held me.

"I don't understand why..." I started saying before it turned into a moan as another wave of both hit me.

Varrik's arms tightened around me.

"I'm sorry Enola. It is the effects of my blood wearing off." He murmured into my hair.

"What do you mean?" I asked through clenched teeth as I clutched at his arm. I swear it felt like I was going to fall off the bed.

"First we need to get you cleaned up. You are covered in dirt and small twigs and leaves. Come. Let's get you into the shower." He said as he started to move away from me.

Briefly I understood why passengers on the train were staring at me before I started to panic. I knew it was irrational by that point but I couldn't help it.

"Shhh, be calm Enola. I won't hurt you. I would never hurt you." Varrik said gently.

"But you have. Twice." I whispered fearfully at him. The fear wasn't strong as it used to be but it was there.

Varrik reacted like I'd slapped him hard then, slowly and gently wrapped his arms around me again and held me.

"I'm sorry, I truly am sorry. I have no excuse and I wasn't thinking clearly at the time. I give you my word I will never hurt you like that again. I promise." His voice was a whisper next to my ear that sent those pleasurable tingles through me as he held me. Then, after a few moments he stepped back a fraction and held out his hands to me as he gazed into my eyes and nowhere else.

When I looked into his eyes there was no compulsion. As I looked down at his hands I noted once again how alone I felt without him next to me. I hesitantly placed my hands in his as I realised I would have to learn to trust someone some time. So, why not him since he hadn't shied away from me so far.

He assisted me into the bathroom then helped me remove my clothing, after catching me when I lost my balance due to another wave of dizziness.

Then, while he was still dressed, he led me into the shower, turned it on and just supported me while I cleaned the dirt off and washed my hair. His hands on my waist felt nice and I found them a little distracting as I tried to clean myself. Even more distracting whenever he moved his fingers against my skin, sending delightful sensations through me.

However, I was glad my legs weren't obviously dirty. There was no way I was going to bend over to wash them. I also refused to face him for the duration. He did wash my back for me and, as he did so, I realised I enjoyed it.

We didn't speak, I was just too shy. It was a new experience for me to actually bathe with someone and I sort of rushed through it, too nervous to fully appreciate and enjoy it. When I finished...

"I'll let you have your shower without interruption now." I said softly but with a tiny hint of amusement at the role reversal even if he hadn't been shy and full of fear like I had been.

"Just too funny, woman." He said with humour thick in his voice as he slapped my butt on my way out of the shower cubicle. It resounded loudly in the bathroom, making the slap sound harsher than it truly was.

I yelped in surprise.

"Brute." I retorted but with a small amount of humour. I left the bathroom to the sound of his laughter.

It was a strange and new experience to discover my fears weren't as strong and were continuing to lessen while I was with him. With the way he'd treated me in the past forty-five minutes, I'd expected my fear to be out of control. Instead, I found myself teasing him in return, even if it was shyly and hesitantly. The other thing that surprised me was that I liked the way he had gone all neanderthal on me.

I was dressed in a burgundy satin robe and sitting on the bed with my back to the headboard when he walked in with a towel wrapped around him. My breath caught slightly as I gazed at him. Stunning was what came to mind, and while I wanted to see more I knew I wasn't ready. So instead I pointed to a second, bottle green, towelling robe at the foot of the bed.

"That's the only non-feminine robe I have if you want to use it." I said softly as I looked at him briefly then down at my hands.

"Thank you Enola." He said gently.

While I did see the towel drop onto the foot of the bed, I didn't look at him again until he sat beside me on the other side of the bed. Even then it was just a quick glance. I looked at the window and frowned at how bright it was outside when I realised the sun was up but he was still awake.

"Ummm... The sun's up but you're still awake? I thought vampires couldn't be..."

He chuckled.

"Vampires don't need to sleep during daylight hours. We sleep when we are tired or injured. We just have to stay out of direct or reflected sunlight, however."

We sat there in silence for a few moments, then...

"Did you get to complete your... mission?" I asked, confused as to what was the right word to use to describe what he'd had to do.

"Yes I did thanks in no small part to you Enola." He said with a warmth I've only ever heard from him.

Strangely enough, I couldn't think of a single occasion where someone had spoken to me with that level of tenderness since the death of my father.

He paused then said, "The information I carried was needed in the hopes of stopping, or at least be prepared for, a battle for the control of the city amongst the resident vampires." He informed me in a slow and cautious manner as if not wanting to scare me or judging how much he could tell me.

I nodded. It was a scary concept but one I couldn't do anything about.

"How did they keep finding us at each of the apartments?"

"My clothing had been bugged so they could follow me. It had happened when we were at my apartment." He stated in frustration born from hindsight.

"And Wayne?" I asked hesitantly because I thought it would be a touchy subject.

"He was... dealt with." Was all Varrik said in a rather toneless and clipped manner. I could only imagine how the man had been dealt with.

"Did you know him long?" I asked softly.

He didn't answer straight away and when he did there was a hint of the betrayal he must have been feeling. "I... saved his life when he was a child."

I was sorry I'd asked and didn't press the matter as it must have been hard to have a so called friend betray him. So, after a pause, I changed the subject.

"How did they know we would be there in the city that night?"

"They didn't. They were just cruising around. It was a spot of luck for them but not for us."

"Varrik? How did I survive?" I asked, after a few moments of silence, in a small voice as I stared at my hands.

"It was a combination of the stake not hitting anything vital as it went in and... my blood." Varrik responded in a gentle tone full of caution. I think he was worried how I would react. When I glanced at him, even his gaze was cautious.

I let what he said sink in before moving on to the next logical question. Hitting nothing vital and his blood... I could understand the first part but needed clarification in regards to the blood thing.

"I see. What is the deal with your blood anyway? Is it to do with that bonding you and Darius were talking about that night?" I asked slowly as I tried to remember exactly what had been said but things were a little hazy.

"Do you not know about vampire's blood?" He asked in surprise.

"Only that the exchange will turn a mortal into a vampire." I said softly as I looked at my hands again.

"That only happens if the vampire drinks the mortal's blood first then feeds the mixed blood from the vampire to the willing mortal..."

"Some mortals aren't always willing though are they?" I asked without accusation, just a question of curiosity.

"No Enola, some aren't. Binding is where the mortal drinks the vampire's blood before the vampire has drunk theirs. If the vampire wishes to partake of their bonded's blood then they must do so after the bonded has fed then wait a minimum of two days before the binding sharing happens again." He paused while I thought about what he said.

"Okay, I understand that. Why bind in the first place? What does it gain either person?" I asked in confusion as I looked at him.

"A vampire will bind a willing mortal to be their day servant, or a friend and/or a… lover who do not want to be vampires but wish to spend their existence with the chosen vampire…"

"Can't that be done without the binding anyway?" I frowned in continued confusion.

"The servant/friend/lover would still be mortal and live only to their mortal life span if they weren't bound to the vampire…"

"Are you saying that if the mortal drinks the vampire's blood then they become immortal without becoming the full vampire?" I asked slowly, knowing I sounded incredulous but since I've never read or watched vampire stories, I wouldn't have a clue as to what is or isn't possible.

"Among other things, yes." Varrik said neutrally.

"What 'among other things' happen?" It sounded so ominous when he had said it I just had to know.

Varrik paused for a few moments, looking like he was trying to work out how to word what he wanted to say.

"For as long as the bonded drinks the vampire's blood they will gain long life, as already stated, as well as fast healing and vampire's presence in the mind. However, the following is subjective as it is different with every binding and the person could receive any one, few or all: strength, speed, the depth of the vampire's presence in the mind, faster healing than normal and talk mind-to-mind..." His voice was calm as he spoke carefully.

"And what does the vampire get out of it? Other than a permanent food source that is." I frowned as I tried to take it all in. It was a lot of information and I was starting to feel tired and sick again and that made it difficult to think clearly but I wanted, needed, to know.

"Actually, the bonded becomes more of an occasional snack than a meal because the vampire would not want to drain their bonded anywhere near dangerously low levels. If a vampire were to drink larger quantities then they either have to wait two to three months or run the risk of killing their bonded.

"As for what a vampire gains from the bonded is a trusted partnership – if they aren't lovers – as the bonded is then entrusted with the life and protection of the vampire for the duration of the vampire's existence.

"If the vampire drinks the mortals' blood after the mortal drinks from the vampire then the bonding between the two deepens. This deeper bonding only happens when there is a personal interest between the two. Also, there is the mind-to-mind, but whether it incorporates the telepathy is 50-50. If there is no sharing then the bonded is usually a friend/servant with fringe benefits."

"Okay, what are the downsides then?" I knew there had to be and I suspected what some of it may be.

Varrik let loose a soft sigh.

"The downside is once the bonded stops drinking the vampire's blood then they usually suffer from any or all of the following: nausea, weakness, dizziness which could inspire nausea, excessive tiredness and the sense of loss when the vampire's and the bonded's minds are no longer connected. Some may never mentally recover from such loss of the mind-to-mind connection.

"If the bonded stops taking the vampire's blood past their natural life expectancy then they age then die rather quickly and painfully. Re-bonding won't prevent the process once it has started. The mortal has to be absolutely certain that bonding is what they want because of that time factor."

I suddenly understood why I had been feeling those symptoms since he and I had met. I had thought it was because of the flu I had.

Varrik paused then, "You need rest now Enola, not more information. Besides, I'm tired as well. We can talk more about it this evening if you want." He finished gently.

I nodded, paused a moment then removed my robe to reveal I was wearing lavender singlet and panties then crawled under the covers. It was what I normally wore to bed when I was alone and since he had seen me already I'd thought why not.

While I didn't watch, I realised that Varrik had taken off the robe he was wearing when he snuggled up behind me with his arm around my waist. Again, I could feel his heart beating slowly.

"I didn't think vampires had heart beats." I murmured sleepily.

"We normally don't, but we can just after we've fed. We can also make our hearts beat if we concentrate. Now, no more questions. Sleep Enola."

With a soft sigh, I settled in his arms. As far as I knew it was the second time we shared a bed and the second time was a little better for me than the first time. It didn't take long before I fell asleep.

# Chapter 7

It was still daylight when I awoke. Varrik was still asleep and I was snuggled into the back of him, my hand on his bare chest. It was still another three hours till sunset by the time I'd slowly and carefully extracted myself away from him. I needed the time out of his presence so I could think about what he'd told me earlier that morning.

So, I put on my robe, went to the bathroom then sat out in the completely clean sitting room after having made myself a cup of tea.

While making myself a cuppa, I looked at my laptop, which was still running and hadn't gotten busted during the fight that night, and saw the night of my kidnapping had been ten days ago. I shook my head in amazement that it had only been ten days and not two or more weeks. It had emphasised the healing rate of the 'staking' I'd suffered. I shook my head again and went back to thinking about my current situation.

First point... Is my attraction to him because of him or because of him kidnapping me? I thought long and hard about everything I had been through since that evening at the night club. I chose to ignore how he had treated me when he had thought I had betrayed him. I would have acted the same way if I thought someone had betrayed me. If I was a stronger person, that is.

I finally came to the conclusion it had nothing to do with him kidnapping me. I had been attracted to him before that. Then there were the little things in regards to the way he thought of me. Of how he treated me.

Next point... I didn't want to become a vampire. That I already knew. Did I want to become bonded to him? In reality, even without the blood, I think I already was even if I didn't fully understand how but that could wait till later. So, did I want to become bonded to him via *blood*? I could feel the emptiness within me where he no longer was and I missed him being there.

Now that I knew he'd been a part of my mind, I recognised what that emptiness was. I knew I wasn't going to go insane if he wasn't a part of me ever again, but if he wasn't then I knew I would always have that bleakness within me for the rest of my life. Not only that but I know I...

"Enola!" Varrik called, interrupting my thoughts, from the bedroom sounding rather urgent and worried... panicked.

Then he practically bolted from the room, sounding like he'd tripped out of the bed in the process – never thought a vampire could stumble but it certainly sounded like he had, only to stop short in the hallway when he saw me.

I hadn't realised he'd slept naked. That fact surprised me and couldn't help staring at him from head to toe and gloriously back again. Definitely a very fine specimen of male standing before me. There was a short scar on his chest that I hadn't noticed before because I had been staring at the fresh slashes at the time.

There was also a long one low on his left hip tracing its way down to the front of his upper thigh. He'd obviously gotten them before becoming a vampire, if what I've recently learnt about his healing abilities is true. To prove my new knowledge correct, the two wounds I'd tended to had left no proof of their existence on his skin.

"You could have taken the time to put the robe on you know." I said quietly as I did my best not smile and forced myself to look him in the eyes. I never knew just a simple act could become so difficult to complete. Especially when that male appendage was impressive.

"What? Can't handle it?" He asked teasingly with hands on hips and fingers splayed, a raised eyebrow with eyes sparkling and a smile tugging at his mouth.

"I just don't think it is very gentlemanly of you…" I started to respond with instead of answering his question.

His smile disappeared only to be replaced with a look of shocked surprise as he turned around and headed back into the bedroom when I said the word 'gentlemanly'. So I finished off by murmuring to myself.

"…when we don't know what we are to each other." as I stared at his breathtakingly retreating form.

He came back out in the robe he'd worn earlier that morning and knelt in front of me once he had reached me.

"I thought you had gone." He said quietly.

"This is my home Varrik. Where am I likely to go? Even though it won't be for much longer when I can't meet my rent." I said softly with a sigh. I didn't know where I was going to go without work of any kind. He took hold of my hands.

"Relax Enola. Your job is safe. I phoned your employer once I found your identification. It seems you have enough sick pay accumulated to cover the time off, plus more. Besides, it won't take that long to work out what we are to each other." He informed gently.

My eyes widened as I looked at him. I hadn't realised he'd heard the end of my comment. I must remember about the exceptional hearing.

"What did you tell my employer?" I asked incredulously as I leant forward and couldn't help noticing how close we were to each other.

"That you had had an accident and were recovering from severe blood loss and I didn't have the authority to tell him any more than that." He said with a warmth in his eyes. "What is it that you do in your job?"

"I'm the receptionist so I make sure the staff receive their messages in a timely manner and give them reminders they've requested of me. I also make sure the printer, fax machine and photocopying machine are full of paper at the start of business, that staff have access to all stationery supplies they need, order supplies when stocks are low... things like that. Nothing spectacular really." I responded softly, feeling a little embarrassed.

"Well, your boss said sick pay would be paid into your account and to tell you to hurry up and get well so you can come back to work." Varrik stated with a smile.

After I recovered from my surprise at him saving my job for me, I then went back to my original thoughts.

"What do you want with me Varrik? Why did you kidnap me? Why were you even in the club in the first place and why did you come after me this final time?" I asked softly with uncertainty obvious in my voice.

Those four questions were the last of the immediate information I wanted to know before I came to an ultimate decision. His answers would decide one way or the other.

He paused, stood up and went into the kitchen.

I thought he had no intention of answering them. I sat there feeling confused with tears threatening to build and spill. He'd made me feel again, to cry and even to feel happiness, pleasure. I didn't know what I would do if he rejected me. Well, I did know but I didn't want to think about that... yet. Then I glanced up at him when I heard him start cooking then started making a pot of tea.

After about thirty minutes Varrik came back out with a tray carrying the lot. It also included a ruby red glass goblet with gold rim and filigree around the bowl on it for himself. He must have brought it with him because I hadn't seen it before.

He handed me a plate of stir fry pork with a sesame flavour to it, noodles and heated vegetables that were still crunchy. As I sat back, he sat beside me and encouraged me to eat then proceeded to talk as he poured me a cup of tea.

"First, let me give you a brief rundown of our little part of the World..."

"Mmmm... this is good." I smiled around a mouthful. It didn't just have a sesame flavour – which was an oil as well as seeds in the meal – but there was ginger, garlic, lemongrass and a few other herbs and spices I couldn't work out.

"Thank you." He grinned.

"Think of the vampire community of Brisbane, or anywhere in the world really, as a middle ages feudal system. A system where there is a Prince – as in the ruling vampire regardless of gender – and a bunch of Barons/Lords who either want to align themselves with the Prince to glory in the Prince's power, stay neutral and live their own lives, or want to overthrow the Prince so they can become the Prince instead because they get to make the laws and enforce them for the duration they are in control."

I listened because I figured there had to be a point to what he was telling me.

"Those who want to destroy the current Prince do so by waging a war, be it minor or major in size. Success is determined by the change, or lack of change, of the ruling Prince. Each vampire who takes the... 'throne', for lack of a better word, is called 'Prince of the City' and has their own agenda; be it good or bad.

"Orenda is the current Prince of the City of Brisbane. The only way she was able to become Prince was to kill the previous Prince and the only way for her to lose her ruling is for some other powerful vampire to kill her. She came to power as a result of destroying the previous Prince in the effort of trying to save an innocent mortal woman from the brutalities of the then Prince.

"We had discovered she wasn't the only one to have suffered but was the only one we were able to try and save. Unfortunately, we were unable to save her completely..."

"What happened to her?" I asked. I understood that Varrik was aligned with Orenda so I had a need to understand what had happened to the woman they'd tried to rescue.

"The young woman's injuries were too severe to get her to the hospital in time so Orenda gave her the choice of dying mortal and free or be embraced and still live as a vampire. The young woman chose life so Orenda embraced her and she now continues her life but with a few... modifications."

"So she gave the woman a choice... Is Orenda a good Prince?" Again, I needed to know what sort of person this Orenda was. I needed to know whether I would support her or not since her position of power would be no different than the human politicians I voted for.

"Orenda is an exceptionally good Prince as far as I'm concerned. She believes in freedom of choice for everyone whether they be vampire, therian or human. Orenda is also anti killing of humans except in self-defence. Those of us who freely align ourselves to her understand the need not to kill humans as we feed just to keep ourselves alive.

"If we kill humans for the sake of sustenance then, after a while, there will be no more humans to keep us alive. At the same time we do our utmost to never take blood from those who do not freely give it to us." Varrik looked ruefully at me. "There are, of course, times when that rule is unintentionally broken and control is sometimes lost. However, those of us who believe in the same ideals as Orenda do our best to stay in control as much as possible."

I could hear the regret in his voice. I'd never heard anyone sound upset about having hurt me before.

"It's okay Varrik. I don't blame you for what happened when you fed from me that night. While I didn't know much about vampires except them being predators, I knew what the consequences of my actions would be. I'm just sorry I caused you anguish over it though." I said softly as I stared at my hands in my lap after a quick glance at him.

It seemed Orenda would be worthwhile supporting after all. Varrik gently gripped my jaw and turned me to look at him.

"Do not stress yourself over it any more Enola. Circumstances were not ideal for either of us at that point and it is now in the past." He said as his thumb caressed the side of my jaw, sending little tingles through me.

Then he resumed telling me about the vampires of Brisbane. "Anyway, as a result, Orenda's reign comes under threat once or twice a year and she and her followers do their best to keep her in power. My role is that of her primary envoy, a harbinger... a messenger.

"An hour after sunset of the night you and I... met, I had received a phone call from one of Orenda's undercover operatives, and no not a James Bond style spy...," Varrik smiled as he clarified.

I couldn't help smiling back then he continued.

"...telling me he had information which Orenda needed urgently and could he pass it on to me to give to her because he had been discovered and had only just escaped. With two of us knowing the information it would ensure it would reach Orenda. He then proceeded to tell me where he was on the north west side of the city. Twenty to thirty minutes later he and I met.

"As with all things we do, we knew we were risking our very existences so we could keep Orenda in power. It may have been night and the two of us may have been hidden in the shadows, but neither of them guaranteed us safety. Especially if those hunting us are also vampires. Just as he was finishing relaying his message to me, we were jumped by a couple of Norton's goons.

"Following a short ferocious fight he was killed after he had killed one of the goons and I was injured before I could kill the other goon. So, I had made my way back to the coterie..." As Varrik took a breath...

"Sorry to interrupt, but coterie is a group of people united by a common cause or interest yes?" I asked him with a small frown as I placed my tray of empty dishes on the coffee table.

Varrik gazed at me with the beginnings of a smile playing at his lips at my words. Only, he didn't answer straight away as he took my dishes away. A few minutes later, he came back with a fresh cup of tea for me.

"Yes. It is also what we call Orenda's faction because we want to live in peace with all those around us including the humans. Norton calls his a conglomerate just to sound corporate and modern while Cameron, a third faction, calls his a sect."

I just nodded and sipped my tea. I'd sort of figured that the word coterie had had an extra meaning. It seemed each faction had a perception about themselves and use of those names seemed to convey that perception. Each to their own I guess.

"However, when I had arrived at the coterie, some of Norton's people were out the front waiting for me. Also, by that point, I had healed the initial injury. It hadn't been that bad. Because of the importance of the information I was carrying and because there was only one of me and at least seven of them, I couldn't risk confronting them so I left. I had wandered around for a few hours while I worked out my options.

"Just a little after ten that night I ran into another one of Norton's men and we fought. Thankfully, it was in a dark section of the street. He sliced me pretty badly before I was able to destroy him. After I messaged the clean-up crew, I had to stay there till they arrived because the site wasn't secure. Following a brief meet-and-debrief I left."

"Clean-up crew? Is that why my apartment looks like there wasn't a fight or decapitated body in here at all?" I asked in surprise. I never realised they had such a system in place, but then there's a lot I don't know. I mentally sighed.

"Yes. Unlike some movies and television shows, vampires do not disappear into a puff of dust when they suffer final death. Sunlight, fire or decapitation are the only forms of final death..."

"What about staking, garlic, the holy cross and holy water?" I asked, side-tracking the telling since I'd heard about them. I finished my second cup of tea while he continued talking to me.

"No. Staking will place the vampire in a state of suspended animation but not kill and if removed then the vampire will awaken after a period of healing. Garlic acts as a bad smell deterrent if the vampire has a sensitivity to it. Holy water, as long as it has been blessed by a priest without doubt will act like acid.

"The holy cross will only deter us if held by someone with true faith. If they have even a small amount of doubt then it won't work. It will burn us, like holy water, only if blessed by a priest of true faith and in the possession of one with true faith. If the cross is held by one without doubt then the cross loses its power to burn as time passes."

"Oh, I see. Useful to know." I murmured, not that I had any use for such information. Although, I guess the misinformation was necessary for the continual existence of the vampires.

"Therefore, to protect the general public from the violent side of our lives, we have clean-up crews to dispose of the bodies and to make the place habitable again." Varrik stood up and took cup and goblet away then came back and crouched down in front of me and took hold of my hands again.

"I had tried to gain entry to the coterie again but Norton's people were still there. Then I received a call for help from a friend. Once again I was on the northern edge of the city but no one was there. Moments later, I suspected it was a set-up

"Roughly five minutes after leaving the area, I realised I had collected two of them and they were following me. Not only that but the second injury was worse than the first and I wasn't able to heal it as quickly while on the move. With Norton's men roaming the streets I had to evade further north, forcing me to range away from my destination. Where I was at the time there were no public places open so I kept to the well-lit streets when I came across the night club."

Well, that explained why he ended up so far from the city.

"I had taken refuge inside it to try to shake them off and to rethink my options because I had already been injured earlier that evening and my blood was low. With the night half gone I knew I needed some place to rest up as well as find a willing donor. Not long after I had sat myself down at the bar I saw you and watched what your not-so-nice friends did to you."

"They've never been my friends." I murmured as I just stared at him as he finished telling me his story.

What had I walked into? It sounded like a big vampire showdown was about to happen. Did I even wish to be a part of him and his life? Then I remembered my life before he had kidnapped me and my thoughts before he came out of the bedroom. In that moment I knew, depending on his words, what

I would do next. Then, Varrik continued...

"I saw something in you which called to me that night. Something which told me you would not come with me willingly. I knew, for whatever reason, if I had let you walk away then I would never have seen you again. Ever. I had misjudged with the knife as I never intended to hurt you and for that I am truly sorry." I could hear the remorse in his voice over his actions.

I opened my mouth to say something, anything, but nothing came out. I didn't know what to say or do so I just closed my mouth and stared at his hands holding and caressing mine until he gently squeezed them. Raising my eyes to his, I saw him looking at me intently.

"Why the suicide attempt Enola?" He frowned but there was no anger or anything in his voice. His words were gentle in fact.

I figured the question would come up again. I sighed, looked down at my hands in his then back up to his eyes. I moved to the edge of the seat to impress upon him how serious this was to me.

"I'm thirty-five with no friends at all, let alone a lover. After twenty-three years of being by myself, it's an extremely lonely existence Varrik. Until I met you, everyone thought of me as, and treated me like, a freak and that was without seeing my scars." I said, indicating to my eyes and hair.

"That night had been the last straw for me. While I may not have known at that point in time what method I was going to use... you, a wounded vampire, became the worthy way of ending it. Only you didn't." I finished softly. I wasn't ashamed since everyone has that 'final straw' within them. I was just shy at having to put them into words.

"You said you weren't afraid of me that night Enola. What

created such fear in you if it wasn't me or what I was?" He asked in a voice thick with confusion as he gazed into my eyes. His thumbs were caressing circles on the back of my hands sending little tickling shivers through me.

"My number one fear is being with a man who would see me, all of me, and reject me. I've been rejected all my life by my mother, foster parents, other kids and people in general. So the thought of revealing myself to a man who would show even the smallest attention to me has been a powerful terror within me. I only had to think of that, and with you standing there in front of me with an expression of interest in me, it made that fear so much stronger and so easy to call up. Add the struggling and I knew, with the condition you were in, you wouldn't have been able to resist."

Again, I wasn't ashamed. It was just so difficult to admit to it all out loud. I've never had to talk so revealingly to anyone before. When I looked at him, I saw compassion in his eyes at my having revealed my inner-most horror to him. A horror which, I was pleased to note, was slowly fading away thanks to his reactions upon seeing me. I knew I still had a long way to go but it was a start.

"I am more than interested in you. I want you Enola. I came back for you and I want to discover more about you. I am sorry I doubted you but when the attack happened here, I thought you had been behind it. It hurt me to think you were using me. I didn't want to believe it. I am also sorry for the way I treated you after the third attack..."

It hurt to hear him agonising over his treatment of me in that moment.

"Don't Varrik. If I had been in your position, I would have done the same. I don't blame you for that, honest." I stated softly as I let my voice and eyes convey the truth of what I was saying.

He cupped my face and answered with a small gentle smile as he caressed my cheek. Then he continued.

"That aside, your strength and reactions under the circumstances of your time with me have been amazing and impressed me immensely. When you bit me, I discovered we had the beginnings of a bonding. It was subtle and I couldn't read your thoughts at first but I could feel you without us touching.

"When you forced me to feed from you, that bond became stronger. Your emotions were scattered and fleeting, tainted with nervousness and attraction, and I would catch glimpses of them. I was intrigued which was why I encouraged the second bite. That and it gave me an excuse to have you in my arms while you were awake and somewhat alert.

"The second bite strengthened our link but I couldn't hear your thoughts until I fed you a third time. When I had slammed you against the wall, it had split the back of your skull and I had to lick it to close to heal it. That and the third sharing completed our mental bonding.

"Besides all that, I happen to think you are beautiful. I love the colour of your eyes and hair, and your quiet strength. How you don't panic and are willing to strike back in a fight, even when they are stronger than you, and... your 'fudgerigars'." He chuckled as he said the last part.

He laughed when I blushed at his words. My heart was almost bursting with happiness over what he was telling me. Some of it also made so much more sense now than it did before.

I slipped off the lounge so I was kneeling in front of him and his hands gently held my arms, with his thumbs caressing me. I only had to tilt my head back but a fraction and we were gazing into each other's eyes. I never knew what it meant to drown in someone's eyes until that moment.

"I don't want to become a vampire Varrik." I said softly and saw disappointment and sadness flit briefly in his eyes before his expression turned neutral.

"But, I am yours."

The warmth in his eyes returned.

"Even without your blood, I am bound to you. In our time together I couldn't stop it from happening. I didn't understand it during that time but I knew it was there and that it was growing."

I paused for a moment to calm myself, not from fear but from my need for him. He's been the first man to show interest in me not based on my appearance. I gazed at him and let him see what was in my heart.

"However, without your blood I am not complete, will never be complete. I will always be empty without you." I leant against him with my cheek against his.

"Complete me Varrik, please." I whispered. My heart pounded so hard I thought it would smash its way out of my chest.

"Enola?" He murmured against my cheek as his arms wrapped themselves around me.

"Yes Varrik?" I whispered and that whisper contained my love for him.

"Bite me." He smiled against my cheek.

With an answering grin I nuzzled his neck for a moment or two, letting my lips, tongue and breath tease him then sank my teeth into his neck.

With a groan, his arms tightened around me and his body jerked ever so slightly. Then I felt his pleasure flood through him and into me at the same time as his blood filled my mouth like liquid velvet and I drank. As his blood flowed into me, it wasn't long before I felt whole once more. And so, I drank like he was my life, and he was from that point on and forever.

*I love you Enola*

*I love you Varrik*

After a few long moments, the wound on his neck healed. Then I transferred my lips to his and we kissed, but eventually I broke that off as well as an important question popped into my mind.

"Varrik? What is to happen now? With the information you had to give to Orenda that is." I was worried and knew it could be heard in my voice. I was anxious because I didn't know how any of it affected us, if at all.

"Now? Now the preparation for battle will commence." Varrik stated bluntly.

I just held onto him as my mind refused to deal with any of it at that point in time. However, I knew I... we, would have to deal with it soon.

No matter what, I knew I was going to resign from my job within the next month or two. I wanted to be a partner to Varrik in all sense of the word. With my near future decided – even though I knew I would have to discuss it with Varrik – I decided, from this point on, no more negativity like *them* in my life any more.

Until then and the coming battle, I would use that time to get to know him and work on reducing my fears further. For the first time in a long time, I felt like I had something worthwhile to live for.

Then, Varrik apparently had other ideas as he lifted me up into his arms and carried me back to my bedroom.

# Part 2
# The Mark

# Chapter 8

The early July breeze blew around and past me causing me to hunch in on myself as I snuggled deeper into my jacket. As the wind howled with a noise that would do an old time spooky movie proud, I thought about how I would've preferred to be at home with a hot chocolate and curled up on the lounge watching one of my favourite movies or reading a good book.

Instead, I was… maybe illegally… on the top of an old building looking through the scope waiting for my mark, my target, to make an exit on that cold winter's night.

The night isn't as dark as it should be thanks to cities and their invasive bright lights of all varieties. The street below me was buzzing with vehicles and people as they went to dinner, a movie or some other social outing if not home. I sighed and forced myself to relax against the hunching-against-the-cold instinct.

Meanwhile, I just sat there watching all who came into my line of sight. At least it wasn't raining like it was over a week ago, but I'd heard we had a dust storm heading our way from out west within the next day or two. Fun! NOT! There didn't seem to be much in the way of clouds, not that it would have mattered because I wouldn't have seen the stars where I was anyway. Too much electric lighting around the area.

I picked up the photo again and cursed the idiot who included it with the hit information. It looked like it had been taken by a surveillance camera that was forty to fifty years old – it was that grainy – and couldn't distinguish any clear facial features to guarantee a successful hit of the right person. All I had was that the target was male, somewhere near six feet tall, slim to medium build and dark short hair.

It was 2200 hours and I'd been sitting on the roof of the building, freezing my butt off, since just before sunset. So far I'd seen at least half a dozen men who could have fitted the vague description in the file I'd received, let alone the photograph. What a load of crock all of it was.

I was just glad it was the first night the job had been placed. Since it was, I still had plenty of time to do a bit of surveillance of my own before the ultimate deadline in nine days' time. Pun not intended. Since they'd so kindly supplied an itinerary, I could try to shorten the list of candidates to less than I currently had. 'Try' being the operative word.

I cursed again as I packed up my gear and headed down the stairs to the alley where my car, a 2009 Jaguar XK convertible in a deep red they called radiance, was parked and waiting for me. It had a mixed coloured interior of ivory (cream) seats and part of doors, and slate (a somewhat dark grey) dash and rest of doors with burr walnut (smooth polished wood) trim that was simply gorgeous.

It was the interior that I fell in love with which had made the decision for me in buying the car.

It was a classic now – twenty years old and still running as good as the day it was created – and all I could afford for its age. I really wanted one of the E types from the late 1960s-early

1970s, but they're truly rare now and so much out of my price range when some collector deemed to sell theirs.

Once in the car I opened my laptop, went into the preferred IRC chat program to start laying a complaint to my middleman. Just have to love the simple things in this technology crazed world.

<LaMuerteViene> this job is crap

<Helmsman> are you renouncing it?

Didn't take him long to respond back.

<LaMuerteViene> never have before so not going to start now but honestly...

<Helmsman> but honestly what?

<LaMuerteViene> *sigh* with the one chronically blurry photo provided, a psychic might be the only way to identify the correct person

<Helmsman> it truly is that bad?

<LaMuerteViene> you've seen the image

<Helmsman> yes

<LaMuerteViene> Honestly, start putting your foot down over shit like this

<Helmsman> careful of what you say!

<LaMuerteViene> *sigh* while the itinerary is one thing, so far I have seen over half a dozen who could easily be the one

\<Helmsman\> I see; and yes I can see the… problems that could arise from that. What are you going to do now?

\<LaMuerteViene\> I'll have to spend the next three to six venues snapping pics just so I can try to reduce some of the potentials

\<Helmsman\> I see

\<LaMuerteViene\> I have no choice. I have a reputation to uphold just like you do

\<Helmsman\> I'll make sure the notice goes out. Keep me informed

I sighed in frustration and ran my fingers through my hair. I'd wanted to ask him to try to get a better photo of the mark from the client/s. As per usual the Helmsman had gone off-line regardless of whether I was finished or not. That really annoyed me. One day soon I was going to tell him/her off for it.

I sighed again as I knew I wouldn't do such a thing any time soon. I shut the program down then headed home. For a Thursday night, at 2245 hours, Brisbane city was still fairly busy.

.o.O.o.

Home. My home. A huge modern ground hugging, single storey, five bedrooms plus study, a rumpus room and three bathrooms, tan coloured brick house with a terracotta tiled roof. It has a triple car garage and a neatly manicured garden full of flowers, flowering shrubs and Australian natives that we pay to have someone come in to maintain. We: as in I share with three other people even though the house is mine. Paid a damned fortune for it too.

While two of the other three house mates had a licence I, however, was the only one with wheels. I owned my Jaguar and a Yamaha YZF-R6 in racing red. Both of them live in the garage when not in use. The third I owned was a dark blue Ford Falcon station wagon. That was the one the others used whenever they needed to go out or gear had to be moved. They just had to pay for the registration, fuel and maintenance.

My Jag and Yamaha took up half of the garage space while Zeaya, my weapons expert, had the other half. The Ford was parked outside of the other half of the garage so I still had room to come and go. Just like the garage's altered usage, each of us had turned various rooms into more than one function or from its original function. Like turning the rumpus room into a mini workout room which only Zeaya and I used for the most part.

Zeaya stands at 178cm of lithe build with obvious muscles as she has almost no body fat at all. She has sandy light brown short stylish hair, flat expressionless hazel eyes and a tanned skin from standing out in the sun shooting more than sunning herself at the beach or by the pool. At thirty-two years old, she has a hard and cynical attitude that has lost her more potential friends than gained; except when it comes to weapons.

When it comes to weapons, she's like a woman on a super-hot date. Then, her eyes come alive and you know something softer is in there somewhere. I told her I would put up with anything from her if she didn't hit on me. She agreed. Yep, her preferred partners are women. Each to their own.

She and I met at a gun range a few years ago. She looked at me as a love interest who had a thing for guns, only for her to realise

I just used them and not adored them slobberingly like she does. So, I employed her instead.

The other two of my house mates are Maisie and George. Out of all three I have known Maisie the longest.

I was in the state library having troubles with my laptop when the, now, twenty-five year old came to my rescue. Even to this day I still don't know what she did to fix my laptop. We'd started talking and I discovered she was being forced to live away from home 'for her own good' her parents had said. I took pity on her and she's been with me ever since.

Maisie is the complete opposite of Zeaya.

She's shy, only 157cm tall of medium build with a few extra kilos that gave her generous curves which make her look really cute, shoulder length wavy hair so dark brown it looks almost black. She also had the most amazingly expressive emerald green eyes I have ever seen. She's also sweet and unassuming.

She's a recluse and is my tech geek. If the item that needs to be built or fixed, has computer components and needs software written for it then she's my girl for the job. I know how to turn my laptop on and off, and how to use the few programs Maisie installed for me, but she does the rest for me. Her workspace is in the second largest bedroom of the house because the study was too small.

I know her bed is in there somewhere. I saw it once.

The last of our little family is the ever petulant twenty-six year old baby, George. I have never seen anyone who sulks as much as he does. In fact, he never stops sulking unless we praise him vigorously for a job well done in cooking and information research. That's what he does for me; cook and research details and information whenever I'm in need of them, whether it be via internet or books. When he wasn't cooking or researching then he was out shopping for food and books the way most women shop for clothing.

George is a typical carrot top redhead with messy hair down to his collar. Fair skinned with a mass of freckles over every part I've ever seen of him – boxer shorts and singlet is thankfully the least amount of clothing I've seen him in – and medium to light brown eyes. Anyway, he's 176cm tall with enough extra weight as proof positive of how good his cooking really is.

While he's not as active as the rest of us, he's exceptionally good at what he does.

I'd met him at the state library almost three months after Maisie when he helped me find some information I couldn't seem to find no matter what I did that day. I couldn't remember how he ended up moving in but he works out of my kitchen for both his cooking and any research the rest of us need.

Although, he had claimed the third largest of the bedrooms to act as a library – to make up for it he took the smallest as his bedroom – for all of our books and he maintains it like a strict librarian. He also behaves like one and chastises us if we mess it up in any way or place a book back in the wrong spot. Heaven forbid.

Then there's me. Since I own the house, I claimed the master bedroom.

I'm twenty-eight, 170cm tall, of medium build and average weight because I constantly exercise to keep the weight off. I run daily, not so much as to keep fit but to be able to run from any danger if I happened to have run out of ammunition; I'm not proficient at unarmed or close combat or fighting in general. The odd thing or two is instinctive but if I have to think about it then I'm hopeless.

My short, medium to thick brunette – almost a chestnut I guess – hair has golden highlights and brushes the nape of my neck in layers stylish and feathery. My eyes are grey and not one of my best features and I'm a Caucasian who has lightly tanned skin that's more of a natural colouring rather than being out in the sun.

I'm lazy if left to my own devices, quiet, quick to anger and just as quick to calm down, but am immensely patient and rather good at waiting.

My number one job is that of a hired hit man and I'm good at it. Not the best but I do my best. My second job – day job so to speak – is that of a personal assistant to the manager of an advertising company. If I need to leave early or can't turn up for work I use my ailing mother as an excuse. Shocking I know. However, Mum is actually dead from heart failure a few years ago but she's become a convenient pretext (but suffering cancer instead) when number one job needs me.

Thankfully, that doesn't happen too often even though Charles, my immediate boss, is very understanding. Never met, or even seen, the owner of the company. I wouldn't even know if they were a he, she, it or a multiple even.

Outside of my number one job I'm known as Sonja. When I first started my number one job, I used the boring alias of Sights2020 because I couldn't think of anything interesting at the time. Then one day Zeaya said, as she looked at me, "Death comes." with a grin on her face. I didn't like it in English so George researched it in other languages for me. Showing me options, I fell in love with the Spanish translation. So, I became LaMuerteViene and have been known as that ever since.

.o.O.o.

It was 2320 hours by the time I pulled into the garage and closed the automatic door. I was exhausted but still had a bit to do if the gang were still up. If I was lucky they wouldn't be. After locking up the car – from habit, I locked my gear in the 'to be cleaned' safe. I then went inside.

I was partially lucky. George was still up.

"Hey Baby." I greeted him tiredly by the nickname I'd given him. He thought it was cute but that was only because he didn't realise I called him that because that was the way he acted. However, I always said it nicely. No way was I going to tell him the reason behind it.

I then slid the file gently towards him.

"Apparently we're expecting a dust storm tomorrow sometime so make sure the house is secure before it hits. Listen to the radio if you have to. When you have time, but before tomorrow at 1600, I need you to find out whatever you can. Any expansion would be wonderful as I know nothing beyond what's in that file. I am now going to crash for the next five hours."

I yawned big time as I gave him a farewell wave. I hadn't given him the chance to do or say anything as I hadn't stopped as I made my way to my room.

# *Chapter 9*

I rolled over and lazily glanced at the clock.

"Shit!" I exclaimed as I bounded out of bed. I was so late for work.

Unexpectedly, there was a knock on my bedroom door.

"What?" I snapped as I started grabbing what I needed for a hasty exit.

The door opened and Maisie came in.

"Morning Sonja. You have a message here. It would seem you called Charles when you got home last night." She said in that timid voice of hers.

The other two sent her in because they know I try to rein in my anger whenever I have to deal with Maisie. I love her like a sister but I can't handle her crying and she'll cry at the drop of a hat.

Her comment got my attention, however, as I reached out for the message.

*While I really do hate those late calls, I'm sorry to hear about the bad spell your mum's going through. Let me know if you can make it to the party for the clients, which starts at 7 tonight. You'll have to attend one sooner or later.*

*Charles*

I stared at the message dumbfounded. I must have been more asleep on my feet than I'd thought when I arrived home because I didn't remember calling him at all.

"Thanks Maisie." I said softly. "Ummm... Can you get George to do me up a plate of bacon and eggs, toast and a cup of Irish Breakfast tea with cream please? I'm starving and will be out shortly."

"Of course Sonja." Maisie murmured on her way out.

I picked up my mobile phone and dialled.

"Hi Charles."

"Hi Sonja, you get much sleep?"

"Yeah I got a bit of sleep."

"Is your mother really bad?" His concern was genuine and it made me feel bad about the lie.

"No, she only had a little turn, not gotten worse thankfully..."

"That's good to hear."

"Yeah, she calmed down a lot once I got here..."

"You must be relieved on that point."

"Yeah. Oh, and I should be there tonight..." I informed him. He was right. I would have to attend one eventually. Maybe it could be a diversion for me from the lack of details for the *job* I've got.

"You sure? If your Mum isn't well..."

"No, no problem Charles, honest. She's mostly calm now so I'll stay with her for a few more hours before going home to get ready for tonight…"

"Well as long as you're sure. Oh, clothing is semi-formal."

"Yeah I am and okay re: dress style.

"Then I'll see you tonight Sonja."

"See you then…"

"Bye."

"Bye." Well, that's done. Good thing I kept the situation with 'Mum' simple. Nothing worse than making the lie complicated and then not remembering what the hell had been said. I sighed.

There were times when I found the idea of the two jobs tough to deal with but I really do enjoy them both and I don't get enough in the way of 'work' from my number one to support all four of us even though Zeaya, Maisie and George do their own sideline jobs. Not that theirs earn them quite enough either.

Then, surprising myself, I thought that if I had to give up one of them then it would be my number one job. That thought stopped me in my tracks. I never realised I would ever consider giving up my hit job. What would happen to the other three, since it was my number one job that had brought us together?

Then I mentally shook myself and decided to deal with it when the time arrived; if it should ever do so. I dressed in grey track pants, a wine/burgundy long sleeved poet's-like shirt and black slippers then made my way out to the kitchen.

My kitchen was a standard kitchen with beige coloured floor tiles, white walls with white splash back tiles, white appliances, pine cabinets and ivory coloured marble counter tops with salmon coloured veins through them.

"George, any info yet?" He was going to bite. I just know it.

There was no way it would ever occur to him not to, that I might be teasing him, and I worked hard at not to smile.

"Yet?! I've been feeding everyone else since I woke up this morning then you ordered your breakfast as if this is a café then you expect me to have found your information already?! What am I? I'm not superman you know…" He bit hook, line and sinker, and whined the whole time.

I laughed. "Easy Baby, I'm just teasing you."

Maisie ducked her head to hide whatever expression was on her face while Zeaya openly smirked.

"Not very nice of ya this time of the mornin'." George grumped petulantly.

"You know I'm rarely disappointed with what you've come up with in the time allotted you. I'm feeling good despite the crappiness of this particular job and I get to go to a party tonight." I said in the effort to pacify him as I grinned big time at him. Damn but he was an easy target.

He glared at me and I watched the huffy expression disappear off his face little by little as he served my breakfast. By the time I got my cup of tea he was smiling a little. Maisie managed to control whatever expression she had since she was facing the rest of us again.

"Zeaya, I put the bag from last night in safe 'D' for you." I said between mouthfuls of tea and toast.

"Huh. Guess I'll go clean them then so they can be transferred to safe 'C'." Zeaya grabbed her coffee and headed towards the garage.

Safe 'D' was for weapons not yet cleaned after having been out, while safe 'C' was for the ready-to-use weapons. Apart from being labelled they were also different colours to tell the difference between them. When I'd discovered her cleaning the weapons after I'd already done so, I decided to leave it all to her. It seemed my cleaning wasn't good enough for her so I didn't need the hassles, or the extra expense. I just let her do it from that point on.

"Maisie Sweetie, I have need of the digital camera for night surveillance. Is it available for tomorrow night onwards?" I asked her gently. Being highly emotional as well as being agoraphobic meant I had to work at being nice as much as possible.

"Umm... I'll check it over after I've had breakfast if that's okay?" Even after all these years she was still a mouse around me, but she smiled like a child who'd been told they were getting what they wanted for Christmas.

"Sure Sweetie, not a problem at all. After I finished breakfast I'm going to sleep a little longer then exercise on and off throughout the rest of the day. Will see what you've found by 1530-1600, George." I took my cup and plate to the sink, rinsed them off then placed them in the dishwasher. That was one machine I was more than happy to buy as none of us liked doing the dishes.

George grunted to let me know he'd heard me.

I walked up behind him and blew in his ear. He knew I saw him as a brother or cousin and not anything more than that. I'd made that clear a few months after I'd met him.

"Breakfast was perfect as per usual George." I said gently to him then headed back to my room.

"Glad you enjoyed it." He called after me in a happy tone. I just smiled and shook my head as I lay down to get more sleep.

I awoke just after midday and, because I woke up later than I'd expected, I'd decided on a slow workout for the next hour and a half instead of smaller rounds throughout the afternoon as I'd initially intended.

To start off: a leisurely bike ride next to a set of weights followed by slow ambling on the treadmill by the glass doors looking out over a wildly waving (wind-blown) mix of ferns, wattles, and palm trees muted in colour slightly by the dust storm gusting about outside. Then I treated my eyes to a bunch of eye candy posters of both men and women plastered to the ceiling while hefting the weights. Finally, I finished off with another stroll next to the glass doors and the crazily dancing plants outside.

Afterwards, I had a wonderfully warm shower. Well... a quick one as I would have a bath before going out later that night. I dried, dressed then headed out to the kitchen.

"Well, in the few hours I've had there is nothing about this guy so far." George greeted me in a semi-sulky tone and glanced at me sideways.

"Relax George." I sighed. "I sort of figured you wouldn't find anything. The only thing I need back out of all that is his itinerary. While I'm on surveillance work you keep going with the research and hopefully between us we will find something out. I'll give you whatever photographs I take tomorrow night so you can see what you can come up with in regards to them. In the meantime can I trouble you for a chicken and lettuce sandwich please?" I asked him nicely while he photocopied the itinerary then handed it to me and slipped the original back in the folder.

Why did I ask him to make me a sandwich since I'm more than capable of making my own? To save the peace of the household is why. He sulks if we don't ask him as he thinks we don't like his cooking and food preparation if we do it ourselves. So, we ask him just to keep all happy.

"Chook coming up. Glass of milk as well?" George asked hopefully.

I grinned at him. "Sure." and I got a smile from him as he happily pottered around the kitchen.

Out of all of us we had to keep him happy the most. I'd swear we're a bunch of neurotics with the way each of us behave. I ate the sandwich and drank the milk he'd handed to me then headed back to the bedroom to find something evening-like to wear. I just loved to play dress up; I never grew out of it really.

On the way to the bedroom I saw Zeaya. "Hey Hon, what you say you and I go to the gun range tomorrow?"

Her eyes lit up. "You serious?"

"Absolutely. You still have time to phone any of them to see if we can play with our weapons of choice, of which you can choose." I offered with a grin as I continued towards the bedroom.

My grin widened when I heard her whoop of joy. My day was complete. I'd made the three of them very happy for the time being. I shook my head in amusement. Honestly, neurotics I swear it.

Despite being winter I ended up choosing a pair of multi-layered black chiffon straight cut pants with an ivory and gold vine and leaf embroidery detail up the outside of the legs from hem to waist on the outer layer. The outer layer of chiffon was split up to the upper thighs on the outside seam, while the middle layer was split to just above the knees and the inner layer was split to mid-calf.

I next chose a dark chocolate brown velvet sleeveless corset which had a similar ivory and gold coloured embroidered vines with flowers design to the pants, while top and bottom hems had golden brown satin trim. The front of the corset had busks with gold hooks and loops, while the back had ivory cord lacing; both in keeping with the gold and ivory theme of the embroidery.

I decided I would just wear a long black velvet coat over the top between houses.

To finish off the outfit I found a pair of black leather strappy shoes with ten centimetre high stiletto heels. Since it had been a while when I'd last worn them, I spent the next hour or so practicing walking in them so I wouldn't fall on my face or look like I was teetering on a knife's edge.

As for the make-up I would wear tones of browns, gold and ivory with a reddish brown lipstick. And my hair? Since I washed it earlier all I had to do was run my fingers through it, give my head a shake and it would be done.

By 1700 hours I was relaxing in the bath full of deliciously hot water that would leave me smelling of mango and frangipani. I didn't get out of it until it was too cool to be enjoyable in the winter coldness.

By 1830 hours I was dressed – with Maisie helping me with the corset, made up and ready to leave. Just a quick programming of the GPS, since I'd never been there before, and

I leisurely made my way to where the party was being held.

The night was beautiful and clear, despite the dust storm, even if it was freezing cold. The dust storm had died down just before sunset and with no clouds the heat disappeared rather quickly. The dust storm obviously hadn't been too bad since the air wasn't thick with dust. Despite that, the air did have a slightly dusty taste to it.

Regardless of all that, the drive was pleasant and I hadn't rushed. When I arrived, I was neither disgustingly early nor fashionably late. I was boringly on time.

The house, I should say mansion – even though I couldn't tell what it was made of other than it wasn't timber or brick – was two storeys, huge, white with large arched windows and lit up like a Christmas tree but without the colours. It was also surrounded by a combined white painted concrete and black metal spiked fence where the front gate had impressive security measures in place; such as cameras and a buzzer to request entrance. I also expected to find electrified wiring around the fence if I looked hard enough.

I was met at the gate by a man with a guest checklist. "Name?" He was dressed in a black suit, white shirt and black bow tie.

"Miss Sonja Reilly." I stated. I could hear the plovers acting up as they flew around. Just by following their cries one could tell where they were. For some reason one was subjected to stereo surround sound whenever they cried out while flying.

"You may park over there Miss." He stated as he indicated the way.

So, I parked where he'd pointed. The driveway and parking

area were all paved in terracotta pavers. I'm sure if I looked hard enough I would see the pattern was unbroken from front to back and side to side. However, I couldn't be bothered straining my eyes in the dark. Not that it was that dark with all those lights on.

Glancing around I saw there were over half a dozen vehicles parked already. Not one of them were the same; except a few of similar colours. A car enthusiasts dream I'm sure. I could see that Charles was already inside. I headed to the door only for it to open just as I started to walk up the concrete and tiled stairs.

After I entered, the doorman took my coat. He too was dressed in the same manner as the gateman.

"Just go right through Miss." He said politely with a smile as he indicated to the right.

"Thank you." I smiled. So I went.

In the quick glance I'd gotten of the entry, the floor tiles were of a dark ivory/light salmon colour (not up on building materials so couldn't tell what they were made of) while the walls were a pale ivory with some sort of generic two tone blue trim. There were two dark wood display tables; one on the left had flowers while the one on the right had a statue. Both had matching mirrors above them. For that evening a long table had been place near the front door to hold the coats of the guests.

Ahead of me was a staircase which led to an upper level and was done in the same (or similar) dark wood as the display tables. The stairs were carpeted in a multi toned blue that seemed to match the trim on the walls. There were no rugs on the floor of the entry area. There was a double wooden door in the same timber as the stairs and tables on the left before reaching the staircase. The doors on the left were closed while to the right was open to a social/living area overlooked by the balcony above.

Entering the living area, I caught a hint of similar colour scheme as the entry before my attention was taken up by the people in the room.

Charles was the first person I saw and he was with some of the advertising staff who'd already arrived, along with some of our top clients with more of both yet to appear. While I didn't deal with the clients directly, either by phone or person, I did recognise them since I had to deal with their files whenever Charles had need of them or required them to be filed away. The client's files had their photographs attached inside.

That night was the first time I'd ever been to one of the work's parties; all the others had been when I was 'out of town'.

"Sonja, pleased you could make it." Charles greeted, dressed in a dark blue suit with a normal but silk multi toned striped blue tie, as he took my hand, gave it a gentle squeeze and a kiss on the cheek. Then he gave me a rather appraising look from head to toe and back again.

"You look wonderful. Nice to see you out of office attire for a change." He said quietly with a smile. He still had a hold of my hand.

Charles stands about 169cm tall and of roughly medium build but was starting to gain a few extra kilos ever since he hit thirty-five two years ago. His greyish hazel eyes were both observant and expressive and appeared darker than they were because of his light honey blonde hair. I had to admit that he was pleasant to look at. He was generally a quiet man but I've never really seen him outside of work.

I suspected, but wasn't positive, that he was interested in me beyond the boss/personal assistant relationship. However, he's never pursued it. Yet. Besides that, I didn't see him that way. Definitely my boss and maybe a friend to me.

"Thank you Charles and thank you for the reminder about tonight because I'd forgotten. Nice to finally be at one of these. The way things were going I thought I was going to miss this one as well." I smiled.

"How is she?"

"She's doing as well as to be expected. I'm just glad it wasn't anything serious this time round." I said, lying through my teeth.

"Let's hope she stays that way for a while, yes?" Charles stated kindly as he looked at me intently but I couldn't read his expression. Not completely anyway. It seemed to be a mix of concern and… suspicion? I just wasn't sure.

"Yes, I do hope so." I answered gently with just enough concern to make it all believable.

Charles proceeded to escort me around the room to introduce me personally to the clients since they and I had never truly met before. By their reactions it would seem Charles had mentioned me to them more than once. The most common response I got was "Ah so you are the elusive Sonja. Was beginning to think you were a figment of Charles' imagination."

For the past hour I'd mingled, greeted, chatted and was totally bored out of my brain. More clients and staff turned up during that hour and it was still another half hour or so before the main course would be served. I had to meet and greet the new arrivals as well and that was just as boring. However, still no sign of the big boss person/s.

Throughout all the small talk my mind kept going back to the 'job' I had since it wasn't kept busy enough to stop it from wandering.

A single photograph of the subject that was useless so a visual of the subject was unknown. Name of the subject unknown or had been refused to be given; unsure which. Residential address of the subject also unknown it would seem. Occupation was also unknown or withheld.

I really didn't know how the one who'd ordered the hit expected anyone to be able to carry it out without any of the vital details. Too many damned unknowns. Except his gender and his itinerary. Even then I didn't know how they'd managed to obtain those two facts without a name at least. Someone was holding back details and the more I thought about it the more that point bugged me.

It was just so damned frustrating.

I was grateful for the little nibblies sitting on a sideboard as they stopped my stomach from becoming overly noisy. Also, during that time, I'd pretty much seen all of the ground floor of the house. It was decorated fairly similarly as the entry. A fully equipped bathroom with a separate toilet done in black, silver and ivory was downstairs. The house had an impressive kitchen. I wouldn't mind having a go in it. Despite having George, I do love to cook. I just don't get the chance any more.

After that first hour of trying to be nice and interested in all the small talk and praise for the previous campaigns – as the current business wouldn't be discussed until either during dinner or after it – as I mingled, I decided to go upstairs and sneak a peek around. I wanted to see if the downstairs theme was continued upstairs.

For some reason, tonight, I was feeling lonelier than I usually did and it was annoying. I'm guessing it was also the reason why I was feeling so restless, a little frustrated – more than the number one job really caused, and bored with what was going on around me. However, I just couldn't reason any of it out.

Once upstairs, I saw the colour scheme from downstairs was continued. However, the hallway was like an art gallery. One wall had a number of paintings between windows. One was a generic landscape but beautifully done in summer colours which could have been anywhere in the world. The second was a seascape that was simply gorgeous on a windy almost stormy looking day and made me feel like I was looking out a window at it. While a third was of Newstead House in Newstead, Brisbane. Just a simple pencil sketch but so full of detail it was lovely. Hell, it could have been one I'd done when I went for a school visit there in grade six.

There were other works of art but those three were the most eye-catching to me.

I then made my way back along the hallway. The wall opposite the windows had statues and sculptures. In between those I casually opened doors in the wall opposite the paintings. In each room, colours were the curtains, bed linens, the pillows and the lounging chairs. Furniture frames were all a rich dark wood. I didn't really turn on the bedroom lights. I just let the outside lights show me.

But what I saw was: bedroom with double bed, bathroom – WOW! *Very* impressive in black marble with silver fittings (just like down stairs but grander) and what a massive bathtub as I could almost swim in that. Bedroom with queen bed, bedroom with another queen bed, a second bathroom as impressive as the first. Bedroom with a king bed this time and lastly a fifth bedroom with a huge bed – as in way larger than a king size, a door that might lead to an en suite and a…

…a butt naked man who was leaning his right arm against the sliding glass door frame to the balcony. His left arm was down by his side and both hands clenched in a fist. Curtains were opened on either side of him as he gazed out at the darkness outside. I saw all that in barely a second or two before he turned around to face me faster than I could even begin to think about back peddling and closing the door.

I received a full frontal view of him then quickly raised my head, followed a fraction slower by my eyes, to look him in the face… only to discover it was completely in shadow. I couldn't see any part of his face at all. I frowned.

"I'm sorry." I murmured then, with my heart pounding, quickly closed the door as he called out – I think he said wait – and headed towards the stairs.

In the space of a second or two my mind and body fought, with the mind winning, but only just. There was no way I was going to wait even if my body wanted to. God! Did my body ever want to.

However, as soon as I'd opened that door I'd sensed frustration stronger than what I'd already been feeling and had no idea where I was getting that from because as far as I knew I wasn't a sensitive. The feeling of frustration lessened some, but still more than before I'd gone upstairs, after I'd closed the door and continued to lessen as I moved away from the room.

It was only then I realised I'd been sensing the frustration faintly ever since I'd walked in the house over an hour ago. While I had thought it had been too intense to be mine I'd still thought it was mine, but now it seemed not to be.

Without making it seem like I was rushing anywhere, since I didn't want to break an ankle or my neck in my high heels, I leisurely made my way down the stairs and to where my coat was waiting for me. The man who'd taken my coat earlier picked it up without a second guess and helped me into it then held open the door for me to walk out.

I thought I heard a door close somewhere in the house behind me. No way was I going to turn around to find out for sure as I rushed out the front door to my car. Of all the times to end up fumbling for my keys, but I eventually found them and unlocked my car. I thought I heard Charles call my name but, again, I didn't stop or look around as I got into the Jag and drove off. I almost sped out of there faster than was wise. The gate was still open thankfully as it seemed there were still a few more guests to arrive.

I headed for Mount Coo-tha because the long drive gave me plenty of time to calm down from my embarrassment. Being Friday night I was glad of the distraction of party goers' traffic to concentrate on as I didn't want to have any accidents right then. The traffic and the winding road of the mountain also gave my mind a temporary break from the turmoil it was in.

Finally at the lookout, I was leaning on the railing at the lookout and just stared out over the city night lights. However, I wasn't seeing them as my mind kept flashing (pun in no way intended) on the wonderful bod I'd seen earlier. There are times I have perfect recall. Sometimes it's a gift while other times it's a curse and that evening it just so happened to be a delightfully torturous curse.

His muscles were subtle and moved effortlessly when he faced me. His dark hair looked soft as it freely moved when he'd turned his head. His skin. His skin appeared smooth taut and young as it covered chest, arms, hips, thighs. Hell, his physique in general. Oh god was he well endowed! What would he be like when aroused?

I groaned with a new sense of frustration as thoughts of him wouldn't leave me alone. I wasn't a virgin. I'd had a few guys over the past ten years, even if it had been a couple of years since I had last been with one. But just the sight of him like that had me reacting like a virgin.

Mind you, I didn't know if not seeing his face was a good thing or not. I sighed as I leant over and rested my forehead on the cold railing, hoping it would numb the mind enough to stop those thoughts. I didn't need them right then as I had to concentrate on the hit. Not on some delectable male I would more than likely never see again.

Suddenly I was tired so I headed home.

"You're back early." George said as I stalked past him.

I hadn't even realised he was there until he spoke because I hadn't been looking as I made a beeline straight to my room. I didn't even know if the other two were there as well. No matter what, I ignored him and everything else in my effort to escape to the sanctuary of my room.

Once in my room, I changed into something more comfortable then flopped onto the bed in the hopes of falling asleep. I was tired but the sight of him, all of him – except his face, kept popping into my mind. Thumping the pillow over my head, I groaned in frustration again.

Eventually, I fell asleep but not before hours of tossing and turning and growling at anyone who knocked on my door, telling them to go away in no uncertain terms.

# Chapter 10

Maybe the one who'd ordered the hit was a middleman himself. A middleman dealing with another middleman and that's why we have so little information about the target.

When I awoke Saturday morning that was my first thought. I laid there thinking it over and decided not to let the Helmsman know at that point in time as it served no purpose. Besides it was only a thought. I sighed and got up, dressed into jeans and polo shirt, and made my way into the kitchen.

Zeaya, George and Maisie were sitting there without looking at me as I walked out.

"Morning." I greeted them.

All three looked at me at the same time and said "Morning." All at the same time.

I understood what was going on. After my grouching the previous night, my house mates decided to tread egg shells until they knew my mood. While sleep hadn't improved my mood from last night, I'd accepted that I couldn't continue to take it out on them. So, as much as I wanted to be crabby, I decided to be nice instead.

"George, can I have the same as yesterday please?" I asked gently and with a smile.

"Uh, sure." and he started pottering around organising it for me.

"Are we still going to the range today?" Zeaya asked while trying to keep her attitude to a minimum. To which I was immensely grateful for because I didn't have the patience for it at that point in time.

"Sure are. I have this need to demolish some targets for a while." I answered with a grin.

"Sweet. We can leave about... 9:30 if you like." She said after looking at the clock.

"Sounds good to me." I responded just as George handed me my cup of tea. "Maisie Sweetie, how's that camera for this evening?" I asked her as I smiled. Sometimes I just wanted to be grumpy as, but I couldn't with her. I mentally sighed.

"All ready to go. All old photos taken off and stored for later inspection, camera cleaned, AstroScope cleaned, fresh batteries in, no problem with the software and plenty of memory. I tested it out last night and everything works fine." Maisie rattled off for me, sounding only half shy. It was the only time her real personality shone through: when she talked about her specialities.

An AstroScope comprises of three pieces which are attached together and then is attached to the front of the camera with the lens attached to the AstroScope. It turns an ordinary camera into a night vision camera.

During Maisie's rundown, George brought me my breakfast and I started eating.

"Excellent. Thank you Sweetie." I then turned to George.

"While I would like you to keep hunting up whatever info you can find about the subject, I'm not expecting you to find anything because I don't think we have enough clues or information to lead us anywhere. So, while you're looking, don't stress too much about not finding anything, okay?" I looked at him intently as I kept my tone calm and pleasant-like. I just couldn't put up with one of his carry-ons today.

"Okay." Was all he said in a cautious tone as if he was expecting me to snap at him.

I let it ride as I wasn't in the mood to soothe his delicate ego. His petulance was easier to handle than Maisie's crying. After I'd finished eating...

"Breakfast was good as always George. Oh, yesterday I started a money tracer program in the hopes of finding out who'd placed the money for the hit. So, can you keep an eye on that please George? I'm not expecting results from it any time soon but if something does happen then please let me know." I commented.

George said sure then Zeaya and I left.


The day was cloudy and a bit breezy with a bit of dust still in the air, but generally fine. A good day for shooting. At the Belmont Rifle Range – it was an outdoor shooting range. We hadn't bothered with pistols and decided to stick to our rifles.

Our 'out of the box' toys of choice were the Remington 700 XCR Tactical Long Range, the Sig Sauer SSG 3000 and the Weatherby Mark V Accumark with plenty of ammo to have fun for half a day. However, my preferred while on the job – the Weatherby Mark V Accumark – was fully customised to suit me; stock, barrel and attachments.

After a rapid fire session...

"I still don't know why you won't do more competitions than you do, especially nationals. You could be as good as or better than me if you tried a little harder." Zeaya stated for the umpteenth time since she and I started shooting together years ago.

For some reason she just couldn't let the subject rest, she just had to keep going on about it every time we went shooting.

"Hon, I'm just not interested. I do well enough in the state comps. Besides, one of us in the top five is more than enough. I'm perfectly happy to be within the top ten." I responded with a smile.

Zeaya just grunted as she took a swig of water from the drink bottles we always carried with us. It became a habit during summer and just turned into common practice all year round. I chuckled at her.

"You so need to get a girlfriend." Then took a mouthful of my water.

"You offering?" She asked in a half teasing and half hopeful tone.

Then I did laugh.

"You wish. Just shoot woman." I said and we practiced some more, but at a slower pace, before heading home to clean up.

A little after midday we packed up and had lunch at a little café half way between the range and home. While we ate we spent the time rehashing our practice session at the range, receiving the odd glance or two from others around us when we couldn't contain our enthusiasm to a murmur.

After that we then went to our favourite beauty store, had a look at what they had, buying anything we found of interest before finally heading home.

"Would you like me to help you?" I asked Zeaya even though I knew she would more than likely say no, but I had to offer.

"Nah, I'll do it all. Thanks for the fun day out, it's been a while." She said with a smile.

"Any time Hon. Just going to get cleaned up." I said with a smile as I walked into the main part of the house.

I first had a shower to wash my hair and get all of the grime off then I had a beautiful long soak in a hot bath with my usual scents of mango and frangipani. At the beauty store I'd managed to find a mango bath salts and frangipani bubble bath, along with more mango and frangipani body wash. As the tub filled, I added the bubble bath to it.

I'd relaxed for so long I jumped in fright when there was a knock on my en suite door.

"Yeah?" I called out somewhat sleepily. Seemed I'd dozing off.

"Thought you might want a wake-up call." Maisie called with a hint of amusement in her voice.

I chuckled rather sheepishly.

"Thanks Sweetie. I'll be out shortly."

Pulling the plug, I gave the tub a quick clean then dried and dressed in black jeans and a dark blue long sleeved polo shirt, and was sitting in the kitchen with a cup of tea in hand soon after. On the back of my chair was a jacket to keep the cold at bay while taking pics.

"I'll leave at sunset as each of these meetings is after the sun has gone down."

"Yeah, what is it with that?" George asked me.

I raised my eyebrows at him. "It could be because the subject is a vampire." I said with a slight smile. At first I was teasing but then the thought stuck.

"You know that for sure?" Maisie asked in a slightly squeaky voice. Even though she'd never met any she was afraid of vampires and therians.

Therian is short for therianthropy from the Greek words therion meaning wild animal or beast, and anthropos meaning human being. The word therian generically covers all forms of were-creatures while lycan and lycanthropy refers to just the were-wolves. The therians themselves voted on that one quite a few years ago.

"No. It's either that or he really likes night meetings." I responded with a grin. After I'd finished my cuppa, "Well Kiddies, since sunset is a little over ten minutes away I'll get myself organised now so I can leave. Be good and have fun."

"So which is it to be? Be good or have fun?" Zeaya piped up.

I laughed. "Have fun and be good at it?"

"Woo hoo" "Yes" and "Cool" were the responses I got back as I walked out with a backwards wave.


Zeaya and I had scouted the area earlier that day after coming back from the rifle range and there was no decent vantage point, high or low, to take photos of those in the café without being seen. As it turned out, that particular café catered to vampires so that had to be the reason why they were meeting there. If they're vampires that is.

The vampires ran their own blood bank and it was surprising

how many people actually donated to it compared to the Red Cross. However, the vampires handed off their excess: half to the Red Cross for free and the other half was sold to mortals who hosted vampires and to cafés and restaurants that catered to vampires. It was a pretty smart business move really and it seems to work well.

So, I was sitting in the café roughly in the middle against a side wall. I watched people come and go for the first two hours before a larger group arrived. During that time I'd consumed two pots of tea, while reading, so the staff wouldn't think about kicking me out.

At a table near the entrance, but against the wall opposite the one I was against, three women and four men sat down and gave the impression they were waiting for more to arrive. All were wearing business suits, men in pants and women in skirts – despite it being winter. I naturally discounted the women since my mark was male. Of the four men, two of them looked like they could have been my mark. Dark hair, slim to average build, roughly six foot and pale skin.

A waiter went over to them to see if they were ready to order but they sent the waiter away.

To me that suggested they were definitely waiting for others to turn up. However, I didn't miss seeing the two non-vampires who'd taken up guard duty at a table outside the café not far from the larger group. Both from the Americas and both natives with long dark hair.

The waiter then came to me and I ordered a Chicken Caesar Salad and a sparkling apple juice. I quietly, slowly, ate and drank while I continued to read. At the same time, I covertly observed the group. After a few minutes I worked out that one of the two possibles could be my target as I'd seen him at the last venue on Thursday night. I just had to wait for the last of their party to arrive.

A short time later another man did arrive. He too fit the bill and had also been at Thursday evening's event. I was now back up to two possible targets. While 'reading' my book I listened to what they were talking about. I had to concentrate because their voices were low. Thankfully, being winter, the café wasn't that crowded.

"Orenda, while we know there will always be challenges to your rule it doesn't mean we can let things relax too much. So far you have had a serious challenge each year since you became Prince of the City. This next one by Norton, Varrik had informed us about over a week ago, will be the second for this year." Stated the man who was the last to arrive.

While his voice was one that could be classified as average, it resonated within me. Much to my surprise. With a quick glance I noted he had dark, neat hair that brushed his collar. It was somewhat longer than most men in suits have theirs but it suited him. He was wearing a dark suit just like all the others at the table but wore a gold coloured silk looking shirt with no tie.

When I sneaked a second peek at his face while he talked I couldn't see anything remarkable but, for some reason, I knew I would never forget his face. Without taking a longer look I couldn't work out why I wouldn't forget.

Then my mind snagged on something he'd said...

Huh! Orenda, Prince of the City. Never thought I would ever get to set sights on her. She's Native American with long dark straight hair and stood about 165cm. The lighting wasn't good enough to tell the difference between dark brown and black hair. However, what surprised me the most was her deep voice.

Then the waiter arrived to take my plates away and I ordered a slice of citrus tart with a large dollop of real whipped cream and a hot chocolate thick with froth and a couple of marshmallows to prolong my stay. At least, that was what I was telling myself.

"Hence the reason for this meeting, Darius. Damn it! Just when I needed Varrik to be surrounded in secrecy. I wonder if we can slowly, covertly, arrange the deaths of those who have seen him?" She shook her head then glanced around the table.

"We need to ensure we stay in power to make certain the mortals stay safe. No matter where we have been established, we have had many years of relative peace with the mortals so far and Brisbane is no different. I would like to keep it that way." Again, she gazed at each in turn around the table before continuing.

"We all know the consequences if we fail and I am destroyed. It will not be just a blood bath on our side of the war. For some stupid reason all challengers so far have wanted to make it open season on the mortals. We can not have this. Safety and free choice must continue in the mortal world.

"While humans breed fairly quickly, our kind can drain them even faster and thereby leaving us without a source of willing nourishment. The majority of our kind has fought hard to live in peace with the mortals over the centuries just to let it all go to ruin because of a few stupid dead-heads. While I have no problems warring with those who oppose me, I draw the line at it spilling over into the mortal's lives.

"What we need are early preventative measures. Better than we already have in place. So, ideas people." While her voice was low and almost impossible to hear, I could hear the earnest tone in her words.

Wow! If what I was hearing was true then she had my vote. However, I almost choked on a sip of water when she'd said 'dead-heads'. A funny pun to call other vampires to be sure.

So, where did my mark fit into this? Was he a spy trying to bring her down or was he one of her people and the other side wanted him eliminated because he would be a problem to their plans?

Damn! I hate it when a simple hit suddenly becomes complicated. Not that this one had been simple from the start. I know it shouldn't matter. That I should just do the hit and that's that. However, I'm one of those mortals their war will spill over to and the lesser of the two evils will need all their people to stop the worst of them. I frowned, as I stared at the book in my hand, over the unexpected complication to the job.

My thoughts were interrupted when I sensed surprise and curiosity while I absently finished up my dessert and hot chocolate. When I glanced up, I saw him looking at me. Darius I think Orenda called him. He was frowning at me. I just blinked at him.

Blast! Had I done something to give myself away? I didn't think I had.

His frown deepened slightly.

I gave him a blank look in return. Not a difficult thing to do since I didn't have a clue as to why he was frowning at me in the first place. Then I turned away from him as I put my book in my backpack and went to the counter to pay for my meal.

Having come to their notice, or his in particular, I couldn't risk staying any longer. I grabbed my helmet and left with one quick glance back at him, making sure I kept my expression neutral the entire time.

While confused, I was flattered he was still watching me. Even if it was with a frown of curiosity.

I went to my bike and had to ride past the café to head to the next destination from where I'd parked. He was standing on the footpath watching me as I rode past. His reaction to me confused me.

Thinking about it, I could only conclude I hadn't done anything to give myself away. Maybe he recognised me from somewhere. Only... I hadn't seen him before where we were in each other's line of sight. I would certainly remember someone like him. He was attractive enough. To me at least.

I shook my head and concentrated on riding to my next destination.

My target had a second event on that night. So, I set myself up in the shadows, across the street from where they were meeting. With camera in hand, I snapped away as each possible arrived. Which was three so far.

The wind whistled past and around me and I'd come to the conclusion that it was too damned cold to be doing surveillance work at night during winter. However, it seemed as if my target might be a vampire after all, so I had no choice unless I wanted to give up the job. No way was I going to do that. Yet.

I paused slightly as I saw... what was his name...? Ah, Darius...

when I saw Darius step out of one of the cars. He made a fourth possible as he obliged me by turning to face me as he helped Orenda out. Perfect as I snapped a series of photos of him.

Lowering the camera slightly, I watched him. Damn but he was good looking. With a shake, I resumed taking photos.

He went still, peered intently out and around him like a good little guard dog and I took a few more photos until it seemed like he was looking straight at me. I tilted the camera down to hide any possible reflection and stayed very still while holding my breath. He wasn't blinking as he stared at where I was. I thought I'd been spotted when he suddenly blinked then walked away.

Keeping to the shadows, I made my way to my bike then headed home as I wasn't going to risk getting caught just yet and hopefully not at all. That was getting a bit too close for comfort. Sometimes I didn't understand how the bounty hunters were able to get up close and personal to fight rogue vamps and therians. They had to be vicious to fight with. No way was I going to get up close and personal to fight with the non-humans.

The evening was still early. When I pulled into the driveway, I saw the Falcon gone and the house dark so the three of them – hopefully – were still out. Once inside, and leaving all the lights off – I didn't see or hear anyone else in the house, I went to my room and changed into my nightie after I left the camera on the breakfast bar. Thankfully, I didn't have to leave a note as Maisie would know what to do once she saw it sitting there.

One of my weaknesses is my love of floor length, long sleeved, old styled, pre-nineteen hundreds, loose fitting nighties. I have them in pastel colours of blue, lavender, pink and yellow, as well as white. Usually they're made of a light-weight cotton with satin lacing ribbons. Winter ones were made of a thicker cotton with lace at the cuffs and velvet lacing ribbons compared to my summer sets.

My summer ones were spaghetti-strapped, instead of sleeves, and had splits up both sides to the upper thighs. My only modification to them.

The one I chose to wear was a soft yellow with matching velvet ribbons.

I stood at the glass sliding door in my room that looked out over one of the gardens at the front corner of the house. I just stared out into the distance without really looking at anything. Because the night was clear it was also cold since there were no clouds to hold the heat of the day in. I felt the cold, I was in just a nightie after all, but my thoughts were far away making me forget about it.

My mind just kept going over the lack of specifics regarding the hit and it was beginning to feel like flogging a dead horse, with my mind being the dead horse. No matter how much I went over it I couldn't make sense of what details there were. And with three to four possible targets, I was still just as confused.

When I wasn't thinking about the hit, I was thinking about Darius's reaction to me at the café and the way he looked. Very pleasing indeed. However, while I was tired, I wasn't tired enough to go to sleep.

I didn't know how long I had been standing there but I... *felt*... something... not sure what. Vaguely, I was aware of opening the glass door and shifting position to change my line of sight and just stared... at what? I wasn't sure. On most levels I wasn't really aware of what I was doing at the time but was able to remember parts of it later for some weird reason. Then my mind was no longer thinking about the job or the incident at the café. In fact, I couldn't remember what I was thinking about as I stared out that door.

However, the feelings... I couldn't tell if they were mine or not. I first felt anger then frustration, loneliness followed by want, need, subsequently desire then attraction.

While I knew they hadn't chased each other in quick succession, I didn't know how long each emotion held me in its grip as I just stared off in that one direction. I still couldn't tell if they were my feelings or not but they could have been for all I knew. I knew I'd been feeling each of them on and off over the past few months but it seemed strange at how frequently, and strongly, I was experiencing them lately.

Then I blinked, and was shocked to discover the sky was starting to lighten. Dawn was on its way. I blinked again then shivered violently from having stood there in the cold for hours on end. I closed the sliding door and stumbled to the bed. I painfully, and stiffly, crawled into it, turned my electric blanket on high and fell asleep.

I slept a restless sleep where I couldn't remember if I dreamt or not.

# Chapter 11

I rolled over and looked at the clock and it read 1400 hours. I groaned. Not so much because of the time but because my mind felt battered and bruised. Also because, even though I didn't remember any of my dreams, my sleep hadn't felt restful. I crawled out of bed, dressed and decided to head out to the kitchen to tell the guys about the two meetings the previous night.

As soon as I'd opened my bedroom door I could hear Zeaya and George arguing rather loudly. Unfortunately. On their usual topic. I groaned. All thoughts about the night before flew out of my head the moment I heard them.

"...you could have a woman if you got off your fat arse, you stupid git." Zeaya growled.

"I'm not stupid! I'm..." George whined huffily.

"So you don't deny being fat..." Zeaya interrupted him.

George opened his mouth to complain as he puffed up like a puffer fish. Only I beat him as I interrupted Zeaya...

"Both of you shut the fuck up or piss off out of here." I snapped at both of them as I entered the kitchen while I rubbed my temple in the attempt to relieve the building headache. I was so not in the mood for their bickering right then.

There was sudden silence from the both of them. Maisie was hunched in on herself just sitting quietly off to the right at the breakfast bar. Poor thing didn't do so well with confrontations. While I just wanted to grab a gun and go postal when I'm feeling crappy like I was at that moment.

Standing on the left of Maisie, I reached for the pain killers when I saw a red dot on my right hand and it started travelling up my arm. I shoved Maisie to the right, away from the breakfast bar for her to fall to the floor with a squeal as I yelled.

"Hit the floor now!"

I'd just started to drop to the floor when I heard a clink of glass cracking then a 'thunk' into the wood top of the breakfast bar where my mid lung had been in line of. Then I felt a burning at the top of my left shoulder. My headache disappeared in the surge of adrenalin that flooded through me. My brain started racing and I had to slow it down just so I could see the options it threw at me.

Zeaya had hauled George down while I kept my hand on Maisie's foot so she wouldn't get back up.

"Zeaya, safe 'C'. One for you and one for me, and keep your arse down. In fact, everyone stay flat to the floor until I say otherwise." I ordered as I watched the red dot travel around the room.

"Shit! Shit! Shit!" I muttered as I crawled to the windows at the front of the house.

"W-wh-what's g-g-going on?" Maisie whimpered.

"I've become a target." I stated bluntly as I watched Zeaya rush back into the room. "Hit the floor you silly cow." I snapped at her.

Zeaya stared at me in surprise as she complied then crawled the rest of the way to me. She handed my rifle to me and we both cautiously peered out two different windows to see if we could spot the shooter. I glanced back at the dot but couldn't tell which direction it was coming from other than from the front of the house.

"George, without getting yourself shot I want the flour please." I stated as I belly crawled back towards the breakfast bar.

Once he'd handed it to me I went back to the centre of the lounge room and started throwing flour into the air. "Zeaya, see if you can follow the trajectory." I just kept throwing handfuls of flour around the room for the beam to travel through. Those old crime shows were good for something after all.

The beam travelled slowly and methodically around the room.

"Got it, I think." She stated and I made my way over to her. She proceeded to point it out to me. "That house across the street, in that front room off to the left... our left that is."

"Yeah, okay, I see it. Damn! We can't just go shooting into the house. Do you know if the Carters are home or not?" I asked as I looked at the window of that room through my scope.

"Nah, no idea. If they are then they're probably dead."

Maisie let out a little whimper at Zeaya's comment. We ignored her as I ignored the ache in my heart at the thought.

"Okay, I can see a partial of a dark shape of a person, just a shoulder perhaps. We can't take the chance of just wounding the hitter just in case the Carters are alive." Then without turning around...

"Maisie, crawling on your belly, get to your room and activate the surveillance system you have around the house and stay out of view of your window. George, slide me the two-way so Maisie can let me know what's going on. Zeaya, help me close all these curtains so the hit man doesn't have a view in."

I didn't wait to see if Maisie and George did as I instructed, as Zeaya and I set about drawing all the curtains closed. Once done, she and I sat beside each other with our backs to the wall. The shooter was good. They were calm and hadn't rushed the shot nor wasted any ammunition when we were drawing curtains.

"Well, looks like they know who LaMuerteViene is." Zeaya murmured.

"Damn it! This is so the last thing I need right now." I muttered.

"Cow huh?"

"Yeah sorry. I didn't want you getting shot." I responded with a shrug then winced as it hurt.

"You're bleeding." She frowned at me.

"Just a flesh wound. It'll stop soon enough."

Out the corner of my eye, I saw her do a 'eh okay' type movement of head and one shoulder.

"Charles called earlier. He wants you in the office by 1530 hours today."

If it wasn't for the fact that I was used to dealing with weird, I would have thought our switch in discussion was strange. However, I was used to this sort of thing and just went with the flow. I peered at my watch.

"Ah crap." I pressed the button on the two-way. "Maisie, call triple zero and tell them you saw someone with a gun creep into number 15 and that you don't think it was the residents, and you heard what sounded like something breaking or a loud noise of some sort but you aren't sure what it was. Then let me know what you see outside Sweetie."

"Saw a gun huh?" Zeaya gazed at me with a small smile and a raised eyebrow.

I shrugged then regretted it as it intensified the pain in my shoulder.

"Fastest way I know to get the cops here. As soon as they arrive in the street, dash out and lock these away. We don't need the extra attention if we can help it. When they turn up I'll wheel my bike through the back yard, through the back neighbour's yard and head to work that way. Sorry to ditch you guys with the police but I can't afford to lose my 'day' job."

"Don't worry about it. We can handle it. Go and get yourself ready now and I'll put the babies to bed." Zeaya stated.

With a slight smile I handed her my rifle then crawled to my bedroom after thanking George and shoving the two-way into the back pocket of my jeans. When I arrived at my room, while still low to the floor, I reached up and opened the door just a crack as I couldn't remember if I'd opened the curtains or not. Now would not be a good time to get myself severely wounded or, worse, dead.

After a pause I then lay back down on the floor and slowly pushed the door open. I chose only to open it half way. Wide enough for me to get through without bumping into it, but not wide enough to advertise the door opening.

"Sonja? There is no movement outside at all." Maisie's voice came from my back pocket.

I was so tired that the irrelevant thought of 'talking out of my arse' came to mind and I had the stupid urge to giggle. A bullet whizzed past me to 'thunk' into the wall behind me at hip level if I'd been standing., My urge to laugh was instantly gone as I reached for the two-way in my back pocket.

"Sonja, you okay?" Zeaya instantly called from the lounge room. With the house so quiet at the moment, it's not surprising she heard it hit the wall.

"Yeah it missed." I called back then grabbed the two-way. "Thanks Sweetie, just keep monitoring. As soon as we hear the police arrive I'm off to the office." I responded back as I crawled forward and closed the curtains of the front windows. Then I crawled over to the sliding door and closed its curtains as well. While sitting on the floor I got dressed.

Very briefly I looked at my injury and noted that while it stung like hell, it was only a graze like I'd originally thought. So I put a big band-aid on it. While dressing, I heard the sirens of the police arriving. I headed to the garage.

"Okay kiddies, I'm out of here. Call me if you need to." I said as I threw the two-way to George as I passed him.

Grabbing jacket, helmet and gloves, I donned them then wheeled the bike out the back door of the garage. Continuing to wheel it until it was on the street behind our place, I then slowly rode off so as not to call attention to myself. For once I was grateful for the broken fence between the two houses.

"Afternoon Charles. Sorry I'm late; there was a drama at home." I said as I entered in a slight rush.

Charles looked at me from head to toe and back again. "Not your mother is it?"

"No, nothing like that." I answered as I placed my helmet, gloves and jacket on the floor between my desk and the wall.

"Not your usual attire for the office." There was a hint of amusement in Charles's voice.

"I had to make a quick getaway and bike was better than car." Now that I was away from the situation at home the adrenalin had worn off and I was feeling tired again. I could feel the headache once more and the bullet graze burned like hell. I also realised I was starving as I hadn't eaten since at the café the previous night.

"Are you okay Sonja? You don't look so well." He asked with concern.

"Yeah, I'm fine. I'm just tired. I didn't sleep all too well last night." I responded as I sat in my chair but only giving him half the truth.

Charles just stood beside me without saying a word.

I gazed up at him in silent questioning confusion.

"Go home Sonja. This can wait till tomorrow. Don't come in till ten and you can leave at four. However, there's another business dinner tomorrow night at the same address and time as Friday just gone. Be there please."

"Are you sure Charles? I can still do my job you know." I frowned at him.

"As much as I'm enjoying seeing you out of your usual office attire, yes I'm sure. Go and enjoy the evening off and I don't want to see you until ten tomorrow. Now go."

I started to open my mouth to say something. Instead, he placed his hands on the back of my shoulders and just hauled gently me out of my chair and shooed me out. I was stunned at his first non-professional treatment of me, just because I looked tired.

I decided to stop trying to argue. I grabbed my gear and headed out the door. In reality, I was pleased to be going home. I planned on an early night.

By 1638 hours I was back home – having been caught in the weekend traffic returning home from a weekend away, but the police were still there with the street blocked off.

"Sorry Miss but you can't come through here." An officer stated when he stopped me.

"I live just there. What happened to the Carters?" I said as I pointed out my home while looking at the house, which was swarming with police, across the street from mine. I could see the flashing of cameras going off in a number of rooms.

"Proof of address please. You knew the Carters?"

"Knew?" I'd just gotten my answer. I dug into my pocket to grab my licence. "We're neighbourly friends to the point of sharing a barbecue or two every few weekends. The children as well?"

"How many lived in the house?"

"There was Jackie and Len Carter then there was Alice, Benny and Lenny, their three children. Please, what happened?"

"I'm sorry Miss, I can't give out any details but all five are dead."

I closed my eyes and hoped it'd been quick for all of them.

"Can I go to my home now please?" I asked as tears thickened my voice.

The officer checked my licence front and back then handed it back to me. He stepped aside and unnecessarily motioned me forward. I rode the few metres to my driveway and into the garage. Once in the garage, with its door closed, I just sat on my bike with my helmeted head against the tank. I couldn't believe they'd been killed just so the hit man could get a shot at me. It was stupid and reckless and brought unnecessary attention to the situation.

A hand touched my shoulder and I jumped in fright. After the initial scare, I peeled my gloves off then took off my glasses then helmet. I looked at Zeaya.

"It's not your fault Sugar and you know it." She said gently to me.

"I know. Doesn't make it any easier to bear though." I said bleakly. Not all assassins are cold hearted killers.

"Come on, George has food and a hot cuppa waiting for you." She said softly as she took my helmet and gloves from me.

I hopped off the bike, took my jacket off and placed it where it belonged then went into the kitchen. Once there I found the aforementioned food and drink, as well as an extra little plate.

"Have you guys touched these with your bare fingers?" I asked as I stared at the two bullets.

"No. I wore gloves when I dug them out." Zeaya informed.

I sighed. I had no choice. Despite my number one job, I was still law abiding.

"Good. Because we're about to have the police in here. Make sure our licences and memberships are readily accessible should they search, discover and request." I stood then went outside.

In Australia civilians can't own guns, even with a licence, if they weren't a member of a gun club. Hence the need of the memberships.

In less than a couple of minutes we had two detectives in the house examining the bullet holes in the windows, kitchen and hallway, asking whose bedroom the bullet hole was outside of, etcetera, etcetera, etcetera. Until...

"This bullet has blood on it." Detective Martin, the younger of the two, stated.

"The blood's mine." I informed. That was one of the reasons why I had no choice. I had no idea if they would be able to trace it back to me or not. I couldn't afford to be caught out like that. The death of the Carters was the other reason. Regardless of what Zeaya and I said in the garage, their deaths were my fault.

Detectives Harris and Martin gazed at me in surprise as Harris asked, "Where?"

I pulled the shoulder of my t-shirt aside to show a large self-adhesive band-aid on the shoulder. "It's just a graze. I was standing at the breakfast bar and I was in the process of crouching down when I felt it graze me."

While I was mostly law abiding, I still couldn't reveal the red dot. To me it screamed assassin and would hint that there was something more to me than I was admitting to the two men in front of me. So, I omitted that little detail.

Harris's expression became unreadable while Martin appeared hostile.

"Why did you leave the scene of the crime?" Harris asked.

"While it isn't a reasonable excuse, I had to go to work."

They stared at me in disbelief.

"My manager had left a message telling me to be in by 3:30 this afternoon. I was late but that wasn't a problem. He thought I looked tired so he sent me back home. You can call him if you like. Except, I didn't tell him anything about this."

"We'll do just that and he will know by the time we've spoken with him. Please provide his details. Is there anything else you've neglected to tell us about?" Harris asked sternly.

"No. I have told you everything. Honest." I said.

"How did you manage to leave without getting shot again?" Detective Martin asked in a slightly less hostile tone that before, but not by much.

"I wheeled the bike out the door at the back of the garage then cut through the back neighbour's yard via the broken fence line and onto the street back there." I answered as I handed them Charles's details.

Detective Harris was making notes when he looked up at me with a frown of curiosity.

"*When* did you leave here?"

"As soon as I heard the sirens." I responded ruefully.

"You know you've done the wrong thing, why did you do it in the first place?" Harris asked.

"As lame as it might sound I didn't want to risk losing my job. I happen to enjoy it and even though the money isn't fantastic it's still good enough."

"Don't go anywhere Miss Reilly. While you may have been another victim, your actions were not entirely responsible. We'll be talking to you again soon." Harris instructed.

I just nodded. I was exhausted and not from the shooting or the third degree; even though they did add to it. After the two men left, I sat down and had my dinner after George reheated it and made me a fresh cup of tea. Then I chased it all with a second cup of tea and some pain killers.

Fifteen minutes after I'd finished, I'd crawled into bed and fell asleep.

I jerked awake to the intense emotions of anger, frustration and concern. And my mobile ringing.

At first I'd thought the emotions had been part of the dream, but what I could remember of it there was nothing in it to warrant those particular feelings. I glanced at the clock and discovered I only had roughly thirty minutes of sleep.

I fumbled for the phone and slid it open.

"I'm not alive. Go away." I muttered into the phone. Only to have to wrench it away from my ear as the person on the other end started yelling at me.

"WHY THE HELL DIDN'T YOU TELL ME YOU'D BEEN SHOT?!"

"Charles, you scream at me like that again and I'll hang up. Boss or not." I muttered sleepily. "Besides the bullet missed me. It was just a graze, a bullet burn so to speak..."

"You should have told me about it when you were in earlier..."

"I take it the police have talked to you then..."

"Of course they bloody well did..."

"Fine. I'm going back to sleep Charles. I'll see you tomorrow. Bye." I said as we kept interrupting each other and I hung up without waiting for him to say 'bye' back.

As sleep sucked me under, I had a feeling I was forgetting something.

# Chapter 12

I awoke at 0600 hours, showered, dressed and had a light breakfast by 0730 hours. Five minutes later, while still sitting at the breakfast bar, I was on the laptop hoping to catch hold of the Helmsman.

<Helmsman> what's wrong and how's your mark going?

<LaMuerteViene> what makes you think something is wrong? The mark is still alive and well as I've only managed to narrow it down to three, possibly two, men

<Helmsman> I don't normally hear from you during a job. So, what's wrong? Don't make me ask again

I took an unhurried deep breath then let it out slowly.

<LaMuerteViene> I've become a target to another hit man

There was a short pause...

<Helmsman> since when?

<LaMuerteViene> yesterday

<Helmsman> were you hit?

<LaMuerteViene> grazed, just a bullet burn, nothing else. I'm fine honest


Another pause of almost three or so minutes...


<LaMuerteViene> Helmsman?


He was still listed as being in the chat.


<Helmsman> I'll try to find out who's taken a hit out on you and let you know so check in again tomorrow

<LaMuerteViene> I'm suspecting it is just a 'I'm better than you and I'll prove it by killing you' type hit

<Helmsman> either way, be careful


Then the Helmsman was gone.

After shutting the program down, I then perused my mark's itinerary and was relieved he had nothing down for the previous night. Looking at the clock I realised I still had over an hour before I could leave to go to work, so I decided to organise what I would wear to the dinner party later that night.

I'd decided on a simple ankle length, long sleeved, 1950s styled royal blue cotton velveteen dress with a heart shaped bust line. I then searched for, found and dusted off the velvet colour matching high heeled court shoes. After a bit more digging around I found a navy blue knitted shawl. I set the lot aside then set about sorting out the make-up I would wear and organised everything ready for my bath for when I got home. Since my hair was short, I thankfully didn't have to worry about a fancy hairdo of any kind. Hairstyles are so not my thing.

After all that, I still had fifteen minutes so I decided to fill the gang in on what happened on Saturday night and handed Maisie the camera where it was hidden on the far right of the breakfast bar between a cream coloured ceramic cookie jar and a matching bread box. By the time I'd finished my report to them, I then left for work.

When I first arrived at work, Charles noisily fussed over me in regards to me having been shot. I had to show him the graze just to shut him up so we could get some work done. Because it looked like I was about to strip, to reveal the minor wound, the rest of the office knew within five minutes or less as to what had happened to me. Unfortunately.

As a result, for the rest of the morning, I was bombarded with questions as to what had happened. It was beside the point that the deaths had been on the news, I just didn't want to talk about it any more. While Charles either hovered around me or stared at me, appearing to be thinking hard. About what I didn't know.

Despite my hours at work being shorter than normal, the day was long and a struggle for me for some reason. I was tired even though I'd had plenty of sleep, my mind hadn't seemed to want to stay on track and I generally felt listless. Maybe I was coming down with a cold, maybe it was the lack of details of the current hit driving me crazy or maybe it was something else altogether I had no clue about. I mentally shrugged as I had no idea what the reason was.

I was certainly pleased when the day came to an end and I headed home.

"Wake me up at 1830 hours please." I requested from my three house mates as I passed them. I stripped out of my work clothes, placed them on the chair then crashed on the bed and that was the last thing I remembered.

After sleeping late and deliberately soaking in the bath for a little longer than usual, I arrived well and truly fashionably late at the time of 2000 hours. The gateman was the same one as last time and he recognised me.

"You can park over there Miss Reilly." He informed me with a smile.

"Thank you." I blinked at him in surprise and did as I was told.

As I was getting out of my car I felt anticipation. I paused slightly. I hadn't been feeling anything remotely like it at any time since I heard about having to be back at the house which loomed over me. My mind started to conjure up the image of the last time I'd been inside.

Oh what a mistake that was as I worked quickly to squash it. I managed to do so before it could fully form as heat of a blush rushed up my face. The last thing I needed was certain set of hormones waking up.

Then I experienced amusement and I didn't even know why because I didn't even feel remotely amused about anything. I frowned then gave a slight shrug of confusion and continued up the steps into the house.

Even the doorman was the same man as he too greeted me with a smile while he took my shawl. Charles practically pounced on me as soon as I entered the living room.

"I didn't think you were coming." He stated as he gently but firmly grabbed my arm. His fingers curled around my upper right arm and gave no indication of letting go any time soon.

"I overslept." I looked at him with raised eyebrows, not expecting the attitude.

"Are you sure you are alright?" He asked in concern after gazing at me harder.

"Yes, I'm okay. Honest. I just haven't been sleeping well since Saturday that's all."

He was about to say something but my attention was captured by the sight of the door near the top of the stairs opening. The door to the room I'd discovered more than I'd bargained on, on Friday evening.

"Dumb fucking luck!" I whispered in shock. My heart started to pound a little harder as realisation hit me and two plus two were equalling a shockingly jolting four.

"Did you say something?" Charles asked me in a quiet tone as he glanced at me before turning his attention back to the person exiting that room.

"I said who is that?" I couldn't take my eyes off the man who'd paused at the top of the stairs. I stared at him with a mixture of embarrassment, surprise, and desire. With the desire inspiring more embarrassment.

He gazed at his guests then our eyes locked and he chose that moment to leisurely descend to join us in the living room. Without taking his eyes from mine. Talk about a grand entrance.

"That's right, you haven't seen him before. That's our boss Darius Guillaume." Charles answered.

I mentally groaned as I thought 'So dumb fucking luck.'

Darius Guillaume was the same Darius I'd seen in the café with Orenda Saturday night. Also, if him coming out of that room was any indication then he was the same delectable 'bod' I'd seen Friday evening. No wonder he'd stared at me in recognition Saturday night.

The way things were going for me lately. he would also turn out to be my target since he did fit the vague description of my mark and he had been at all venues so far. Always in threes.

"Evening Charles. And you must be the ever elusive Sonja Reilly." Darius's deep-ish voice said. His voice had the same effect on me as that night in the café.

Charles chose that moment to let go of my arm. For some reason I got the impression he didn't want to but seemed to have no choice in the matter. Not that I understood why.

"Must I?" I asked in glib surprise. "Well, I would hate to be responsible for creating any disappointment and therefore ruining the party. So, I guess I'll just have to be her for the evening." I surprised myself at sounding normal while my insides felt like a hormonal teenager.

Charles quietly chuckled at my flippancy.

Darius had to be about ten centimetres taller than me, making him roughly 180cm I guess. His shoulders were slightly broader than mine but had narrower hips. He has an exceptionally pale olive complexion, but I suppose that's typical for a vampire.

He was wearing a suit similar to Saturday and it wasn't an off-the-rack suit with the way it fitted him. He seemed to have a thing for gold silk shirts because he was wearing one again. Darker and with a pattern compared to Saturday's though and it too hugged his torso rather snuggly.

166

However, I knew what his body looked like without and I had to fight another blush at the thought.

He had straight brown hair with gingery highlights which was neatly trimmed and just brushed the top of his collar, and intense dark blue eyes. Nothing really stood out on him at first glance. His lips were characteristically male and chiselled along with his squarish jaw. His nose was mostly straight – had been broken at least once – and was neither too large nor too small. While his eyebrows were a little heavy and thick for his face but not obscenely so.

I still thought he was attractive to gaze at and his voice still did wonderful things to me. I was so in trouble if we stayed in each other's company for too long.

Darius grinned at my comment and I felt amusement. A moment later I frowned at him with a dash of panic. It was his feelings I was sensing? I didn't understand and I didn't think I had the time to try to work it out.

His smile mostly disappeared as he gazed at me intently. Then he placed my hand on his arm with his other hand firmly on top of mine, effectively trapping me. Then he sstarted circulating throughout the room, taking me with him. I had no choice with that grip of his or I'm sure I would have been dragged along and I hate making a scene. Especially at my expense.

Mentally, I was barely there as my mind reeled from trying to comprehend what was happening to me. As I'd mentioned before, as far as I knew I wasn't a sensitive. I'd certainly never experienced anyone else's emotions before Friday night, so why was I tuning in to his emotions and no one else's? I had no answer and didn't know who I could turn to, to ask.

Something I was blindly gazing at brought me out of my mental freeze. I frowned a little as I watched a woman stagger slightly in our direction. Darius, Charles, three clients and two staff were talking away.

While I was spacing out with incomprehension when something about her caught my attention. I watched as she wove her way towards us like she'd drank too much. In her ten centimetre heeled stilettos, I was surprised she was still on her feet.

Then I looked into her eyes again and that was where I realised something was not quite right. For a little longer, I observed everything about her to confirm my suspicion.

Her eyes weren't those of someone who had imbibed too much alcohol regardless of her actions. They were too clear and watchful. Looking at her I then realised she wasn't staff or client, and all guests were either staff or client.

She staggered up to us so she was between but behind Charles and Amanda who was one of the clients.

Since Darius had released his grip of me while he was talking, I removed my hand from his arm – now that I was out of my mental haze – and casually walked up to Charles. I put my hand on his arm as if I was going to say something to him when the woman pulled out a gun and aimed it in my direction. Such a fucking reckless bitch!

She wasn't after Darius as I'd first thought because he was off to my left a little. Our eyes locked and a number of things happened at once...

I shoved Charles and Amanda in opposite directions away from her and I.

"Sonja!" Darius called out as I started to reach out to push her gun hand up towards the ceiling.

The gun went off and I was falling backwards instead.

Two men rushed in to disarm and restrain her before she could pull the trigger again.

"Call triple zero and tell them to send the police and an ambulance immediately." Darius ordered as he bent over me. "Sonja?" I could hear the frown and the concern in his voice.

I just blinked then, "Shit! That hurt!" I groaned through clenched teeth as my shoulder – the same freaking shoulder as the day before I might add – burned. I frowned at Darius.

"You've been shot. When did she fire a second round?"

"She didn't. The bullet went through you and hit me." He stated quietly.

I fought to keep my eyes open as I heard the arrival of sirens. Either they were quick or I had lost some time.

He stared at me intently then his hand gripped my wrist rather firmly, almost bordering on painful.

"You and I need to talk when you get out of the hospital." He said in a quiet, intense tone that brooked no argument.

I looked at him in confusion as he was moved away by the ambulance attendants.

"Slowly breathe this in until I say otherwise." One of the attendants ordered and I was given something to inhale, that left a horrid taste on my tongue, while they started treating my injury.

"You again." Said the voice of Detective Harris as he crouched down beside me.

Whatever I was inhaling may have tasted horrible but I wasn't feeling much in the way of pain. I wasn't feeling much of anything anymore in fact.

"The bullet that hit me is in Darius." I murmured as I fought to stay awake but failed.

# *Chapter 13*

Waking up, I realised two things at the same time. My shoulder hurt horrendously and the typical hospital smell. Why is it that just by smell one can tell they're in a hospital before visual confirmation?

I groaned. I wasn't sure if it was from the pain or the smell or both.

"Sonja?" Maisie's soft voice squeaked fearfully beside me.

I opened my eyes and took hold of her hand. "I'm okay Sweetie. Just hurts like hell that's all." I said with a half-hearted smile.

She wiped at her tears as she smiled back. Then I noted she was the only one at my bedside.

"Where are the other two?" I asked.

Maisie opened her mouth, but...

"They are waiting outside which is where you can wait." Harris stated as he walked in.

I took hold of Maisie's hand to prevent her from leaving.

"Detective, while I understand you have a crime to solve, that doesn't mean your manners can go by the way-side. I'm responsible for Maisie and it's actually a very big deal for the effort she's put in to be here with me." I stated as I kept eye contact with him.

Harris looked like he wanted to explode but instead he breathed slowly then said, "You're right, I apologise for my lack of manners." Then he turned to Maisie, "Maisie, can you please join your two friends in the corridor while I talk to Miss Reilly?"

Maisie looked like a scared little mouse as her eyes locked with mine. I gave Maisie's hand a squeeze and a small nod and she left.

"Thank you Detective."

"Why would someone want to kill you Miss Reilly? I don't think you've been very honest with me." Detective Harris questioned.

I had to lie. While I didn't like lying to the police I had no choice as I couldn't afford the discovery of my number one profession.

"I have no idea why someone would want to kill me. Does your question mean the bullet from Darius is the same from my house?" The moment I'd asked, I knew the answer was no. Rifles and pistols use different ammunition. However, I also realised my question aided in me appearing innocent of such knowledge. Therefore, it diverted some of the suspicion from me.

Hopefully.

"No. The two bullets from your house were fired from a rifle while the one that hit you then lodged in Mr Guillaume was shot from a handgun."

"So not the same person then?" I frowned as I thought it would have been the same person since she seemed to have targeted me.

"I didn't say that. The bullet removed from Mr Guillaume was fired from the same gun as the one used to kill the Carters." Harris was watching me intently.

I closed my eyes. There was nothing I could do to change what had happened but I couldn't suppress the couple of tears that managed to escape.

"Apart from being my boss, you know what Darius is?" I asked as I looked at him again.

"Why don't you tell me." Harris said with deceptive politeness.

Again. I closed my eyes in annoyance while biting my tongue. The last thing I needed was to turn him against me just because of what might come out of my mouth. Even though I understood he was just doing his job, I didn't appreciate the round about ways the police have.

"Miss Reilly."

I sighed.

"Just for the record... Things would go faster and smoother if you guys didn't beat around the bush with your twenty questions. It wouldn't hurt for you guys to actually answer questions in the effort of speeding things up. I'm the victim here, not the perpetrator." I stated tiredly, but before I could continue with his request...

"Just tell me Miss Reilly." Harris stated with a hint of well-rehearsed boredom.

"Darius is a vampire who seems to be highly placed in Orenda's entourage. I discovered that fact quite by accident on Saturday evening. However, I'd never met him before even though I'd been in his house for another work related party the night before that. I hadn't seen him that night.

"I'd left before he'd made his appearance... after embarrassing myself by accidently walking in on a naked person in one of the bedrooms. Even though I'd seen Darius at a café on Saturday night, I didn't know who he was other than being a vampire and aligned with Orenda. I didn't connect two and two until... last night?"

"Yes, you were shot last night. Who was the naked person?"

"I don't know, his face was in shadows."

"Then how did you know it was a he?"

"The face was in shadow but not the rest of his naked body. I didn't stay beyond the couple seconds while I was shocked over my discovery."

Harris never gave anything away other than disbelief at certain points, or boredom.

"How could you not know Mr Guillaume was your boss?"

"I'd never seen him before. My office hours are always during daylight and Charles was the one who'd employed me since the position was for his personal assistant."

"What about previous business parties?"

"Friday's was the first I'd ever been to. I arrived at seven, mingled, got bored, checked out the house, discovering more than I bargained for, and left roughly round eight before Darius had decided to join the party."

"What has any of this to do with why you were shot?"

"What if Darius was the real target? What if the shooter thought I was *attached* to Darius in a personal way? They would have had no knowledge that I didn't know him..." I offered to the detective. I knew it was a stretch since Darius was right there in the room as well.

"Are you attached to Mr Guillaume in a... *personal* way?"

"No." At least that was the truth... As far as I knew it to be.

"Thank you Miss Reilly. If I need to clarify anything then I'll be in contact." Then Detective Harris left.

As soon as he walked out, my three house mates walked in. The four of us smiled at each other then I turned my attention to the iv dripping blood back into me. The bag was almost empty so I reached up and closed off the drip, detached the tube from the cannula then ripped the cannula from my arm. There was a slight sting of the syringe coming out but nothing too bad.

"Sonja, what are you doing?" George asked in surprise.

"Yes Miss Reilly, what *are* you doing?" The Doctor asked when she walked in. She was about my height with naturally blonde hair and suntanned skin. Her pale grey-blue eyes frowned as she stared at me.

Out of the corner of my eye I saw Zeaya stare at the doctor with avid interest. I secretly hoped the doctor was single and preferred women as a love interest. Anything to take her interest off me. Other than that I didn't let on I'd seen Zeaya's reaction.

I then noted the doctor gazed at my three friends. I wasn't sure, but it seemed as if her steel grey eyes lingered on Zeaya a little longer than the others before looking back at me. Maybe my private little wish was going to come true. I could only hope.

"I'm checking out of here whether you like it or not Doc. Sorry." I stated bluntly.

"While I believe it's pointless of me saying so, I would prefer if you stayed in for another day or two. However, I can see by your expression you have no intentions of staying. Just stay there till I get your release forms." She turned around to leave.

"Five minutes max Doc and then I'm going home." I called out as she walked out the room. I then threw the covers back. "Clothing?" I asked the three around me.

Zeaya handed me a bag.

"George, go outside please while I change."

"Sure." George said then left the room.

With Zeaya's and Maisie's help I was dressed by the time the doctor came back. I signed where she told me to then she place my arm in a sling to help support the shoulder muscles for a few days.

"I still think you should stay but don't do anything else stupid."

"Thanks Doc." Was all I said as we grabbed whatever belongings I had then walked out. As I dressed, I found my mark's itinerary. I shoved it into a pocket in my jeans.

With Maisie beside me and the other two behind me, the walk to the car was quiet. After we got in and left the hospital...

"Take me to Darius's place then you three go home. My car's still at his house I believe, so I'll drive myself back after he and I have talked."

No one argued with me and the rest of the drive was done in silence. When we arrived, after directing them there, I got out and waved at them as they left.

I turned to the gate and started to walk towards it as it opened. Well, that saved me from having to use the intercom and proved my point about hidden security measures. I slowly continued to the front door and it also opened before I could knock.

As soon as I stepped through, I noted how dark it was inside. Then a hand gripped my upper left arm – sending pain through my shoulder, the door closed and I was swung around till my back slammed against the wall.

I briefly registered Darius in front of me as I rammed my knee up between his legs only to drop us both as his pain ripped right through me.

"What have you done to me?" I gasped at him in a barely audible voice as I curled into a foetal position.

He recovered quickly, far faster than I could, and grabbed me by the throat. He lifted me to my feet and slammed me against the wall again.

"Who paid you? You were also at the second venue Saturday evening so who paid you?" His voice deeper than usual snarled.

"Don't know, middle man." I managed to croak out in a whisper as my feet dangled slightly. I had to grip his wrist with both my hands in the effort to ease the pressure of being hanged by his strength alone. The sling hung uselessly around my neck.

"What do you mean a 'middle man'?" Darius demanded in a fading voice, my hands dropped away from his wrist as I was losing the fight with the encroaching blackness.

Suddenly he let go of me, an instant withdrawal of his hand and arm, and I crumpled into a heap on the floor gasping for air. Then his hand was pressed against the base of my neck after he shoved me hard against the wall once more.

"Start talking if you wish to stay alive." He snarled again with his fangs flashing mere centimetres away from my face.

"I didn't know who you were until last night…" I wheezed out as I fought past my pain and his anger pounding within me.

"You saw me Friday evening when you entered my room." He frowned.

"But I didn't see your face…" I whispered. His comment confirming my suspicions about him being the one in that room.

"How could you not have? We were just metres away from each other." He demanded.

"Your face… it was in shadow. I didn't know who you were until last night." I repeated softly as I continued my fight with my pain and his anger.

Unexpectedly, his hand removed itself from me and I collapsed the rest of the way to the floor.

"Then why did you save me last night?" Without even looking I could hear the frown tainting his confusion.

"I didn't. I was the target. Are you truly aligned with Orenda or spying against her?" I murmured as I closed my eyes.

"I am her General." Despite his surprise, he was still frowning. His emotions were now drowning out my pain and I was becoming lost in them.

Being battered by my own pain and his emotions caused me to be rather uncoordinated. I fumbled my hand into my pants pocket, pulled out the itinerary I had and slid it over to him.

"Yours or someone else's, fitting your general description?" I whispered, too weak for anything more.

After a pause of paper unfolding and a few moments silence.

"This is mine, no other. How…" Abruptly, he swore and lifted me up so I was sitting upright but leaning against him. He then pressed my face against his chest.

"Drink Sonja."

Darius had said it with such command I couldn't resist. Not even a token struggle. Even mentally I couldn't fight. It was in that moment that I realised I'd never been challenged in such a manner before and therefore wasn't as strong as I'd always thought. I never realised I was so weak minded until that moment, so I drank. I drank deeply until the cut healed itself.

He bound me to him.

As soon as I felt the compulsion release me, I'd started to slide away from him to the floor. Only he stopped me and ripped the shoulder of my shirt away. Then I put up more of a struggle as I finally realised what he planned to do. Even as I did so, I knew I couldn't stop him.

"No, please." I pleaded in a whisper.

I knew I'd left the hospital too soon but I hadn't expected to be fighting off a vampire once I was at his place. He'd seemed so civilised, I'd momentarily forgotten what predators vampires are.

"Be still Sonja. You are bleeding too much." He murmured.

Then slowly, tenderly, he lapped up my blood around and over the entry wound while his hands and arms held me as a lover would. As pleasurable little shivers went through me I fisted my hands in the side of his shirt unable to do anything more than that. Once done, he then pulled the remains of the top of my shirt away from my left shoulder and his mouth worked over the exit wound.

As much as I hated myself for it, I whimpered with my pain, in weakness and from his combined need and pleasure. A small part of me whispered to me, if I was honest with myself then I would admit that I too enjoyed the feel of his need and pleasure.

With a final flick of his tongue he moved away from my shoulder. A moment later I was cradled in his arms as we sat on the floor.

"I am sorry Sonja. I had not intended on reopening your wound." He said softly as his finger feathered along my cheek.

I stared at him as I felt his emotions deep within me instead of just brushing my mind. His presence in my mind was an almost solid thing now, I could feel it. While I knew, I couldn't stop myself from asking.

"What have you done to me?" I whispered. I stared at him for a few more moments before I slowly moved into a seated position.

"You were bleeding too much, I had to stop it." Darius said quietly.

Despite the pain I couldn't stop myself, I didn't want to stop myself. I kissed him. I wrapped my arms around his shoulders and kissed him deeply. I held him so tightly one would have thought I was trying to physically merge with him. While I felt his need, want, of me all I really understood was how badly I wanted, needed, him right then.

Darius curled one arm around my back then moved us both slightly and slipped his other arm behind my knees then stood so he was carrying me. With my arms around his neck and my head on his shoulder, he then proceeded up the stairs to his bedroom and huge bed.

Lying in the middle of his enormous bed, I was feeling both

happy and content. Both his and my own. I was snuggled against his side with my head on his shoulder, a leg draped over his and a hand on his chest.

When we had arrived in his room, he'd forced me to sleep for a few hours. After waking up, I'd just spent the most amazing afternoon with the delectable bod that had invaded my thoughts for the past half week. He was better in the flesh than in my imaginings. My blissful thoughts were interrupted when my stomach grumbled rather loudly. I flushed with embarrassment as I buried my face against his chest.

"Come on, let's get you something to eat." Darius laughed.

"Only if I can cook in your amazing kitchen." I said with excitement building within me at the thought of having free rein in that wonderful kitchen of his.

"Of course you can." He responded with a big grin as he handed me a dark blue velveteen robe then dressed into a black one himself.

We both left the room bare footed. Once in the kitchen I started going through everything.

"While you have an awesome house, you're a vampire. Why would you have a kitchen such as this?" I asked in amazement as I checked it out all over again.

"Just because I can not eat does not mean the food has to be prepared elsewhere whenever I host dinners or parties. I have a friend who loves to cook even if he too can not eat but there are always mortals around whenever there is a gathering here."

I just stared at him in surprise then proceeded to do a simple fried rice with bacon, egg and shallots while Darius took it upon himself to make a cup of tea for me. We didn't really talk as he just watched me while I moved around his kitchen cooking.

We didn't talk during dinner either as he just encouraged me to eat. I could sense his joy and amusement as he watched me. While it was embarrassing for me to be watched while devouring food, I continued eating as I was so hungry.

Once finished I started to collect the dishes to wash them when he stopped me and said in a low voice, "There is a dishwasher right there. Besides I can think of other things to do."

Then he started nuzzling my ear and one thing led to another. We didn't get to leave the kitchen.

# Chapter 14

When I awoke, it was Wednesday mid-morning and I was nicely horrified of the past eighteen or so hours I'd willingly spent with Darius. I gazed across at the studly naked vampire who was sleeping beside me on his back with the sheet pooled around his hips. It just barely covered him and I fought the urge to touch him. Anywhere, everywhere.

Strangely, I wasn't horrified at us having spent the time together as that had been so enjoyable. I was horrified at how quickly I'd been willing to have sex with him. Normally I waited until I'd gotten to know the men to work out if it would be more than a one night stand before becoming intimate with them. But not this time.

I was confused at my recklessness as I generally wasn't like that. However, I knew I would continue, that I wouldn't restrain myself while I was with him.

Because of that realisation I decided I needed time, space, to think things through. I knew I wouldn't be able to do that once he awoke. So I gently crawled out of bed, put my pants on and grabbed my shirt. Looking at it I realised I couldn't wear it since the left shoulder was torn and all bloodied. I decided to rifle through his wardrobe and pinched one of his to wear instead.

A small price for him to pay for ruining mine I thought.

When I closed his wardrobe door I finally saw my shoulder injury. It looked almost healed. I flexed my arm and shoulder and it didn't hurt as much as it had yesterday when I'd left the hospital. Even the scar seemed a little fainter than before. I just stared at it in amazement then at him via the mirror before donning the shirt. I'd heard about the healing qualities of vampires but had never seen it in action.

Quietly leaving the room, with one more glance at him, I reluctantly and desperately made my way downstairs and out the door. I got into my car and as I neared the gate it opened and I left. I was amazed I'd been able to creep out without making a sound as I tend to bump into things when trying to sneak about in a non-professional capacity.

On the drive home, it barely registered that the day was chilly but beautiful.

I thought I would have some breathing space away from Darius's impressive and addictive presence. Instead, a panic and fear started settling within me as the distance between him and I grew. Panic for being away from Darius and fear in regards that panic.

However, despite our intimacy a few hours ago I was worried about what he would do with the information he knew about me. It would be nice to think after last night he wouldn't do anything but in reality I knew nothing about him. He was Orenda's General and I was hired to kill him after all.

I sighed as I tried to concentrate on my driving but thoughts of Darius kept sneaking in. Like he had since I first went to his house on Friday night. Since Monday, every time I gazed at him, my heart rate sped up and my breathing caught. I couldn't believe how hard and fast I'd fallen for him.

No matter how hard I tried, he kept creeping back into my thoughts. To make things worse, or to emphasise the point, Kylie Minogue's *'Can't Get You Out of My Head'* started playing on the radio.

Once back home twenty-eight minutes later...

"Damn it Sugar! You had us worried." Zeaya snapped at me as I walked in the door.

"I'm sorry. I didn't mean to cause you any concern. Darius and I discussed things..."

"Just what did you pair discuss for the past twenty-four hours?" George asked incredulously.

"It's only twenty hours maximum and I slept in one of his rooms when he invited me to stay. Besides he is my boss after all..."

"What do you mean he's your boss?" Zeaya asked with a frown.

"Discovered that little fact Monday evening while I was there for the business dinner. The house is his and he owns the company I work for." I said with a shrug.

"So, is he your mark or not?" Zeaya asked, still frowning.

"Yeah he is." I sighed. If she hadn't asked the question I wouldn't have said anything, however, she did ask.

All three just stared at me in shocked surprise.

"How did you find that out?" George asked in an incredulous tone.

"I showed him the itinerary and ask if he knew whose it was

and he said it was his."

"And he's still alive?" Zeaya was just full of questions.

"Yes he is." I simply stated, even though the situation was far from simple.

"Let me get this straight... He's a vampire, one of Orenda's people, your boss who you just spent the night with at his house, your mark and he's still alive?" Zeaya ticked off on her fingers as she stared at me in disbelief.

"Mmmm, yep, that about covers it." Was all I said then "George, can I please beg a cup of tea from you? I haven't had anything. I awoke before he did and came straight home." I said imploringly at him in the effort to change the subject.

He smiled and started making me one. George is a funny person. No matter what shit was happening if someone asked him to make something in the kitchen then he was happy. Shame I couldn't please Zeaya as easily. I saw my laptop on the breakfast bar and grabbed it. Zeaya didn't say anything so I opened up the chat program hoping Helmsman would be online.

<LaMuerteViene> Helmsman?

I sat there waiting to see if he was there. His name was listed in the online column. Almost half a cup of tea gone and five minutes later...

<Helmsman> what's wrong?
<LaMuerteViene> the one trying to kill me... is that just another hit man trying to prove themselves or have I

become a target for some reason?

<Helmsman> seems to be just another hit man trying to prove themselves so far as I haven't found out anything else but that doesn't mean there isn't a contract out on you. Now, what's wrong? You know how I hate to repeat myself

I paused a fraction...

<Helmsman> LaMuerteViene??

<LaMuerteViene> I'm compromised

<Helmsman> who by?!

<LaMuerteViene> my mark

<Helmsman> you know who your mark is?

<LaMuerteViene> yes

<Helmsman> who?!

<LaMuerteViene> Darius Guillaume

<Helmsman> Orenda's General? That Darius?

<LaMuerteViene> yes

It was a few moments before Helmsman responded.

<Helmsman> the hit is cancelled! Protect yourself Sonja. Go into hiding as I think you've been made, possibly by Orenda's enemies, maybe because you were taking so long to do the hit. Either way you *are* in danger

The panic that had been subsiding flared instantly as I read his words. To hell with another hit man making out my identity. How the hell had Helmsman made me?!

<LaMuerteViene> how the hell do you know who I am??? I'm outta here

Quickly I shut the chat program down and turned my laptop off without waiting to see Helmsman's response. Then I shoved away from the breakfast bar as I stared at the laptop. A second dose of panic ran rife through me. Who the hell was Helmsman that he would know the true identity of LaMuerteViene? How in the hell did he find out my true identity in the first place?!

I had no answer as I continued to stare at my laptop. And that scared me more than what Darius would do to me.

"Sonja? What's wrong?" Maisie asked in a confused voice.

George and Zeaya looked at me at Maisie's question.

I glanced at all three of them.

"I'm compromised by both my target and my middleman. Helmsman just cancelled the hit after I told him the name of my mark then he used my real name."

My friends looked as shocked as I felt.

"I'm out of here until further notice. I'm going into hiding but will have my secondary mobile with me if you need to contact me. I'll leave my primary mobile here. Just don't answer it. Anyway, it's up to you three to decide what you do with yourselves while I'm gone."

They just stared at me in stunned silence. I then turned towards Maisie.

"Maisie Sweetie, you need to decide whether you are going to stay or go. I'm sorry I can't take you with me. I'm not safe to be around at the moment. Not to mention the mark that seems to have been taken out on me." I gazed at all three of them in turn.

"I'm sorry."

Probably for the first time in my life I regretted my number one job and regretted getting them involved in that side of my life. I knew I was jumping to conclusions and making assumptions but I'd decided not to take any chances. Better that and be alive rather than dead.

I then rushed off to my bedroom, changed into my motorbike leathers and packed four days' worth of clothing into the panniers, hauled them out and attached them to my bike. Next, I grabbed my Weatherby rifle and my Sig Sauer P220 pistol with their appropriate licences, memberships and ammunition, and packed them onto the bike as well.

As the garage door was opening, I gazed over at the three of them one more time. They stood in the doorway of the garage/kitchen looking forlorn (George), lost (Maisie) and angrily worried (Zeaya). With a sigh, I then backed the bike out and left.

First, I went to one of my bank's local ATMs to withdraw enough money to last me more than a week. No way was I going to leave a trail of some kind for anyone to follow. Thankfully, I didn't have to worry about Charles and work as me having been shot took care of that side of things for a few more days at least.

Next, I left the comfort zone of the north side and headed to the south east of Brisbane until I found a little motel that had rooms with a little kitchen section in the Holland Park area. I dumped my gear into my room then headed out again to buy quick, microwaveable food.

I didn't know how long I was going to hide out but I figured a week would be ideal as that would make the hit and anything else regarding that situation over and done with.

Hopefully.

I stripped out of my leathers and boots, redressed into track pants and pullover, flopped down on the bed and stared up at the ceiling. The room was cold and I was shivering. However, the air conditioner looked old, rusty and very dusty so I ignored it. I didn't want to risk a fire in the effort of becoming warm and crawled under the covers instead. At least they were clean and fresh.

Exhausted with a mind that felt abused, I huddled there while I thought over the events since the business party Friday night.

I wasn't surprised over my attraction to Darius; he is a good looking man after all. Well, at least to me. What did surprise me was the connection we had before he bonded me to him. As I mentioned before I'm not a sensitive and yet I felt his emotions from the moment I'd walked in the door of his house Friday evening.

As for Monday evening, it was obvious he sensed my feelings as well. The thing is, how? I didn't think such a thing was possible but we're 'living' proof.

Ugh! I know nothing about the subject of the powers and capabilities of the mind. What little I read years ago, just confused the hell out of me and hurt my head. The thing that shocked me the most was the strength of my desire and need of him. The potency of it bordered on obsession; maybe even addiction.

What surprised me the most at this point in time was how much I missed him. While I did miss Darius, I was more worried about the side effects of his blood when it wore off. How many of the effects would I experience? How severe would they be? How soon and for how long would I experience them? I had no answers.

Even now I could feel his mind in mine and it felt sort of comforting, and scary at the same time. Scary because I would think it was comforting. Just how much of my mind could he see into? I could only read his feelings and knew they were his and not mine or anyone else's.

Strangely, I still couldn't sense the emotions of others around me, so why was I only sensitive to him? Again, no answer. I sighed, rolled over and tried to get some more sleep.

# Chapter 15

By 2200 hours Thursday evening, I'd had a shower to clean myself up after lazing listlessly in a cold locked room for over twenty-four hours. After receiving a call from Maisie, I was on the bike, with everything packed back onto it, and riding the streets of Rochedale.

The information Maisie gave me was of no benefit to me at that point in time. I didn't recognise the name of the man who was fronting the money I would be paid with for completing the hit. Not that that was going to happen now.

I sighed. I was bored and frustrated with staying in the motel room for so long with nothing to do to take my mind from going around in circles.

For the duration of my self-internment at the motel, I felt his anxiety and frustration. I could only guess he was worried and annoyed that I'd disappeared. Also probably because I stayed away, didn't call and that he couldn't find me. However, I wasn't ready to go back to him just yet. Or... his emotions were work related and I didn't factor into his thoughts at all. That last thought hurt.

Strangely enough, or maybe not, Darius was the subject my mind kept going back to and nothing else. I missed him terribly.

I almost lost control of my bike when that thought hit me as I realised the truth of it. While I was riding down Ford Road, it was deserted at that time of night and still one of the sparsely populated areas of Brisbane for some reason. The farms in the area must still be doing reasonable business. It wouldn't do to have an accident along that road with no one in easy distance to help me. Also, it had next to no street lights so it was exceptionally dark.

Suddenly, stomach cramping nausea rippled through me and again I nearly lost control of the bike. It faded almost as quickly as it hit and I felt fine so I continued riding. A few minutes later I was hit with the same symptoms but a little worse than before, only to be followed by more waves of nausea. Again I almost lost control of the bike. When I had a spare moment between the waves of pain, I realised I had to stop before I had an accident. However, the pain was too intense to concentrate on stopping safely at that point.

As the latest round of nausea eased some, I looked up from where I'd hunched over the tank only to see a number of people ranged across the road a few hundred metres in front of me. With me closing fast. Shit!!

Another round of cramping nausea chose that moment to hit me and I jerked the handle bars to the left in an effort to miss the people I could no longer see with my head against the tank. I hit a ditch I hadn't seen in the dark. The bike flipped me off, I went flying through the air and landed against the tree. Back first and upside down, followed by my head, only to slide into an upside down heap onto the ground. Then I felt my body fall some more.

Apart from the pain of hitting the tree then the ground the earlier pain and nausea was gone. I tried to move but I couldn't and panic swamped me like a wave on the beach. Had I injured my spine in the effort to miss the people on the road?

"Do not move her." I heard, a muffled voice called out, through my helmet.

Again I tried to move but it was like I was disconnected from my body and it wouldn't obey me. I tried to talk to let them know what was going on with me but again nothing happened.

Hands carefully moved over me from neck to upper shins/calves. "Nothing seems to be broken and no internal bleeding from what I can see. I am going to remove her helmet."

That was the second time they referred to me as a 'her'. How did they know I was a she? My clothing doesn't give my gender away. Then I felt the strap under my chin loosen.

"Support her neck and head."

I felt other hands gently hold my neck. As the helmet was cautiously removed I felt a hand move to cradle my head.

Once the helmet came completely off, I saw Darius's face close to mine. My heart soared at the sight of him and I tried to smile up at him.

"Sonja, can you hear me?" He asked, frowning slightly in concern.

I tried to nod and say yes. Still nothing happened. Everything felt distant as well as disconnected and I didn't know what to do about it or how to fix it. I couldn't even blink or move my eyes. The fear within me grew stronger.

Darius's frown deepened. His hands gently gripped either side of my face as he stared into my eyes. Then his hands went away and I was rising in the air, only to realise he was carrying me.

"You take her bike up to the house, and you grab her helmet." Darius ordered.

With my head on his shoulder he started walking. Just by the feel of his movements his stride was rather quick, a ground-eating pace. He walked what seemed like ages. There was no talking and no sounds of their footfalls, if the others stayed with him that was. Finally, after what seemed like an hour or more but probably wasn't, he entered a house.

"Please let Orenda know I need to see her. I will be in my room when she is ready." Darius said to someone out of my line of sight.

It's interesting how you can tell the age of a vampire by listening to how they say their words. The older they are the fewer the contractions they use. The only time it isn't an indication of the vampire's age is when it's a person's second language. The learning process tends to be more formal than to those who grow up with it.

Next, it felt like he was climbing stairs and I went back to looking at what I could see. The inability to move was a nuisance. If I hadn't damaged my spine then why couldn't I move or respond? The climb seemed to take a long time.

"Ah Max. Can you open the door for me please?" He asked in a tight voice.

"Sure. She doesn't look so good. Is she okay?" A deep and slightly gravelly voice responded. I didn't get to see him.

"She hit a tree and I do not know." Darius answered.

Once again I heard concern in his voice. How bad was I really? If only I could move or talk then I might be able to find out. I didn't seem to be in pain beyond hitting the tree. Despite the panic running unchecked throughout me, I was surprised I could think as clearly as I could. However, even though I was worried about myself, I wanted to wrap myself around Darius more. Being so close to him, it upset me that I couldn't.

Locked within my mind like I was, all I could do was think about my need for him. Then it just occurred to me that I wasn't feeling his emotions at all. I searched my mind and I couldn't find any presence of him whatsoever within me. I found the place he'd occupied but he wasn't there.

My panic rose another notch as I forced my focus back to the world around me.

Darius had walked into the room and placed me on the bed and sat beside me. He didn't say anything at all. He just sat there and held my hand. There was no expression on his face so I couldn't tell what he was feeling. I didn't know him well enough to read him.

"You wanted to see me Darius?" Orenda's deep voice came from behind him. "Ah, I see you have found her."

"No, our paths crossed unintentionally this evening. What is wrong with her Orenda? She's alive, not responding and I have checked yet can find nothing wrong." He said as she stood beside us.

Orenda tenderly took hold of my jaw.

"I recognise her from the café on Saturday. The one who had captured your attention away from our discussion briefly that evening." Subsequently she stared into my eyes then she let go of me. "You have bound her yes?"

"Inadvertently, yes."

"Inadvertently?" She raised her eyebrows at him.

"In my anger I accidently reopened a wound. With the extra blood loss she did not have the strength to survive a trip back to the hospital. I fed her to help heal her but the wound needed to be closed to be of benefit. As I result I ended up ingesting her blood during the process."

"A complete bonding then." She murmured. "For what I am about to say, do not hate yourself for what you have done. What has happened could not have been foreseen Darius…"

There was a pause.

"She just so happens to be one of the rare mortals who become trapped within their mind when the binding wears off." Darius's face crumpled with what looked like devastation.

So, that was what had happened to me? Nothing more? An instant flood of relief ran through me.

"However, if you bind her again then she should not be ensnared within her mind." Orenda stated softly.

Darius looked hopeful at her words, as was I.

"But there is a catch. You will have to give her the choice of whether she wishes to be bound to you for the rest of your existence or she stays trapped within her mind for the remainder of her days or you end it quickly for her. You see Darius, even though she is locked away in there, the likelihood she is totally aware of what is happening around her is extremely high."

Again, Darius looked distraught.

Oh. Well, that last part didn't sound like fun at all. It seemed like I had a decision to make so, I started thinking about it. However, my thoughts were interrupted as I listened to her speak again.

"You have to give her those choices my friend. I will send someone with nourishment for you in an hour. Deal with this and I will see you at sunset tomorrow." Then Orenda left.

Darius stared at me for a few more moments then positioned himself behind me so I was sitting up. Then he repositioned me slightly so I was leaning against him with my head on his arm so I was looking up at him.

"Please forgive me, Sonja." He murmured, gently opened my mouth, cut his wrist then let his blood drip into my mouth.

I wanted to tell him it wasn't his fault but, of course, I couldn't.

At first nothing happened other than me feeling the drops hit my tongue and start to dribble down my throat. Once it reached my throat there was still nothing. I chose to retreat into my mind and I closed my eyes. I couldn't bear to live like this or look at him as he gazed back at me seeming so upset. Darius's arm tightened a fraction around me.

"Sonja?" His hand caressed my side and it sent little shivers through me.

My eyes sprung open as I felt my body physically move in response to his touch. Then I felt his concern, fear, desire, need around the edges of my mind. I wanted to cry but knew it would be of no use while trapped as I was. The teasing of his feelings was just so cruel. I then saw Darius's hand move to my face and gently caressed my cheek.

"Come back to me Sonja. Please." He whispered.

I swallowed convulsively only to start choking. I felt the force of the choking shake my body and Darius's hold on me tightened some more. He'd started to move his wrist away from my mouth but my hand swiftly latched on to it of its own volition and held it as I closed my eyes and willingly drank. Only then did I fully realise I was no longer trapped within my own mind.

Darius held me firmly against him and I felt his pleasure, desire and relief grow. I felt him in my mind again.

As I released his wrist, I gasped for air like I had been drowning then twisted myself in his grip so we were facing each other and kissed him. While I kissed him I slid my hands up his shirt so I could touch him, only for me to start unbuttoning his shirt. He caught at my hands but held me tight to him.

"We need to talk first. Are you okay?"

With him stopping me, I could suddenly feel how tired I was. How tired he was.

"Yes Darius, but let us rest first please." I murmured as I rested my head on his shoulder. He stilled, gazed at me then nodded.

"Then sleep Sonja." And I felt his compulsion as he laid us down, after he'd turned off the light.

Wrapped in his arms, I snuggled into his chest and fell asleep.


When I awoke I found him watching me as he fondled my hair.

"We need to talk Sonja." He stated as I gazed up at him.

"Shhh... I heard and we will. But first, love me Darius." I whispered against his lips after pulling him down to me.

After an almost frenzied removal of clothing, he laid himself on top of me and proceeded to do just that with a wild abandon as if it would be the last time we would be together. At the moment of his release and my back arched in orgasmic pleasure, his fangs sank into my breast and drank from me until he had no more to give me. Then he collapsed on top of me and just held me.

"Why did you leave me like that?" His voice low but harsh, tainted with anxiety and anguish.

"I'm sorry but I needed time to think and I knew I wouldn't be able to if I had stayed." I murmured as I held him.

I was locked to him for eternity, bound to him. Did I want to be? I did want to be with him forever. But as a bonded? No. I realised... I knew... I wanted more.

"Think about what?" His breath tickled as he nuzzled and murmured just behind my ear.

With the decision made, I didn't answer. Instead, I kissed the outer curve of his shoulder and trailed little kisses along the top of his shoulder towards his neck. I felt his lips curl into a smile as I kissed the base of his neck and continued up towards his jaw. Only I didn't make it to his jaw as I bit his neck hard, broke skin and drank.

"SONJA... NO!" Darius choked out in a harsh whisper.

At the same time I felt his sorrow and regret, I also sensed his pleasure both mentally and physically. I knew, at that point, that his pleasure was greater. He groaned but didn't stop me as his arms tightened around me. Therefore, I continued to drink as I held him just as tightly until he'd healed my teeth marks.

I laid back and gazed up at him through half closed eyes, feeling happy and complete. He turned the light on then his hands gently cupped my face.

"Why Sonja?" He murmured as he gazed into my eyes.

I reached up and brushed a strand of hair out of his eyes.

"Since I am locked to you till the end of time, I thought why not completely instead of just until the end of your life. Trapped within my own mind is over rated. Been there, done that and didn't bother with the t-shirt."

Despite his eyes revealing his concern, Darius grinned at my flippant words.

"This way we can be together without that problem. I don't know if what we have is love, but I know I can't be without you. The overwhelming power of it scares me but here I am anyway." I said softly.

"You reckless crazy woman." He muttered against my cheek as he held me tightly.

I could feel he was both upset and pleased, and I just held him. Besides, the decision wasn't reversible.

I understood what I'd done. I just didn't want to go through the long and, potentially, boring discussion about it. Soon my body would go through the change from human to vampire. I wasn't really looking forward to experiencing it but hoped it would be a small price to pay compared to the alternative. I tried to think of other things as I started to become nervous. Anything to take my mind off it.

It wasn't working.

"I'll be with you Sweetness. You won't go through it alone." He murmured softly against my ear as his arms tightened around me.

I smiled into his neck as I held him just as tightly.

Suddenly, he picked me up and carried me into the bathroom. After setting me on my feet he then turned the shower on and we just stood under it, enjoying it as we simply held each other.

I didn't do anything other than stand there with my face against his chest as I held him tightly. While his arms held me in return, his hands caressed my back and he leant his chin on the top of my head. At the beginning the shower felt like rain.

I didn't know how long we stood under the shower like that when the first wave of pain hit. It wasn't so bad to cause my body to spasm. In fact there were no outward signs at all. However, because Darius and I could sense each other's feelings he knew and gently took me down to the tiled floor.

He was sitting with his back in a corner of the cubicle. Such an inaccurate term for the large rectangular shower recess we were in. While I was sitting on my hip with the top half of me facing him as I leant against him.

When the second round of pain hit it practically doubled me over and pulled a groaning gasp from me as I clutched at Darius. With one arm and hand supporting me, his other was rubbing useless but comforting circles over my back as he murmured in a soothing tone.

The third lot of pain caused me to cry out and tears started to flow as I vomited. It had been ages since I'd eaten anything so very little came out other than more cries of pain and more than a little amount of fear.

My stomach felt like it had been punched, while my chest felt like I'd done twenty rounds of weights after having done no exercise for years. My throat felt like I'd been screaming for hours. All of which left me with a pounding headache. While the shower went from feeling like soothing soft rain to small pellets of hail pelting down on me.

Basically, I hurt from the abdomen up.

I received a small reprieve as I lay panting in Darius's arms and I enjoyed it while it lasted. However, it didn't last for long. But while it did last, I let him support my weight as he soothed me while I tried to calm myself.

Cramping through my intestines had me emitting groaning cries as I doubled over yet again. With more tears streaming, I tried to block my mind to what was to happen next. I concentrated on Darius's arms around me as he held me firmly to his chest. I concentrated on the hairs of his arm pressed against my face and breast as he cradled my head with his fingers in my hair as they caressed my scalp. I concentrated on his heart beating slowly against my ear.

But no matter how hard I concentrated, I knew what was happening to me. I could feel it, smell it because it wouldn't let me ignore it as my body expelled the wastes it no longer wanted within it.

By the time I recovered, there was no sign of having gone through the change at all. The two of us just stayed where we were on the floor in each other's arms as the shower continued to rain down upon us. After a while, once the soreness had eased, Darius helped me to stand then turned the shower off. By that time, there was no hot water left. We dried then went into the bedroom.

On the bed were six bags of blood. Seeing them on the bed, I noted I was starting to feel hungry as if I hadn't eaten for days and I couldn't stop staring at them.

Until Darius let go of my hand.

I glanced at him when he left my side only to watch him to turn off the lights. I stayed where I was while I waited for my eyes to adjust to the darkness. When my eyes had finally adjusted, I saw he was beside me again and holding his hand out to me. I placed my hand in his and he led me to the balcony.

At first I was shy because we were both naked and it was the middle of winter. But then I thought 'Stuff it, why not', and went with him. We stood there gazing out into the darkness with me standing in front of him, my back against his chest and his arms around me. We didn't talk. We didn't have to. I could sense his happiness and peacefulness just as he could mine.

I thought I would have been cold standing there without clothing in the middle of winter but I wasn't. Another bonus to being a vampire I guess. Then he handed me a bag of blood. I hadn't realised he'd grabbed them.

"Sorry I can't present it to you in a goblet. I wasn't expecting to host you like this." He said quietly.

I turned in his arms so I was facing him. "I don't mind. Honest." I smiled up at him.

"Drink Sonja." His tone intimate.

So, we brought the bags up to our mouths and I paused momentarily as I felt my canines lengthen into fangs then I sank them gently, tentatively, into the bag.

It was a different taste to Darius's blood. More metallic, plus something else I couldn't pick up on to be able to describe it. Therefore, I didn't bother and just drank until the bag was empty.

He took the now empty bag from me and carelessly tossed the two of them onto the bed with amazing accuracy. Then he wrapped his arms around me again. We were both feeling wonderful and we just stood there in the darkness of midnight, enjoying the mood. However, it didn't last long as nausea and cramping rippled through me yet again.

"Darius?" I whispered in confusion, pain and fear as another wave went through me. Followed quickly by three more. I pushed away from him only to hang the top half of me over the railing of the balcony as I brought up the blood I'd just swallowed.

Darius was instantly holding me, supporting me as I was left feeling weak and shaking. I was starting to feel almost... feverish.

The bedroom door slammed open, hitting the wall hard, and we both jumped.

"What the hell have you done?! My General or not you had no right!" Orenda exploded into the room. It was the only way to describe her entrance as she stormed towards us.

"Sonja made her choice. I did not know her intent until it was too late. There was nothing I could do. However, there is another issue more important." Darius stated calmly as he held me while I started shivering.

"What is more important than what you have done?!" Orenda snapped. She really didn't sound happy.

"She's not keeping nourishment down." His voice was tight with concern, but I had a tough time concentrating on what he was saying and feeling as I started to feel weak and couldn't stop trembling.

When she next spoke it sounded like she was beside us.

"Sonja, drink from me." She ordered gently and she placed her wrist against my mouth.

Reluctantly I drank but not for long before I vomited again. My shaking worsened to the point I could barely stand.

Thankfully, I didn't have to worry about that since Darius supported me.

"You yourself feed her." Now it was Orenda's turn for her voice to be full of worry. That fact intensified my own fear.

Darius pressed his wrist gently to my mouth. I sank my fangs in and fed as his other arm tightened around me yet again. Sinking into his embrace, I kept drinking from him and the fever-like symptoms, the nausea and cramping started to go away. And I continued to drink from him. The more I drank the better I felt.

"Here Darius, drink this." Orenda said gently.

He moved one arm away from me then I felt him drinking. Once I was feeling better, I flicked my tongue over the fang marks I'd created and moved his wrist down across my chest. When he finished the bag Orenda had given him, he scooped me into his arms and placed me on the bed after Orenda turned down the covers. Once the covers had been tucked over and around me he sat beside me. Orenda sat on the other side of me. Our nakedness ignored.

"Did you choose this Sonja?" she asked.

"Yes. I thought if I was to be bound to him for eternity just to keep my sanity then I'd thought this would be the better way. A choice rather than a necessity. What's happening to me?" I finished fearfully in a whisper.

While I'd never come in contact with vampires before this hit job on Darius, I'd never heard of others having the trouble I was having when they became bonded or as a vampire. I had no idea if what I was going through was normal or not. Although their reactions seemed to suggest it wasn't.

Orenda sighed.

"It would seem you are a rare person in regards to the effects of our blood. Not only did you suffer one of the exceptional side effects of being a bonded, but you suffer a rare outcome as a vampire. I have never seen anyone suffer from this particular affliction before. I have heard rumours about it but never seen it." She slowly shook her head in amazement. She looked at us both before continuing.

"You are one of the rare vampires who can not survive on any blood other than your Sire's."

"I had thought that was a myth." Darius stated as he frowned at Orenda.

"It would seem not." She sighed again. "Care for her tonight. Get some sleep both of you and I will see you both in the conference room tomorrow evening an hour before sunset. Whether you like it or not Sonja, you are now one of my people, therefore one of my soldiers and we have a war to fight." With that she walked out of the room, closing the door after her.

"War?" I whispered as I gazed at him.

"You heard part of the discussion Saturday night at the café right?"

I nodded.

"That war. Ever since Varrik brought us the message almost two weeks ago, we have been moving some of our people here without the enemy factions knowing. While at the same time we have let it be known Orenda and a select few would be 'taking a break' here so she can relax from her 'hectic' schedule."

"What exactly is the war about?" I asked.

"As you know Orenda is the current Prince of the City. Being Prince of the City allows that vampire to be the overall leader of all the vampires within that city. But like everything, there are factions. Those for the Prince, those against the Prince and those who just want to exist without all the excessive vampire politics.

"This war is about one of the factions who are against Orenda and her policies. Norton will try to kill her so he can take over as being Prince of the City. If he wins then the humans are back on the menu as unwilling food source. If he wins then soon after there will be a larger, maybe world-wide, scale war where we will be openly hunted by all humans instead of the select few who police the rogues.

"We are going to do our best to make sure he does not win. Those of us who align ourselves with Orenda agree with her ways, hence why we want her to stay in power. I am sorry to say, my Sweet, but you have walked right into it."

"Then love me tonight Darius and we'll deal with tomorrow when it arrives." I murmured to him as I wrapped my arms around his shoulders and slowly pulled him down to me.

It was sunrise, with the curtains closed, before we finally fell asleep.

# Part 3
# The Challenge

# Chapter 16

Darius and I awoke three hours before sunset. For the first half hour we just laid in each other's arms. We didn't speak. We didn't have to. We knew how the other was feeling. After a while later, and more intimacy, we had a long shower then dressed. Just as we finished dressing there was a knock on the door and Darius went to answer it. We had about twenty minutes before we had to attend the meeting.

There was some murmuring for a few seconds then Darius came back with four bags of blood and two goblets. From somewhere in the house, someone had the music pumped up with it a little heavy on the bass as it vibrated through the place. Currently Justin Timberlake's *'Sexyback'* was playing. Certainly an interesting choice considering what they were planning in the house.

I turned away from him and towards the balcony and the curtains which separated it from us. My mind went numb at the thought of drinking the blood from the bags after what had happened to me the previous night. I was grateful for the numbness as I didn't want Darius sensing my current state of mind right then. I ran my hand along the fabric of the curtains to distract myself.

"Are you regretting your decision?" Darius's rich deepish voice resonated within me as he spoke and I couldn't get enough of it. His voice was like his body. Addictive. However, while his voice was that of a general enquiry, his feelings were one of alarm. I spun around to face him.

"Oh no Darius, never." I said as I rushed to him and wrapped my arms around him. He wrapped his arms around me.

"I thought you were going to step into the sunlight." He stated quietly, relief flooding through him.

"Never. I was just dreading having to drink those after what happened last night." I murmured against his chest.

"Don't Dearest. They're for me. You get to feed from me." His voice went husky at the last statement and I felt his desire, as well as his hunger.

I pushed him back onto the bed, straddled him and kissed him. He wrapped his arms around me again, held me snugly against him as he deepened our kiss. After breaking the kiss for air – more out of habit than necessity, I gave him the blood that had fallen from his hands when he gently gripped my waist. I waited until he had drunk two of them before I gave in to both our desires then to finally drink from him.


We were five minutes late to the meeting. Darius, holding my hand, walked towards two vacant chairs to the left of Orenda. He sat in the one closest to her after placing me on the other one. I sat there with my hands in my lap while Darius's were clasped together on the table in front of him. The first order of business was introductions. From Orenda's right and continuing around the table until Darius and I were reached were:

Itztecpatl who was the head of the were-jaguars and looked to be Native South American, like a Mayan or such with waist length black hair, Anoki who was Itztecpatl's second in command and appeared to be Native North American, also with the same coloured waist length hair. Charlotte who was a European pale, six foot-looking Amazon with thick black hair down to her thighs and straight as well. She was the Chief of Security.

I had never seen so much long hair in one room before.

After Charlotte was Max who's also a Native South American Indian and the head teacher to the newly embraced. He had short neatly trimmed black hair. I wonder if he is the same Max Darius spoke to when I was carried into his room.

Lastly, and beside me, Varrik who was European and the Emissary also had hair that was brown, wavy and just passed his shoulders and tied back at his nape.

So, that was Varrik. He was taller than Darius and just as attractive.

"And this is Sonja our newly embraced. What is it you actually do Sonja?" Orenda asked as she finished off the introductions.

"Well, before becoming a vampire I... worked... as the personal assistant to the manager of Darius's company..." I started saying.

"But it was not in that capacity in which you entered our little world is it?" Orenda asked, our eyes locked.

"No." I responded softly. "When I'm not working in Darius's company, I'm a hit man. My skill is that of a sniper." I continued in the same tone. I knew these questions would be asked and saw no reason why to hide the truth.

213

"I see. Why were you at the café?"

"I was hired to kill someone but the photo supplied made the mark unidentifiable. So, via the itinerary which was also provided, I had to do surveillance to narrow down the possible targets. I found out Tuesday that Darius was the target." I stated quietly without shame. As far as I was concerned I had nothing to be ashamed of.

My words, however, sent a shockwave around the table except for Darius and I, as they stared at me then glanced at Orenda, Darius then back to me.

"Why did you not make the kill once you knew who your target was?" Orenda asked with curiosity.

Something I never knew... A freshly fed vampire can blush if they were that way inclined as a mortal. There wasn't much that caused me to blush but when my heart's involved then I do have a tendency to do so.

I felt Darius's amusement at my reaction while those who saw my reaction smiled and/or raised eyebrows.

"The reluctance came Saturday night in the café when I heard what you'd said. It caused me to think and re-evaluate the reason for the hit. I decided I had to know whether my target was one of your people or an infiltrator. The first motivation not to was when I discovered I was strongly attracted to one of my possible targets. The second came to me when I realised he happened to be in the top ranks of your supporters." Despite my blush I managed to explain calmly.

"I see. Well, I am grateful you chose not to eliminate him." Orenda stated with a hint of amusement then asked, "As a sniper what is your skill level?"

"I rank in the top ten of the state rifle competitions. I don't follow the assassins' rankings." I answered softly.

"Excellent. That gives us three for the roof. Darius, Charlotte... Do we have at least one more for the roof?" Orenda turned her attention to the two of them.

"Adam is willing if no one else can be found because he said he still isn't that great a shot." Charlotte responded, her voice was mid-range and smooth with still a hint of accent as if she hadn't been away from her country for very long.

"Well, unless something changes at the last moment, tell him he is up on the roof and to do the best he can." Orenda informed.

Still talking to Darius and Charlotte... "Remember the big battle out at Helidon about a decade ago?"

They affirmed their remembrance.

"Well, we still have those armbands we used. They are in a box in my office. Issue them out to everyone here regardless of where they will be during the fighting." Orenda then turned her attention to me. "Just so you understand Sonja, you will be on the roof and you are to kill any who are not wearing the same armband as you."

I glanced at the two jaguars then back at Orenda. "Are vampires the only enemy who will be attacking?"

"No. There will be therians as well. Why?" Orenda answered, sounding suspicious.

"First, do you have the capability to create your own ammunition here?" I asked.

"No but we do have a stockpile of ammunition that came with the house when I bought it, why?"

"Do you happen to know what style of ammunition it is?"

Orenda looked at Darius.

"It just so happens to be a mix of pistol and rifle rounds, normal and hollow points. Why Sonja?" Darius asked.

"Do you have holy water and silver nitrate here by any chance?" I'd decided to be blunt about the thought I had.

The room was naturally quiet but it was totally silent by that stage.

"Answering questions with questions is getting tiring... Explain." Orenda demanded quietly.

"I apologise but the answer is simple. You want the enemy dead and those two items are the best way to ensure that."

"You wouldn't happen to have talked to a were-jaguar called Sarah would you?" Itztecpatl asked me with a hint of a smile.

I looked at him in confusion only for the others to chuckle or smile as I said no.

"Yes we do just so happen to have both of those items." Orenda answered with a smile.

I nodded.

"Good. If allowed, I would like to start making the ammunition as soon as possible so as to have as many as possible available. I'll also need the aid of three people please. Preferably those who'll be snipers with me since we'll be the ones to use the ammunition."

"Done." Was all Orenda said. "Anything else?" She asked as she sat back in her seat and gazed around the table.

"Also, I would like to see what your people on the ground will look like with those armbands on and the lights off while I look through the night scope. Reason being, I wouldn't know your people from a bar of soap let alone who're the enemy. I figured me standing at the top landing while a few with armbands on stand in the foyer with the lights off will let me see what I'm to avoid while viewing through the scope." I stated quietly.

"They are your people as well Sonja. You are part of this family now." Orenda informed me patiently. "And yes, I think it can be arranged for you. You will have until the attack starts and that could be any time tonight or definitely tomorrow." She informed me then sighed. Slowly she ran her fingers through her hair while gazing thoughtfully at me.

"Normally, I would have you pledge allegiance to me with you partaking of my blood but, due to your particular affliction, I have to dispense with the usual ritual." Orenda stated. "Do you swear loyalty to me Sonja?"

"Yes I swear loyalty to you Orenda. I heard part of your discussion in the café last week and I'd thought to myself that if what you were saying were true then you needed to be kept in power. Especially since I was one of those mortals you were referring to at the time. If that doesn't convince you then my need to keep Darius alive will keep me loyal. He believes in you and that's enough for me." I stated quietly. I felt Darius's pride in me but I kept my eyes on Orenda. Orenda nodded with a hint of a smile then gazed at each of us.

"If that is all then you all know what you are to do. Dismissed." She concluded.

Darius indicated for me to leave the room while he stayed seated. I did so and, a few moments after the door closed behind me, sensed concern, annoyance, from him.

Once outside the room and waiting, Itztecpatl and Anoki were quietly talking off to one side when the front door opened to reveal it was dark outside. In walked a short, relatively cute woman with black hair and a walking stick, and one of the tallest men I'd seen so far. He was a fraction taller than Varrik and I'd thought Varrik was tall.

For some reason the woman seemed vaguely familiar to me but I couldn't work out where from. After a few moments it started to bug me.

"Sarah, what are you doing here? Kaelan, surely you could have kept her away." Itztecpatl stated with a frown as he walked towards them. So, that was the Sarah he'd referred to?

At that point, Orenda and Darius came out and I sensed amusement from Darius as he watched the three of them.

"After all these years do you really think I could stop her once she'd made her mind up?" Kaelan stated with a tolerant smile and an exasperated rolling of his eyes.

"Such a lovely greeting." Sarah hit both of them since the two men were standing beside her then walked over to Orenda.

"Sarah, so pleased you could come." Orenda greeted.

"Glad someone is pleased to see me here. Hello Orenda, Darius." Sarah stated with a smile as she and Orenda hugged.

"Hello Sarah." Darius grinned at her.

Once she and Orenda completed their hug, Anoki grabbed Sarah from behind in a hug.

"I'm happy to see you even if your brute of a mate isn't."

Sarah laughed as she gave his arms a hug then looked back at Itztecpatl and Kaelan.

"Which one are you referring to?" She asked with a cheeky grin.

Whoa! She has two of them? I glanced at them and saw their devotion to her in their eyes. Together? Greedy cow.

I then sensed amusement again and I caught Darius gazing at me, smiling. Keeping a straight face, I sent him a burst of desire. He grinned. I had a hard time keeping the answering smile off my face but I managed then turned back to the scene before me.

"Anoki! You aren't helping matters any." Itztecpatl growled. But, just by looking at him, I could see he was amused. Anoki just grinned and looked far from intimidated by his leader.

"It's your own fault Love. You're the one who made me co-leader of the jags. Where else did you expect me to be at a time like this?" Sarah asked as she stood there with hand on hip, attitude blaring as she glared up at him.

It was right at that moment that I realised where I'd seen Sarah before. She was the leader of the group who fought the rogues out west at Helidon ten years ago. I'd seen it on the news because I wasn't affiliated with any of the groups to want to join in. But she'd had red hair back then.

"Oh, Thad sends his apologies that he couldn't join in as he was handed a job he had to take." Kaelan informed Orenda.

"Tell him I said thank you for the offer when you see him next." Orenda said with a smile. "So, why are you here Kaelan?"

The question sounded like the pair might not get along.

"Itztecpatl said you were having problems getting sufficient snipers for the roof so I thought I would help out." He stated with a casual shrug.

"I for one am pleased and accept your help Kaelan."

Charlotte chose that moment to come towards me.

"Come with me Sonja and I'll show you where you can make your ammunition." She murmured and started leading the way.

I turned and followed. In a quiet voice from behind me, I heard...

"Ammunition? I'll see you later Baby." Kaelan, at least I thought it was him, had said. The words were then followed by the sound of a kiss. Then Kaelan was beside me. I gazed up (and up) at him.

"Didn't they tell you, you were to stop growing in your mid to late teens?"

He gazed down at me with a grin.

"I have to say Sonja, I'm surprised to see you here. I didn't realise you ran in this particular circle."

I couldn't hide the surprise at him knowing who I was.

"I didn't until recently. We've never met before..."

"No, I recognise you from the state shooting comps. I'm surprised you don't compete in the nationals."

"Thank you but they don't interest me. I'm happy enough in the state competitions."

"So, how did you end up entering this particular little world?"

Figures he would ask such a question. I decided to be blunt. "I chose to become a vampire last night."

"Oh." Was all he said.

"Let me guess... You're a bounty hunter." I said neutrally.

"How did you come to that conclusion?" Kaelan asked just as neutrally.

"Your 'oh' spoke volumes and told me. You're not exactly

pleased with my choice." Then I explained briefly about the accidental bonding, the results after it wore off and my decision as to why I chose to become a vampire. I don't know why but I felt like I needed to explain, to justify myself I guess. Very rarely have I ever felt the need to do so.

"I apologise for being judgemental. I hadn't realised such a thing could happen." He murmured and he did sound sincere.

"None of us realised. While Darius and Orenda knew of the possibility, they hadn't seen it happen before."

"Interesting." Kaelan stated quietly. "So, why are you making ammunition?"

As Charlotte led us down to the cellar, I told him why.

The steps down were concrete, cracked but dry. It was a typical cellar of brick, concrete and the occasional thick timber beams, and it seemed to be the size of the whole house. Once down there, she led us down the corridor passed closed doors, until she finally opened one near the end. Charlotte flicked on a light.

The room had four brick walls, wooden ceiling and a concrete floor. All unpainted. It was full of white topped benches, backless bar stools, pine coloured cabinets and a white metal first aid cabinet, a stainless steel double sink with a drainer-bench on the right and a white painted wooden door in the opposite wall. Looking at the wall next to the door we'd just entered I saw a second switch with the label 'Red Light' under it.

I was guessing the room used to be a photographer's developing room. Only it smelled stale and dusty as if it was rarely used.

Then I started searching the cabinets. At first glance there were a number of different pistols and rifles, and a variety of ammunition, to suit those weapons, all boxed and marked accordingly. The collection also included hollow points which appeared to be about half ml capacity.

Other cabinets revealed various measuring utensils, sticks of red sealing wax, bottles of holy water and silver nitrate. Numerous boxes of latex surgical gloves – medium and large, cotton buds – for some strange reason as I thought they would be in the first aid cabinet, a small gas camping stove with small heating pots and weapon cleaning gear. Everything needed to create the ammunition I was interested in was in the room. It seemed, at one point, it stopped being used as a photographer's developing room as I found no equipment for that purpose at all.

Briefly I opened the other door and discovered it led to a little sleep-out with a single person camping cot and a small square basic table beside it. It smelt better than the outer room as if someone had been in there not so long ago.

Then, closing the door as the little room held no interest for me, I started pulling all the stuff needed out of the cabinets and placing them on the bench nearest the sink.

My idea was to place a quarter of a millilitre of holy water and silver nitrate each into the half millilitre cavity of the hollow point and seal it with the wax. A single round won't kill either vampire or therian but it would be enough to slow them down till either another round was shot into them or someone on the ground could finish them off.

Then, just for curiosity's sake, I did a more serious search of the cabinets while waiting for the other snipers to arrive. Only to make a rather surprising discovery in the back corner of one of them. I pulled it out into the light so I could see it better.

I looked down at the one litre jar in my hands and read the hand-written label…

*Blessed Silver Nitrate*
*Date: 10/2024*
*Note:*
*Therian: 12/2024 – Tested and works*
*Vampire: 02/2025 – Untested!!*

With it in the crook of my left arm and a cotton bud in my other hand I went over to the sink. I opened the jar, dipped the cotton bud in and dabbed it on my arm so that a patch of skin the size of a five cent piece was damp with the stuff.

I had every intention of swabbing more of it on but hissed in pain instead, almost dropping the jar of liquid.

"Fuck! Fuck! Fuck! Fuck!" I muttered as I quickly spun the tap on to run the water. The pipes clanked for a bit then the water started running after it splattered and spurted for a few moments.

"Sonja? What's wrong?" I heard Charlotte ask from behind me as she and Kaelan came over to me.

I didn't answer her as I continued to swear with pain.

The blessed silver nitrate was burning the hell out of my arm and blisters formed while I watched. And it had only been a small smearing. I couldn't place my arm under the tap immediately because the water came out brown from disuse and had to let it run until the water turned clear. As soon as it did I thrust my arm under it as I clenched my teeth against the pain and swearing.

I heard the sound of running feet. Faster than human running.

"Shit Sonja, what the hell did you do?" Kaelan asked from beside me with a frown tainting his tone.

"Sonja!" Darius called urgently as he burst into the room.

The sound and feel of his anxiety hurt almost as much as the burning did. It hadn't take him long to be at my side as he gripped my arm to inspect the burn. It was now the size of a ten cent piece on my left forearm.

"What caused that?" Orenda demanded. She and Darius must have been together at the time Darius sensed my pain.

I didn't say anything. I just lifted up the jar so they all could read the label.

Darius held me as he murmured "You reckless crazy woman."

"Where did you find this?" Orenda asked her tone neutral.

"In the back corner of the cabinet over there. As you can see it works, and that was barely a swab. However, I also didn't get to wash it off straight away." I stated. I looked at Orenda. "How long have you owned this house?" I asked as I started thinking about needing to heal the burn after Darius whispered how to do so.

"Four years and nine months thereabouts."

I nodded. Holy water and other blessed items start to lose their potency after five years. By the date on the label no one here had the bottle of liquid made.

"Blessed silver nitrate. That will certainly make this battle a little easier for us snipers if we have to deal with one type of round only." Kaelan said as he gazed intently at me.

His expression was one of 'why hadn't someone thought of this earlier'. I could see other possibilities going through his mind. Only because I'd been thinking them as well. Then I had to remember that I too was a vampire now. I turned to Orenda.

"Permission to use this in the coming battle?"

Orenda glanced at the jar then at Darius and Charlotte. I hadn't taken my eyes from her so I didn't know what their reactions were. Then she looked back at me and nodded.

"Do it." Then she left the room followed by Charlotte and Darius, after he gave my hand a quick squeeze.

Two other men then entered the room as I put the individual bottles of holy water and silver nitrate back in the cabinet.

"Hi, I'm Lars." Said a tall sandy blonde haired, pale skinned European with blue eyes and what sounded like a German accent. He was a vampire.

"And I'm Trent." Said a deeply tanned, brown haired, brown eyed American who was about the same height as me. Trent was a therian of some sort; I just didn't know which species.

"Sonja and this is Kaelan." I stated as I walked over to close the door. "Here's what we're going to do. All four of us are going to double glove because we'll be dealing with blessed silver nitrate which has the effect of holy water to vampires, as well as the usual effects to therians."

Trent and Lars glanced at each other, at Kaelan then back at me as I showed them the burn on my arm.

"That burn is half healed." I mentioned then headed back to the bench we would be working at.

"As a result we'll have to keep an eye on the condition of the outer glove then change both layers at the same time. Three of us will fill the hollow points with the blessed silver nitrate and the fourth will cap them with sealing wax. We'll continue with this until it's time for the battle. While we need to get as many made as quickly as possible, don't rush as we don't need the injuries."

With that, and after Kaelan and I showed Lars and Trent what to do, we set about the task.

However, just before I started, I grabbed a black marker and wrote on the jar of blessed silver nitrate...

*Blessed Silver Nitrate*

*Date: 10/2024*

*Note:*

*Therian: 12/2024 – Tested and works*

*Vampire: 02/2025 – Untested!!*

*------------ 07/2029 – Tested and works!!*

# Chapter 17

Hours passed and I was concentrating so hard on what I was doing that I was oblivious to practically everything else around me. Other than the vague knowing that it was morning and the sun was above the horizon. On some level I was aware that the other three had left a while ago to eat and get some rest, but that was about it. Still, I went on with the task of filling and capping the hollow points.

So absorbed in what I was doing that I'd forgotten to keep track of the condition of my outer gloves a number of times. As a result I burnt myself. I had to quickly quash the pain of the burns as soon as they happened so Darius wouldn't come running. I would rinse the burns as quickly as possible – hence the reason for working close to the sink, think about healing the burns, re-double glove myself then continued working.

Something touched my shoulder scaring the daylights out of me and, as a result, something primitive rose swiftly within me. Not thinking clearly I'd reacted by raking my nails against whatever it was while snarling as I went into a defensive crouch after stumbling off the stool I'd been sitting on.

I couldn't make sense of what I was seeing as my senses refused to function properly. I bared my fangs and hissed at the other creature. The only reason my brain worked out it was a creature of some sort was because of the blood I saw within it and the slow heartbeat emanating from it. Realising that it was blood that I could smell, hunger cramped through me in unrelenting waves.

It made a slow movement and I growled at it... Similar to the way a domestic house cat growls a warning in the back of its throat. The creature made a soft noise as it moved slowly towards me.

On all fours, I backed up and growled again. I continued backing up until I bumped into something solid behind me and couldn't go any further. I felt cornered, trapped, and threatened as hunger raged within me. I hissed again, followed by another high pitched growl to warn the being away.

Still the creature kept coming slowly towards me making low sounds I didn't understand.

With nowhere else to go, I hissed once more and leapt at it. With my hands bent into claws and my fangs extended, I only had the thought of escape. That and self-protection and to feed if the opportunity arose.

I landed on it, flattening it to the ground as I sank my fangs in deep where the blood was the closest to the surface as well as pulsed the strongest.

Something wrapped itself around me, holding me tightly, as I drank. However, once the blood had entered my mouth I hadn't cared that it had entrapped me. My need to feed had total control of me by that point.

I drank deeply and just kept on drinking as my hunger knew no bounds.

The sound of a door opening vaguely registered in my mind.

I growled, thinking the new creature nearing me was after my food. Hunching ready to defend my food, I dug my claws deeper to keep the creature from stealing it.

The words "GET OUT!" also distantly penetrated my slowly de-fogging brain but made no sense to me.

Feelings of concern, need and desire finally infiltrated my mind. The arms around me eased their hold and became tender and caressing as I became aware of the body beneath me was male and familiar. Realisation hit me like a speeding truck on a highway.

The horror of what I'd just done filled me as I leapt backwards away from the body beneath me and I hid in a semi-dark corner of the room. Tears streamed down my face because of the appalling thing I'd just done.

"Sonja... Sweetness... please, it's okay." Darius called softly as he cautiously took a step towards me. I could feel his distress and worry wash over and through me.

"Stay away from me." I whispered through my tears.

He ignored me, slowly continued forward; only to crouch down in front of me just beyond arms reach.

"Please Dearest, listen to me... What you just went through is normal and I'm not angry or upset with you in any way..." His tone was unhurried, quiet and gentle.

It was true.

I sensed no reproach from him at all and I sensed no anger, feelings of betrayal or disappointment directed at me. Only anxiety, grief, need, and desire from him.

"Normal?" I practically screeched only for my voice to come out hushed after that. "How can it be normal?! I just attacked you like some kind of rabid animal!" I sobbed.

I didn't understand how a civilised person could do such a thing. Even if I was a vampire now. A self-loathing I'd never experienced before flared within me, consuming me, and I couldn't look at him. Let alone want him to touch me. I didn't even comprehend how he could still look at me, let alone still want me after what I'd done to him.

He made a sound as if he'd been hurt.

"Shhh Sweetness. It is not your fault. I should have been down here earlier to feed you. I had not realised you had used up so much blood to heal that burn yesterday." He paused and ran his hand through his hair.

"The frenzy was not your fault Dearest. All new vampires end up experiencing it at some point in the beginning of their new life." He kept his voice gentle and low.

He reached out to me and I flinched away from him again.

"You are not even two days old as a vampire. You can not expect perfect control straight away." Darius said gently as he slowly closed the distance between us.

I cowered as far from him as I could get but he still continued towards me then wrapped his arms around me. I tried to escape him but he held onto me so, I just collapsed into his embrace and cried as he made soothing sounds.

He scooped me into his arms and carried me into the sleep-out room. Darius sat on the cot with me in his lap. He cradled me like a child as I cried. He continued to hold me even after I stopped crying. Then...

"You need to drink some more Dearest. Then you need to sleep." He said quietly as he dried my tears.

"I can't. I have work to do…" I murmured a weak protest against his neck.

"Just a few hours. Sleeping will help you heal without using so much blood. Please Sweetness." Darius implored gently.

I gazed at him and, still sensing nothing negative from him, I kissed him – long and lingering. I still didn't understand how he could still care for me the way he did. But his feelings told me the truth about how he felt about me. And, despite my self-loathing, I couldn't stop how I felt about him. I needed him like I'd never needed anyone before.

Following the kiss we undressed each other. In the process I found a couple of bags of blood in his coat pockets. I handed them to him and waited until he drank them both. Then, lying down with me on top, we made love.

It was almost as frantic and animalistic as my feeding from him had been. We drank from each other at the height of our pleasure. A sharing far deeper than I would have thought possible.

Spent, we finally fell asleep with me still on top of him and his arms around me.

When I awoke, we were laying on our sides with my face against his bare chest. I just laid there without thinking about anything. However, I could feel his contentment as he held me so I knew he was awake.

"The attack was so my fault earlier." I murmured softly into his chest. I still felt really bad about what I'd done.

Darius jerked slightly as if I'd surprised him. I don't think he realised I was awake.

"Why do you believe that?"

"I hadn't been paying attention to my gloves after the guys had left and burnt myself a number of times…" I started saying when he tilted my head back so I would look at him.

"You hid your pain from me?" He asked me incredulously.

"Yes." I whispered as I gazed into his eyes.

"Why Sonja?" He looked as confused as he sounded.

"I didn't want to worry you, to take you away from the work you had to do."

"You reckless crazy woman." He muttered as he held me tightly. "Don't do that to me again. Don't hide yourself from me like that again. Promise me Sonja."

"I can't promise that and you know it. Just as I can't make you promise me the same thing. Both of us will do so to try to protect the other. You know it and I know it." I murmured against his throat as I held him just as tightly.

He sighed.

"In reality, it still isn't completely your fault Sweetness. Hell, you have not had any training yet. Not even the basics of what to expect and not to expect."

Then he went quiet. After a few moments, I snuggled into him and felt his longing. Both mentally and physically. I smiled then sighed and whispered.

"I don't think we should as I'm not the sort to perform for an audience. Especially ones with exceptional hearing."

Darius chuckled as we both heard the other three guys talking and moving about in the outer room.

"Then get dressed woman or they will hear more than you bargained on." He kissed me.

"Later Darlin', later." I murmured with a smile against his lips.

"You can count on it." He whispered as he let me feel his desire.

A few moments later we were dressed. Darius had collected the used bags and we were out the door and in the outer room.

"Kaelan, make sure she doesn't work too hard that she forgets to check her gloves please?" Darius asked the tall man.

I swatted Darius in the arm for his cheek as Kaelan raised an eyebrow in surprise then nodded.

Darius sent me a burst of desire then left the room. I watched him as he left and sent him my feelings that the sight of his retreating form sent through me. He grinned at me as he closed the door.

I started to reach for the gloves when Kaelan stopped me. I gazed up at him in confusion.

"No point. The three of us are doing the last lot now. Why don't you start sorting out the rounds to the relevant rifles while we finish these off then we'll help you complete the sorting. We've done well for eighteen hours of work."

"Eighteen? So... what? It's about midday then?" I asked as I looked at all three of them.

"Yep sure is." Lars chimed in.

"Yeah, you only napped for about four hours." Trent informed.

"Oh." Was all I said. Then I started sorting out the ammunition.

Once the guys had finished filling and capping the last of the hollow points, they then helped me sort out the remaining rounds to the appropriate rifles. Once that was done we stood back and looked at our collection.

"Well... I think we have more than enough to deal with the coming battle." Kaelan stated.

Each rifle had well over a hundred rounds. None of us had actually counted them but I would have to say we each had a minimum of roughly 175 rounds. Give or take a few. And... we still had quite a bit of the jar of blessed silver nitrate left.

"We just have to make sure we don't shoot any of our own." I murmured.

Then I turned to one of the other cabinets, pulled out four small backpacks I'd seen the previous night and handed one to each of the guys. The previous owners certainly were organised for a non-human war. Made me wonder who they were.

We placed our ammunition into the bags, grabbed a bag and rifle each then headed upstairs after we'd cleaned the place up and put everything away.

Kaelan went to find Sarah, while Lars and Trent went their own way. I headed up to Darius's room. Even though I'd had four hours sleep I was tired. It was 1400 by the time I crawled onto his bed.

# Chapter 18

As I started making my way up to consciousness, I could sense it was almost dusk. Opening my eyes confirmed that the sun wasn't far from touching the horizon, along with the view of a bare chest lightly sprinkled with dark hairs millimetres away from my face. I breathed him in. For the living dead, he smelt wonderful. With the intention of going back to sleep I snuggled into him.

"We have to get up Dearest." Darius murmured into my hair as his arms tightened around me.

"Do you know, roughly, when the battle will start?" I asked softly.

"1900 tonight at the earliest."

That was in less than three hours' time.

"How can you know that so precisely?" I gazed at him incredulously.

"Every now and then, when battles like this occur, we set up a little 'free' appreciation dinner for the local farmers and their families. As an extra incentive for them to go, we organise free childcare at the venue and free transport there and back for those who wish to drink but not drive. It allows them to enjoy the evening and we have the surrounding area free of innocents." Darius explained as his arms relaxed around me.

I just stared at him in amazement. He smiled.

"The challenging faction may or may not realise we have a hand in clearing the area. Not that they care. However, we do care about whether the innocents are hurt or not. Either way, sometime tonight we will fight."

"Will Norton be here?" I whispered.

"Yes. If Norton wishes to become the next Prince of the City then he's the one who has to kill Orenda. He has no choice because the one who kills the current prince becomes the new prince." Darius informed me.

For the first time in my life I was truly afraid. I'd never been in a situation like the impending battle and, to top it off, I was addicted to – in lust with – the Prince's General. I wasn't so sure about love at that point, but lust most definitely. Burying my face against his chest, I held him tightly as I wondered what I'd gotten myself into.

"Sonja? What is wrong Sweetness? Why so afraid?" Darius's concern flooded through me as he held me in return.

It took me a few moments before I could answer as I let his gentleness and strength seep into me.

"I've never been in a situation like this before Darius. One target who will never get the chance to retaliate against me is all I've ever done." I paused for a moment or two as a self-realisation hit me.

"Shit! In reality I've never been tested like this before." I murmured against his chest as I admitted out loud something I'd never let myself think of before, let alone admit to myself before.

And I was incredibly scared. I'd placed myself into a situation

I knew nothing about. I was so out of my depth. For the first time I realised most things in my life I'd coasted through. Had taken the easy path, the least painful path. Any problems along the way, and there had been some that were merely the occasional bump, I'd managed to skirt around. However, they'd still never been that serious. I guess I've had an easy life. Up until now.

"How hard was it for you to admit all that?" Again, his arms tightened around me as he murmured against my hair.

"Very." I whispered as I ducked my head further against his chest.

Darius traced a finger along my jaw until his finger reached my chin then he tilted my head so I was forced to look at him.

"You will do fine Sonja. I believe in you. Just treat it as 'ducks in a line' at a fete. Do not think of it any other way. You are good at what you do, take your time and trust in your abilities." His finger caressed my face the whole time he spoke to me.

I didn't know what to say as my mind went blank, but his confidence in me pleased me that he thought so well of me. As my mind stayed blank for a while, my emotions calmed down and as they calmed down a question from a few days ago – totally off topic – popped into my head.

"Darius? How did you know it was me at the second venue last week?"

He chuckled.

"Under normal circumstances where you were hidden was perfect. I could not see you. However, the wind was unpredictable that night and, at times, I could smell mango and frangipani on the wind. The same scents in the café. As well as in my room the night before when you had entered." His hands started caressing me. "You were a surprise that night…"

"So were you. I wasn't expecting you when I opened the door. Not physically, nor naked, and that image wouldn't leave me alone." I couldn't stop the feelings of desire that flooded through me at that memory.

"I could not get you out of my mind either and I did not expect to see you again after Friday night last week. So, I had asked Charles about you. Little did I know you would come waltzing back into my life the next night. At least, not in the manner that you did." His voice came out deeper and huskier than before as he rolled me onto my back.

He opened his mouth as if he was going to speak again but I reached up and kissed him. We still had roughly two hours before we had to join the others. Despite his pep talk, I wasn't sure if either of us would survive. If he died then I definitely would. All talk was forgotten for a while as my need for him overrode everything else.


By 1800 hours we were fed, sated, showered and dressed, and leaving the bedroom with the backpack over my shoulder and rifle in hand. Both of us were dressed in black. Black jeans, him in a black turtleneck shirt while I was in a black long sleeved polo shirt, and accessory clothing like shoes and socks also in black. My hair was covered in a black knitted cap.

"Ah Sonja… Good, if you would like to go up to the next landing you will see us from a reasonable height with the armbands on." Varrik called up to me when he saw us reach the stairs.

I nodded and made my way up to the next landing as I dug out the night vision scope from the backpack. Darius continued down the stairs. The lights were turned off as I made my way up. Once there, I stood at the railing and looked down at them through the scope. There were a mix of those wearing the armbands – on both arms – and those not.

"Thanks." I said quietly as I put the scope away. As I walked back down the stairs the lights came back on.

Standing next to Varrik was a rather tall, and human, woman holding his hand. It seemed they were a couple.

She had black hair that had blue or purple or both highlights. I couldn't tell which. Were they natural? I had no way of knowing without sunlight and that was never going to happen for me now. Her eyes, however, were incredible. I couldn't tell if they were blue or black, but seemed to have what appeared to be flecks of grey and... purple?

Ookaaay!

While her face appeared average looking, the colouring of her hair and eyes made her stand out and seem attractive. So it wouldn't appear as if I was staring, I glanced around at the others on my way down.

"You are welcome. Here are your armbands. You and the other three snipers might want to head to the roof now and get yourselves settled so you will not be spotted by Norton's people too soon." Varrik informed as he handed me two armbands.

I'd just finished settling them on my arms when Kaelan, Sarah, Lars and Trent entered, followed by four others. Kaelan and Sarah kissed then she went and stood beside Itztecpatl.

Darius lightly touched my arm.

"These four Jags are going to protect the four of you from any aerial attacks. That way, you will not have to worry about anything but killing the enemy on the ground." Darius informed us.

We nodded then Kaelan and I followed Trent, Lars and the four Jags.

As Darius's touch lingered as I walked away from him, he sent me a burst of confidence. I smiled at him then went back up the stairs.

I've only been among them for a short while but the few lovers I've seen don't seem to hide their feelings from those around them. That knowledge pleased me immensely because I didn't think I could keep my feelings hidden whenever I was within touching... no... within sight of Darius.

Trent led us into the attic and from the attic, up two spiral staircases through two trap doors that exited onto the roof. When the doors were closed they couldn't be distinguished from the rest of the tiled roof.

The night was dark. I noted that the majority of the lights in the house were off. Especially on the two upper levels. Either the moon hadn't risen or it was a new moon. With no lights shining in the near vicinity, it made the night even darker. One consolation was that the stars were exceptionally bright. I like looking at the stars.

Once all of us were on the roof we split up. Kaelan and a jag called Michael went to the rear side of the house. Trent and Tony went to the left side of the house. Lars and Bart went to the right side, while Frank and I went to the front of the house. Kaelan was the only unaltered human among the eight of us on the roof but he didn't seem to have any problems with that.

With rifles loaded, silencers attached and ammunition in easy reach, we sat back and patiently waited.

For forty-five minutes, the eight of us sat on the roof waiting. Out of the eight of us, Kaelan and I were the only ones who sat silently. I guess he and I were used to waiting. Goes with our jobs I guess. Gazing quietly out at the front of the property I saw movement at the perimeter. I double checked through the scope.

"They're here." I murmured softly, knowing the other six altereds on the roof would hear and Michael would let Kaelan know.

I then sent a burst of alertness to Darius and received a sense of gratitude from him. I brought my rifle into place ready. We had to wait till they were half way across the open space before we could shoot. I took a slow deep breath then let it out just as slowly to ground myself while I waited.

Once in range, I started killing them.

With my first shot, my target screamed, fell to the ground and rolled in agony. It was a gut shot so I fired a second time and the target went still. There were other shots sounding out as my fellow snipers started shooting as well. The enemy scattered and started running towards the house. With each shot there were more screams. By my fifth shot – all in a matter of seconds – the others in the house came out.

Sniping just became harder.

Not only did I have to hit a moving target, but I had to make sure I didn't hit my own people. I did learn that if I hit the enemy in the heart or head then I only needed the one shot. Anywhere else and it required a second round. A third if the first two were away from anything vital.

Not long after the others had come out of the house did the therians change, as well as the vamps. Some of them changed into wolves and the bigger cats and into predatory flyers to attack each other. There were eagles, owls, falcons, kites and any other birds along those lines.

It wasn't long after that that the enemy flyers discovered us on the roof and started attacking us as well. Knew it would be too good to last. Staying hidden that is. I just did the best I could and kept firing at the enemy.

At one point I felt the sting of pain as somewhere down there Darius had been hurt. However, even I could tell it was more of a glancing blow than a serious injury. He sent me a small burst of calm to let me know he was okay. That injury wouldn't be the only one he would receive throughout the night.

Gratefully, though, none of them were too bad.

After a while I lost count of how many of Norton's people I'd shot. However the battle didn't get any easier.

In the one slight break I had, I watched vampires rip heads off and hearts out, I saw therians slash at each other and tear each other into shreds, as well as limb-from-limb. It was both clean and messy and all I could think was thank goodness it was dark and that I was on the roof and not down there.

The ground glistened but it still looked dark. I was ever grateful that the blood didn't show up red on the ground in the dark. From my vantage point the battle didn't seem quite real and I felt rather detached from it except whenever Darius received an injury. Then it felt very real.

My unexpected break came to an end when sharp pain lanced through my left shoulder and my eardrums felt like they were going to burst when a bird screeched piercingly loudly next to my ear. I screamed with the pain. Frank was suddenly beside me and started wrestling with the eagle that had attacked me.

"Sorry for the delay... There were two of them this time." He grunted out in a growly voice as he fought, ripping the bird from me.

The action caused burning pain as the bird's talons tore furrows in my shoulder. A wave of anxiety washed through me and I clamped down on the pain. While I thought about healing the injury, I sent Darius a wave of calm to let him know I was okay. The anxiety disappeared as we continued our respective fighting. All-in-all, Frank did a reasonable job at protecting me.

Bodies littered the ground. Thankfully, more of Norton's people than ours, but some of those bodies were definitely ours.

I caught sight of Orenda and Norton fighting at the front of the house, off to the right, so I kept their little battle on the up-and-up whenever someone tried to sneak up behind Orenda. Couldn't have such an unfair fight between the two leaders now could we? Thanks to my sniping, I kept their fight private.

To me, they seemed to be evenly matched as they traded blows and clawings in between their circling of each other. I didn't get to watch all of their battle due to keeping it on the up-and-up, only bits and pieces of it. Then the balance between them changed as he slid a little on the blood that covered the ground.

Orenda took advantage of his unbalance as her fist smashed into his chest. When she pulled her hand out, his heart came out with it. I don't know what she did but she dropped it to the ground in pieces. Then she ripped his head off. Orenda stood there, turning slowly in a circle with Norton's head raised high and hissed at any who thought they could take her. Norton's people thought better of it and left her alone.

It was over.

Those who saw Norton die, retreated. Orenda held back her people when they had started to give chase. Once the enemy had disappeared, Orenda started issuing orders to tend to the wounded, to dispose of the bodies and to clean up the mess so everything would look normal come daylight. The fighting was a couple of hours long, give or take a few minutes.

It was at that point I discovered I had run out of ammunition. Perfect timing. I sat there and just stared at the devastation on the ground. I could think of better ways for claiming the proverbial throne. One that was less costly in lives, as well as less messy. It was almost as if they had forgotten how to be civilised once they were no longer strictly human. However, humans weren't exactly civilised when it came to wars either. My ideas would work for them as well.

My musings were interrupted as pain ripped through my throat then chest. I screamed as I fell backwards onto the roof. Another slash went through me as Frank tried to find out what was wrong with me.

"Darius..." I managed to gasp out before a third, fourth, fifth and sixth attack had me writhing in an agony I never wanted to experience ever again.

The attacks were so quick I didn't have a chance at controlling the pain. As a result it was looping back between Darius and I, making it seem worse than it truly was. The others were around me now as Frank picked me up and they headed to the trap door.

As he passed me down to someone waiting below, the pain vanished so quickly I passed out.

As I regained consciousness, I could feel I was in someone's arms and they were moving. My first thought was Darius but then by the person's scent I knew it wasn't. Then I remembered his pain.

"Darius...!" I called out as I jerked in the arms of the one who held me. My head swivelled about as I tried to see where I was then back to the one carrying me. It was Kaelan.

"They're trying to find him now." He said quietly as he continued to carry me.

"In here Kaelan." Said Max from the meeting. He had a deep gravelly voice like the one Darius had called Max the previous night. Max hadn't spoken during the meeting which was why I had no idea if they were the same man.

As we entered Darius's room the tall woman, who'd been with Varrik, and Sarah entered as well. I'd only been unconscious for about a minute or two.

"Enola, Sarah... please stay with Sonja while we try to find Darius. Enola can you let Varrik know about Darius please?" Max asked, sounding calm the entire time.

"Sure Max." Enola responded.

The men left.

In the dark, Enola sat in one of the chairs and stared at nothing in particular, while Sarah stood at one of the windows. I didn't even want to know what she was seeing out there. As for me, I sat on my side of the bed. A breeze wafted through the open windows bringing the smell of blood and death on it.

"I can't feel him." I whispered as my panic started rising.

"Darius will be okay. He hasn't survived this long just to be easily killed." Enola stated. I just didn't trust the confidence in her voice.

"You don't understand. I can always sense him, I always have since we first met. But I can't feel him at all now. Not even his pain." I whispered, trying to keep the panic under control.

In the back of my mind, I had the thought that maybe he was just hiding his pain from me. Only, my fear of losing him was so strong that surely he could feel it and would therefore try to relieve my worries.

However, my panic overpowered me and I couldn't think clearly. The more I thought about it, the more I was becoming convinced that he was dead because I was sure no one could hide that much pain.

I reached into the drawer of the bedside table and pulled out the pistol I'd seen hours earlier during a curiosity snoop session. My life was over without him.

"Sonja! What are you doing?!" Sarah demanded.

"I can't live without him." I murmured as the certainty of him being dead had grown to the point I no longer doubted it.

"Sonja, you mustn't!" Enola stated as panic sounded in her voice as well.

Just as I was putting the gun to my head, both Sarah and Enola rushed me. They grabbed my hand and the three of us struggled for a few moments as they tried to take the gun from me.

Then I pulled the trigger.

# Chapter 19

Blinking, I looked up at the ceiling as I choked on blood and found it difficult to breathe. There were hands at my throat and the gun had disappeared but didn't remember it being taken away from me.

"Fudgerigars Varrik! Just find him and tell him to let her feel his pain. I don't know what will happen next if she doesn't." Enola muttered next to me through clenched teeth. Then she turned her attention back to me.

"Hold on Sonja. Sarah has gone to get some blood to help you heal."

I wanted to speak, to tell her that I couldn't drink the blood, but all I did was choke on the blood that pooled in my throat. The lights were still out and there was no one else in the room with us. I closed my eyes so I wouldn't have to see Enola's face. Her horror was too much to handle.

Then I heard running feet. After a few moments the light flicked on.

"I've got the blood." Sarah stated breathlessly.

"Shit Sonja, what were you trying to do?" Kaelan demanded as he rushed in behind Sarah.

A third pair of feet stopped near the bed.

"Put the bags over there Sarah. Sonja can't drink them. Darius can however." Max instructed.

My eyes snapped open with a spark of hope at his words and tried to speak, only for the blood to bubble and splatter over my face. I attempted to swallow some of it.

"What a right mess you have made, you silly childe." Max stated quietly as he frowned down at me. "Here Enola, clean away the blood from her throat so we can see how well she is healing." He said and handed her some cloths. "If the bleeding has stopped then we need to change the bed covers."

Enola set about cleaning the blood from my throat and face. I swapped between swallowing the blood and choking on it.

"She's starting to heal..." Enola informed.

"Good. She'll either be a strong one or a fast healer then." Max muttered.

Then Enola's eyes lost focus. "Varrik says they've found him..."

My eyes locked to her face as I waited. The fear resurfaced since I still couldn't sense him. She spoke in a distracted tone as she relayed what Varrik told her.

"He's alive but badly injured... There are volunteers standing by to feed him... Varrik said once Darius is stable, they'll bring him up."

I couldn't help it but I started crying and I couldn't stop. The relief that flooded through me was so intense.

"Shhh, it is okay Sonja. He will be here soon." Max soothed. "Right. Let's get Sonja and the room cleaned up. She needs to sleep to help heal her wound."

For a while there was no more talking as Kaelan held me in his arms while the other three set about cleaning me and changing the sheets. He looked down at me.

"Why Sonja?"

"I can't survive without him." I rasped through my sore throat.

"Can't or won't?" Kaelan asked as he frowned at me.

"Can't. I can't feed from anyone but him." I whispered.

Kaelan's expression was one of surprised disbelief. Not that I blamed him since my… *condition* seemed to be rare. But Max must have seen his reaction.

"She is right Kaelan. She honestly can not feed from anyone else. Not even the donated kind." He sighed. "Good thing the gun had normal ammunition in it."

"I wasn't thinking clearly and forgot I wouldn't die from the normal bullet." I whispered.

"Good thing you did forget that little detail then." Max stated.

Once they had finished, I was settled back on the bed.

"Sleep Sonja." Max commanded. His compulsion hit me and I couldn't fight it.

*

The scent of Darius around me forced me awake. The lights were off and it was still dark outside. By the feel of it, it was in the early hours of the morning with dawn still a few hours away. I tried to sit up to look at him but his arms and legs kept me where I was, they were that tight around me.

"Darius?" I whispered fearfully and hopefully.

His limbs tightened some more.

"Don't you ever do that to me again Sonja!" He was so angry.

Tears trailed down my face.

"I won't if you promise never to hide yourself from me again. I can't live without you and when I couldn't sense you I thought you were dead." I sobbed as I buried my face against his chest.

"You need to feed." For some reason Darius's anger didn't subside.

Despite the hunger building within me, I couldn't bring myself to drink from him just then and kept my face pressed against his chest.

He reached up and, with a roughness born of his anger, he tangled his fingers in my hair. Then, gripping firmly, he pulled my head back so I was forced to look at him.

"Drink damn it!" He growled at me.

As pain tingled across my scalp from his action, my heart broke as I thought our relationship had come to an end with the way he was treating me. Fresh tears fell as I bit my bottom lip in the effort to hold back the sobs.

Darius made a small moan-like sound in the back of his throat as he hugged me to him.

"You reckless crazy woman." His whisper was harsh in my ear as feelings of fear, need, adoration and desire swamped through me.

When his feelings hit me, letting me know we were okay, I started crying again as I clung to him. We stayed that way until I'd managed to calm down.

"Feed Dearest, please." Darius's whisper implored.

Since my face was already against his throat, I softly nuzzled it for a bit then gently sunk my fangs in. His body jerked a little as his breath hissed, but it was pleasure that flowed through him. I drank him slowly and lovingly and hoped we had an eternity together. Once my fang marks healed…

"Now sleep Dearest. You need it to finish healing." He stated as he laid me back down and curled himself around me.

Together, we fell back to sleep.


Only three hours had passed when I awoke again. Glancing around without moving, I could see it was still dark. I snuggled closer to Darius and his arms tightened around me.

"You need to feed again Sweetness. While sleeping reduces the amount of blood used in healing, we still expend quite a bit."

"And what about you? You are healing your injuries as well as feeding me Darius. You must be low as well."

"There are six more bags on the bedside table waiting for me."

"Then drink as much as you need now." I murmured.

"Well, I will drink half now and half later." He responded.

I watched him as he drank them slowly and it seemed to add an extra level to the sexual tension between us. Then he gathered me into his arms. Nuzzling his neck for a few moments to tease…

"Drink woman." He growled sexily in a low voice.

So I did. My fangs sinking in then, sucking longingly, I drank deeply. Naturally, one thing led to another – usually the one thing – whenever the two of us were alone together like that.


Sometime later, just as the sun was rising, and we lay sated and contented together...

"What happened Darius?" My voice was but a whisper. Not because of the damage I had done to it – that was now healed, but because I couldn't bring myself to speak any louder. In that moment, I thought Varrik and Enola's ability for telepathy would be perfect right about now. Not to mention very convenient during a battle.

"Clayton, Norton's second-in-command, jumped me and was vicious in his attack. He was trying to rip out my heart after he had already ripped out my throat..."

Horror washed through me and he held me closer as he tried to soothe me with his feelings. Then he continued...

"...but I am older than him and was able to survive where others would not have. However, I did not get to kill him. The bastard made his escape. He will probably take over Norton's faction now if he is strong enough to defeat the challengers. The bastard let it slip he was the one to take the hit out on me. If he survives then I will definitely kill him next time round."

"Wait a moment..." I started, frowning. "...Clayton? As in Clayton Jonston?"

"Yes. How do you know him?" Darius frowned as he leaned back to stare at me.

"I was running a money tracing program when one of my house mates told me that he was the one who was paying for the hit against you. I didn't recognise the name until you mentioned it." I explained.

"Bastard. At least that answers that question. However, for the time being, I'll let him think I do not know. He can wait until I am ready to deal with him."

"Is the battle truly over?" I nodded then asked. I couldn't quite keep the fear out of my voice. I didn't want to go through all that again any time soon.

"Yes it is over. If we are lucky there will not be another until a year's time. While they were fierce, we were brutal in the hopes of discouraging them from retaliating again any time soon."

I got up on my elbows and gazed down at him. My eyes started to tear up again. As his hand came up to cup my face, I spoke before he did.

"I promise you I will not hide my emotions from you if you promise me the same. Blood aside Darius, I need you and can't be without you. While sustenance was on my mind at the time, it was a small part of the reason why I shot myself." I glanced down at his chest before looking back into his eyes.

"You were my addiction before I became a vampire my Love, so please promise me." My voice came out as a whisper at the end.

Surprise flitted through him at my words then adoration flooded him only to spill into and fill me with warmth and belonging.

"I promise Dearest. But promise me you will make sure I am truly dead first before trying to kill yourself." He murmured against my lips.

"I promise." I whispered then he completed the kiss.

A moment or two later, we were still kissing when the door burst opened and I jumped in fright. Both of us looked towards it.

"See Enola? I told you they would be alright." Varrik stated as he followed Enola into the room. He looked sheepishly at us barely covered by the sheets that had worked their way down with our movements. "I am sorry but she had to see for herself."

Enola swatted him as she spoke to us. "Mind you, he's just as guilty of wanting to know how you pair are." She grinned.

Before they could come any closer, Varrik stepped in front of her, threw her over his shoulder and headed back towards the door. She let out a squeak then slapped him on his snugly clad arse.

"Hey, ya neanderthal fang-face!" Enola growled at him with a smile, even though he couldn't see it, as she waved at us then hooked her thumbs in the waistband of his pants.

We laughed at their behaviour. Varrik slapped her on the butt in return as he walked out the door.

"Close the door after you woman and let's leave them in peace." He gave us a back handed wave as he walked out the door.

"Well fudgerigars!" She muttered as she smiled at us. After the door closed…

"I take it they're friends of yours?" I asked with a smile. It was a pleasant surprise that they included me in their 'checking-up'.

"They will be yours too. Varrik and I have known each other for hundreds of years…" He chuckled.

"Just how old are you anyway?!" I couldn't keep the surprise from my voice as I stared at him.

"I am just under a thousand, while Varrik is a couple of hundred years younger." Darius chuckled at me.

"Oh." Was all I managed to come out with. He looked bloody awesome for an extremely old man.

Darius then made himself more comfortable and dragged me down with him.

"Both of us need more sleep. We will talk more when we wake up." He murmured as he settled me beside him.

I didn't bother arguing.

# *Chapter 20*

It was Sunday and the sun had set by the time I'd awoken. I couldn't believe how much sleeping I was doing over the past couple of days. I rolled over to snuggle into Darius only to find he wasn't there.

Panic flared within me as I opened my eyes and, after a quick search, found the room was empty. I knew it was stupid to jump to conclusions but I couldn't seem to help it. Not after the rollercoaster ride my life had experienced during the past week. I sat on the edge of the bed in the effort to calm myself down.

Then I felt a spike of anxiety that wasn't mine.

"Sonja?" Came Darius's voice from the en suite doorway.

Gazing at him sheepishly, I watched him wipe the remainder of shaving cream from his face and throat.

"Don't mind me. I'm just being silly." I murmured then looked down at my feet. I felt so embarrassed at my overreaction.

He was suddenly in front of me kneeling down and peering into my eyes. He brought his hand up to cup the side of my face and I leant into it.

"You do not get rid of me that easily Dearest. Just remember that okay?" He stated softly as our foreheads touched.

I nodded. Then he was standing up and hauling me to my feet.

"Come on. You will feel better after a shower."

"Only if you join me." I responded softly with desire as I wrapped my arms around his waist and held him tight.

True to form so far, when the two of us were together and naked, our shower took longer than normal as we bathed each other. Among other delightful things.

God! I would never get tired of sex with him if it continued like that.

As we dried ourselves...

"You did say the battle really is over didn't you?" I asked.

"Yes I did Sweetness. You and I can get to know each other better now." He answered from behind me and I could feel him smile.

"I need to go home first." I said softly.

"Oh? Why?" Darius asked with curiosity.

"I have three house mates who need to know what has happened to me."

"Then by all means do what needs to be done."

"Is my motorbike okay?" Now that things had settled down enough, I wanted to know.

"Apart from a few scratches in the paintwork and a broken mirror, it is amazingly fine. The front forks are not even dented let alone bent."

"Surprising... but good. At least I have a way to get home that won't frighten my house mates."

After feeding, cleaning teeth and dressing into my riding leathers, we headed downstairs.

With the battle for leadership of Brisbane over this time round, it appeared quite a few were in the process of leaving. Orenda had her arm around a young female vampire I didn't know and was caressing the young woman's shoulder rather intimately. Okay! Orenda prefers women. I just blinked and moved on.

On the other side of that same young woman Max also had his arm around her. Another threesome? Alright, each to their own I guess. There was also Varrik, Enola, Charlotte, Anoki, Itztecpatl, Sarah, Kaelan and a few others I didn't know yet who were gathered in the foyer quietly chatting.

Darius and I joined the crowd.

"Well, Enola and I are off. Call me when you need me Orenda." Varrik stated as he wrapped an arm around Enola's waist.

"I will my friend. Be well both of you." Orenda responded.

Enola hugged me while Varrik and Darius did that manly arm shake that guys do.

"Call me so we can organise a get-together." Varrik said to Darius.

"Will do." Darius grinned at him.

Then Enola hugged Darius as Varrik hugged me.

"Glad he finally found someone." Varrik breathed into my ear so I was the only one who heard him.

I smiled in response then the two of them left. It made me wonder how long Darius had been alone.

Orenda was telling Itztecpatl he didn't have to come back until tomorrow night when I turned my attention back to the rest of the group. After hugs from Sarah and a quick goodbye by the three of them, Itztecpatl, Kaelan and Sarah left as well.

As they exited I was stunned to see Charles enter.

"Charles, what a pleasant surprise. Are you well?" Orenda greeted.

It took a lot of effort on my part to not let my jaw fall to the floor as I just stared at him. He and Orenda knew each other? Questions swirled in my mind but didn't know what to ask first. Darius gently squeezed my hand as I felt his amusement.

"I'm good Orenda and I am pleased to see you are still Prince of the City." He responded calmly then he turned towards me. "Hello... LaMuerteViene."

My mind stopped functioning totally, along with my breath as his greeting to me sunk in.

"You're Helmsman?" My voice came out so soft it was almost a whisper. I felt Darius's amusement over my reaction.

Charles nodded with a hint of a smile. I blinked then cleared my throat.

"How long have you known who I was?" I still couldn't believe it but it did explain how Helmsman knew my real name on Wednesday. He smiled gently at me.

"Monday morning when LaMuerteViene told Helmsman about the attempted hit on her."

Realisation hit like a blinding spotlight.

"Of course. Sunday evening you found out about me being injured and obviously put two and two together come Monday morning."

He nodded then looked from me to Darius and back to me again.

"I guess you aren't my P.A. any more and nor will you be back at the office come tomorrow."

"Ummm... No. I'm vampire now." I answered gently.

"Did you have to take my best P.A. away?" Charles stared at Darius with a frown.

"Not my doing. She chose all on her own." Darius denied with a grin.

"Do you know how hard it is to find decent P.A.s these days?" He grumped at me but his eyes were gentle with a slight sparkle to suggest he wasn't that upset. Charles just shook his head.

"I'm sorry Charles." I responded with a kind smile. I knew he would find another one without any problems. "Anyway, why are you here?" I asked quietly in confusion.

"I'm a business man not a fighter. As Helmsman I help keep Orenda and her people safe from hits so she stays in power. I came to see if all went well." He stated simply.

"I see." I murmured. And I did.

He was in the perfect position to ensure he grabbed any hits before anyone else did. Then I realised that, him as Helmsman, I could definitely give him a piece of my mind for all the abruptly ended conversations we'd had. But that can happen at a later date.

"We have to go Charles. I'll call you soon okay?" Darius said.

"Sure."

"Call me if you need me Orenda." Darius said as he turned to her.

"I will. Be well both of you." Orenda responded with a smile.

We said our farewells and walked out the door. My motorbike

was waiting for me with two helmets, mine and one other, on the seat. I handed Darius the other one while I grabbed mine. In no time at all, with his arms around my waist and his chest firmly against my back, we were off the property and on our way to the north side and home.

As I pulled up to the gutter, I had to admit to myself that I rather enjoyed Darius's arms around me while I rode. His thumbs had caressed my ribs when I let him feel my happiness of him being there with me on the bike.

Then he tapped me on the shoulder. I lifted my visor and turned my head towards him as I waited for him to hop off.

"My place?" I felt as well as heard his confusion.

"Yeah. I need to talk to them alone. I'll come back here when I have finished." I said gently as I caressed his hand.

"Then be as quick as you can Dearest." He then hopped off the bike and stood on the footpath and watched me ride off as I sent him a burst of desire.

I also had to be honest with myself that I was nervous meeting up with the three of them hence why I wanted to meet with them by myself.

A few minutes later I hit the garage door remote button as I neared the house. The three of them were waiting for me as I slowly rode in then closed the garage door. They were standing in the doorway between kitchen and garage. I sat there for a moment before pulling gloves and helmet off.

"Hi guys." I greeted tentatively.

"You okay?" Zeaya asked as she looked at me, the motorbike then back at me. She'd noticed the damage.

"More or less." I said as I walked towards them.

There was a slight pause then we group hugged.

"You're different." Zeaya stated as we parted. Trust her to notice.

"Come. Let's sit in the kitchen."

"Do you want anything?" George asked hopefully.

For once it saddened me that I had to decline because I knew it would disappoint him. I shook my head. "No thank you George." I said softly and I was right as he pouted.

We sat around the breakfast bar and I started filling them in on when I left the hospital Tuesday, as in Darius binding me to him. Maisie gasped when I told them what had happened to me Thursday evening when the binding wore off and, therefore, my decision to become a vampire. I told of how I was still bound to Darius and why but left out last night's battle.

If they were upset with what I've told them so far then how would they react with that piece of the story? I didn't want to find out.

"Well, no wonder you didn't want me to get you anything." George commented petulantly as he frowned at me.

"I'm sorry George. The whole thing was unplanned and backfired severely. Not even Darius and Orenda guessed this would happen. I guess it's a good thing I'm attracted to Darius since I need him to stay alive." I said softly.

To be honest I was still a little stunned over the strength of my attraction to the studly vamp.

"So, what happens to us now?" Maisie asked in a small voice.

"Whatever you want to happen. I won't be living here

anymore but there is nothing to say you three can't stay here. I'm still a hit man regardless of what my duties may be within Orenda's coterie. I just don't have a day job any more, that's all."

"So I don't have to leave here?" Maisie asked hopefully.

At the same time as Maisie spoke...

"I take it you'll be living with Darius then?" Zeaya asked in her usual gruff tone.

"No Maisie, you do not have to leave. This is your home for as long as you want it to be. Yes Zeaya I will. I can't drink blood from anyone else but him."

"Prove it." Zeaya demanded.

"What?" I asked in confusion.

George thrust his arm ramrod straight at me.

"Yeah, prove it." He stared obstinately at me. He was acting brave as I could hear his heart starting to beat faster with nervousness and/or fear. I wasn't sure which.

Maisie sat there watching us with her eyes wide.

"You can't be serious." I stated as dread started to build within me. I remembered that one time all too vividly and didn't want to experience it again.

"Very serious. Prove what you've been telling us, that you aren't just ditching us." George stated with a stubbornness I knew only too well.

After a pause I swallowed then stood up and moved the two of us over to the sink.

"You sure?" I murmured.

"Yes." He responded gently.

I hesitated for a moment then bit his wrist. I took a couple of swallows before licking his wrist to close the puncture marks. I was swamped with his memories of how we first met. The first time he stood as close to me as we were right then.

"Cool." George stated as the three of them watched the marks heal and vanish.

A moment or two later the memories disappeared as nausea twisted through me then I was bent over the sink and brought up what I had drank. A spike of concern went through me and I knew it was from Darius. When I'd finished, I rested my forehead on the tap as I rinsed the sink out.

As I tried to regain my composure, my mobile rang. I dug it out of my side pocket and accepted the call.

"I'm okay... No don't. I'll be there soon and I'll explain then... Bye." I then hung up. I stayed where I was for a moment before I straightened up and faced the others.

"You okay? You brought up more than you swallowed." Zeaya asked. I could hear the worry in her voice.

"Yeah, that's the way it was last time as well." I murmured as I waited for the last of my stomach to settle.

"How did he know something was wrong with you?" Zeaya asked with a frown.

"He and I can feel each other's emotions. He'd sensed my distress from the sampling of George." I responded quietly then looked at all three of them.

"I just need to know two things from you. Are you going to stay here and, whether you do or not, will you still work with me?" I hoped they would say yes to both questions.

"Well, I don't know about the other two but I'm staying and I'll still help you when you need me." Maisie's shy timid voice never sounded so good as it did just then.

"Thank you Sweetie." I said softly to her as I hugged her.

"Ah what the hell. As put out as I am that you never came across to my side I'm yours until ya tire of me." Zeaya grumped with her hands on her hips and head down as she peered through her fringe at me.

I gripped her arm. "Thanks Hon."

Then I looked at George.

"Where else am I gonna go where my habits are tolerated as much as they are here?"

I laughed.

"Thanks Baby. I'm glad the three of you are choosing to stay. I didn't want to either sell the house or rent it out to strangers. I don't know for how long but your time is your own. I have a new life to settle into as well as to work out what I'll be doing with my time. I'll take my bike when I leave in a few and will come back for the Jag in a day or two then you can park the ford where I used to park."

"Does that mean you won't be coming back here?" Maisie asked with a hint of fear.

"No Sweetie, I'll be back and forth. I just won't be sleeping here unless I have to do to a job. Oh, here is the key to the motel room I was staying in. Can one of you check the room to make sure I haven't left anything behind and hand the key back please? I think there might be some food at least."

When they nodded...

"Thank you. Well, I've got to go. Enjoy your few days break and don't get up to any trouble." I said with a grin. "Oh, once I'm settled I'll introduce you to Darius."

And my grin widened at Maisie's wide eyed response. The other two just looked dubious.

"Sweetie, when I do he'll be the second vamp you'll know." I stated as I winked at her.

Maisie gave a shy smile of realisation.

I hugged each of them and they followed me to my bike. Helmeted, gloved and on the bike I gave them a wave, backed the bike out then rode off to Darius's.

The trip back to his place was quick yet seemed to take forever as I had to stop for lights, signs and give way to other traffic and pedestrians. Then finally I was in his street.

The gate opened as I pulled into his driveway and I saw him in the open doorway waiting for me. After parking, I sat there for a moment as I gazed at him standing there and I just let myself enjoy the sight of him. My eyes roamed his magnificent physique as he stood there in jeans and a grey turtleneck, both of which fitted him snugly.

Then I slowly removed the helmet, gloves and key from the ignition. After shoving the gloves and key into the helmet, I didn't rush as I got off the bike and made my way up the stairs. We never took our eyes off each other.

Darius took my helmet and placed it on a little display table without looking. Putting his hands on my waist he pulled me inside, closed the door and lifted me up against him so we were face-to-face. I wrapped my legs around his waist as he kissed me. Then he turned around and made his way upstairs to his massive bed.

Once there, he still hadn't put me down or onto the bed as he gazed at me longingly.

"I have been waiting for you for a very long time. You are my life, my light. I love you Sonja." He murmured against my lips in a feathery touch.

I felt the truth of his words as he let me sense his emotions. I tightened my arms around him.

"And I love you Darius." I whispered against his lips then I closed the almost non-existent distance between us and kissed him hungrily.

They were the last words spoken between us for a long, long time.

## The End

Want to read more about Sarah's story?
Read on to find out the details.

# Extras

## *Bio*

Back in 1967 KC was born on the morning of a black Monday on the Sunshine Coast north of Brisbane, Queensland, Australia. KC is the first to admit that her life was nothing special. She has worked as mechanic, in a book shop and in an IT company. Her interest in computers led her to do volunteer teaching online within the graphics community. Her internet time also sparked her interest in puzzle based games, graphics and internet communities based around her pastimes. Eventually, her pastimes led to the first in her Unnaturals of Brisbane series. She is an avid reader and a cat lover.

Below are ways to follow KC. While she's slack with posting, she uses her facebook author page as her blog.

http://www.kcrileygyer.com/

https://www.facebook.com/KCRileyGyerAuthorPage

https://www.facebook.com/KCRileyGyer

https://www.amazon.com/author/kcrileygyer

https://www.goodreads.com/KCRileyGyer

# Meeting the Characters

I rushed around like a headless chook. Well, I would have, if I was at all physically capable of rushing. I was just glad I didn't have to use my crutches so I had both hands free for setting things up. Glancing at my watch, I let out a groan as the start time ticked closer. Everyone would be here soon. Real soon.

Stopping in the middle of the room, I looked around. Info sheets for playing the part of the host? Check with no small thanks to my behind-the-scenes friend. If it wasn't for him, I think I would still be totally disorganised. Chair for host? Check. Seating for guests? Check. Chairs for audience? Check. Refreshments for everyone? Check. Small tables for host and guests to set their refreshments onto during the Q&A session? Check. Lighting?

I rushed over to the light switches and played with the dimmers to set each control to the right brightness. I didn't want us to be blinded by glaringly bright lights but needed them to be bright enough that we could see each other clearly enough.

There, done.

Closing my eyes, I stood there and took a slow deep breath in, held it for a bit then slowly let it out. I was trying for calm and it worked. A little. Geez, despite Skipper organising my notes into some form of coherency, I'm so nervous. Never have I done anything like this before.

Opening my eyes, I looked around. The walls appeared to be a mix of Victorian wallpaper and wood trim, with some Grecian-like decorative elements at the top of the walls where they meet the ceilings.

As for the seating, they were a mix of different styles and fabrics. Where they did match was the colour of the reddish brown wood and the mid to dark teal fabric. Thankfully, there are two doors into the room. One at each end. The door at the back of the room is hidden by a sparkly midnight blue velvet curtain, from which my guests will come out from behind of. While the door at the front of the room is where the audience would come in.

I guess I should be grateful that the audience is going to be small. Just a tad larger than the number of guests I have arriving. Others could still arrive but that's all I know about at this time.

And then, my time was up.

A knock on the door, the audience would enter through, sounded. Grabbing my crutches and the audience list, I opened the door. A pretty young woman with straight brown hair stood before me.

"Hi KC, I'm Emma Jane." She greeted shyly but had the most amazing smile. Ah, the beauty of social media; where one doesn't have to introduce one's self to their followers.

"Hi ya Emma, welcome." I smiled back as I ushered her in.

As I did so, I noted more guests coming down the corridor. One by one, I placed a tick beside their name and pointed them towards the refreshments and their seats. Once all had arrived, had a drink in hand – nothing alcoholic since we can't have me falling asleep half way through the event – and were sitting in their seats, I made my way up to the stage and stood by my chair.

"Welcome to an evening of Meeting the Characters. Tonight, our four guests played an integral role in keeping Orenda, the vampire Prince of the City, in power. One is the Prince's General and the other is her Harbinger, an archaic word for messenger-slash-envoy. And, with them are their bonded life partners. Please welcome, from Objective: Crimson Empire... Enola, Varrik, Sonja, and Darius."

As the audience and I applauded, I turned towards the curtain on my left and in walked our guests. They smiled and waved to the audience then gave me a hug before sitting down. With Sonja and Darius sitting on the sofa on my right, Enola and Varrik sat in the one on my left. A moment later, with grins and thank yous' from the four, the audience quietened down. Then I continued.

"For those of you who are unsure, you the readers have this opportunity to delve deeper into the lives and minds of the characters in the 'Unnaturals of Brisbane' series. Our guests have generously given up some of their time to be here tonight so let's make it worth their while! Without further ado, it's question time from the audience." I stated and hands rose into the air. I pointed to one woman and she stood up.

"Hi, I'm Emma Jane."

"Hi Emma." Was the chorus from the stage as all looked at her.

"Varrik, how long have you been a vampire?"

"Oh, ahh..." Varrik frowned in concentration.

Darius sniggered and threw a small ball of paper at his friend. Where he got it from, I had no idea. It hit him in the side of the head and Varrik grinned sheepishly. I couldn't help smiling with a slight shake of my head at their antics.

"Roughly 800 years, give or take a few years." He chuckled with a sideways glance at Darius.

When Emma sat down, hands rose into the air and I chose the next person.

"Hi KC and all, my name is Jayne."

"Hi Jayne." We greeted.

"My question is to both Varrik and Darius. It's easy to see that you have been friends for a long while. How did you meet and how did you become friends?"

"We were on opposing sides on a battlefield when I was attacked by a vampire." Varrik started.

"Only, that vampire was on neither side, a vulture of our kind that battles tend to attract. So I saved Varrik's sorry arse instead." Darius continued as he chuckled with a shake of his head.

"And we've been friends ever since." Varrik finished with a grin.

Just for a change, I chose one of the few guys in the audience.

"I'm Robert."

"Hello Robert." We chorused from the stage.

"My question is for Darius. Do you ever get nervous or anxious before a battle?"

"Oh, good question Robert." I stated quietly in approval.

"Hmm, yes and no. There is always a degree of reservation as to what the outcome of a battle will be. And anyone who isn't nervous doesn't know what is ahead of them, but I try to not let it rule me. To combat it, I just concentrate and fight."

Smiling, I pointed to another lady this time.

"Hello, I'm Ann."

"Hi Ann." Everyone greeted.

"This question is for Sonja. How long have you been a hit man, are you selective about the hits you accept? You made a choice with Darius, have you ever not completed a hit before?"

"Well, I've been a hit man since I was twenty. Until the hit where Darius was a possible target, I've never had to be selective. Until that hit, I guess I had been lucky that those who had become targets were not nice people. I think that had something to do with my middle man and the jobs he gave me. So therefore, until Darius, I had completed all jobs. As to the choice of not going through with killing Darius, I honestly can't say I made that choice solely because of him..."

"Oh, how you wound me Woman." Darius quietly growled teasingly.

Sonja laughed, nudging him with her shoulder then continued.

"When I'd learnt that my target... please remember that I didn't know it was Darius at that point... could have been on the side of keeping unattereds off the menu, I had a serious choice to make. Also remember that I was unaltered at that time so it was in my best interest to think hard and make the right choice."

Having a new hand up in the audience, I chose her to be next.

"Hello, I am Susanne." All eyes turned to her.

"Hi Susanne."

"I would like to know why Sonja, you choose to be an assassin by night and a mild mannered personal assistant by day?"

"Well, now I'm just a sniper for Orenda. But you know what? That is one question I'm unable to answer on a truly personal note because I've never thought about it. However, I enjoyed both jobs but, each by themselves, didn't pay enough to keep the house and the three who still live in it. Each are dysfunctional enough to not be able to hold down a full time job, so it was no biggie for me to earn the money. That and I enjoyed the diversity of the two."

I couldn't help smiling as I selected Jayne again.

"Enola, my next question is for you. Do you think that you would ever want to become a vampire?" Jayne asked the quiet Amazon looking woman.

"At this point in time, my answer is still no and I have no idea if that will ever change."

Varrik turned towards her and laced his fingers with hers. She smiled tenderly at him.

When Robert had his hand up again, I selected him to ask his question.

"Enola, what would you like the future to be like for you?" Robert asked.

"I would like less fighting and drama that's for sure, but I don't think that's going to happen. So, I'll settle for just a long and happy life with Varrik." Enola responded with a happy smile at Varrik.

After Robert sat down, I nodded at Ann.

"My next question is for Darius and Sonja. Although it's very rare the bonding you have, have you come across any others with the same needs as you?" Jayne asked.

However, her question brought on a seriousness over the room as Sonja gazed at Darius and he took hold of her hand.

"No we haven't. A number of us have researched the subject and tried to find others with this same situation, but all to no avail so far. While we, ourselves, do not advertise our particular bonding, we do monitor for other possible pairs." Darius answered seriously.

Jayne nodded and sat down. I then indicated to Emma to ask her question.

"My next question is for Darius, Sonja, Varrik and Enola. Do you have any hobbies or interests?" Emma Jane asked.

"Darius and I love cooking..." Varrik started.

"And we love watching them work their sexy butts off while they cook." Sonja piped in with a grin.

"Oh most definitely." Enola giggled, as the two women seemed to share an inside joke.

With a small shake of their heads, the two men just grinned and rolled their eyes.

"Seriously though, we do love to cook. Believe it or not, so do the ladies. Just like anyone else, we read, go to movies, night hiking and swimming..." Darius answered.

"We also try to spend as much time together getting to know each other as much as we can." Enola added. "Despite us having a long life, with the life we lead, it can still be cut short."

The other three nodded in semi-solemn agreement and the room lapsed into momentary silence.

Despite there being others in the audience who hadn't asked any questions, our time had run out.

"Unfortunately, we have to call an end to this evening. You have been a wonderful audience. Please give a round of applause to Enola, Varrik, Sonja and Darius for sharing themselves with us."

As we applauded, we all stood. Our guests smiled and waved then each hugged me and left. One by one, the audience grabbed their belongings and said farewell to me then went home. They chatted merrily as they exited the room.

I plonked myself down on the lounge. It was over. My first of hosting a crowd seemed, to me, to be a success that went off without any hitches despite my nervousness. Glancing around, I noted there was no rubbish lying around. That pleased me since I was too exhausted to clean up.

"Come on KC, let's get you home. You did well kiddo."

I smiled with happy tears welling in my eyes as I grabbed Skipper's hands. With a small shake of his head as he smiled at me, he helped me stand and handed me my crutches.

He flicked the lights off and closed the door as we left.

# *Excerpts*

Turn the page for a sneak peak at
the next book by KC Riley-Gyer...

All novels are available in both paperbacks and ebooks.
However, the paperbacks have an extra
that the ebooks do not have.

*Changes in Degrees*
*Sarah's Story Part 1*
*Now available*

# Chapter 1

It was a sunny and brisk winter's day and it was a perfect day to play now that he and his men were on leave. While the kiosk was playing some music which barely registered to him, he was leaning against the Jeep waiting for the rest of his players to turn up. He surveyed the area, sizing up the various people who came to play: the wannabes – more danger to themselves than to anyone else, the possible threats who obviously knew enough to hit only their intended targets and not everything else, and the kids wanting to have fun. However, pretty much all of them ignorable. Until...

He first saw her at the paintball range as she hobbled from the ladies rest room and everything else around him was momentarily forgotten. He watched her walk towards him, her head down with the occasional glance up as if to make sure she was on track to her destination.

A slightly overweight young woman, standing 156cm tall, in her mid to late teens – early twenties maybe – leant heavily on her darkly painted metal adjustable walking stick. Then she slowly veered to her right towards the picnic tables. She was dressed in a navy blue simple heavy cotton dress with little purple and red flowers and black open toed slip on shoes.

'Her feet must be freezing.' The trivial thought caught him by surprise. Deciding to ignore the thought, he continued his inspection of her.

Her dull dark brown hair was tied back away from her face with a thin layer acting as a wispy fringe partially covering her forehead. Even though her hair was tied back he could see it was long, past her shoulder blades. Despite its length there didn't seem to be much of it, as in not thick. The one thing which saved her hair from being bland, in his opinion, was the faint red highlights that shimmered occasionally in the sunlight as she walked.

Regardless of her weight and dull looking hair, her face was cute in a plain sort of way even though it was etched with pain at that point in time. She wore no makeup as if, maybe, she didn't care about how people perceived her and, strangely for him, it added a level of attractiveness to her. He hadn't realised that could attract his attention.

Letting his eyes travel slowly down her body – while he could see she was over-weight the dress fitted her well and showed off the potential for a reasonable figure – he noted her left hand clenched, emphasising the pain he was seeing in her face. Then, he continued down her legs to her feet.

'There's the problem. She's obviously been in an accident of some sort, maybe recently. Her feet don't sit flat anymore.'

However, while she was wearing shoes, he realised one would have to really look at her feet to notice the problem with them. He noted the weight seemed to be on her heels and on the outer side edges of her feet, and that they turned in slightly. A few of the toes on her right foot were partially clawed and it looked to be permanent.

'With some nerve damage perhaps, in some way. It would seem she has lost some mobility, flexion, to her ankles.'

In checking her over, he realised she was no threat. She was out of condition – the effort of walking from the ladies to her destination left her sweating despite being winter. Disabled and definitely feminine in her ways, she looked like she didn't know how to fight back. The young woman was a victim, not a predator. With that assessment he had every intention of dismissing her from mind and sight, but...

Watching her, she joined five other people at one of the tables nearby. He had just started to look away when their eyes locked briefly. Her hand paused in mid motion of taking her drink to her lips. Her lips, minutely parted, were a little pale but looked rather nice with a noticeable cupid's bow on her upper lip. Now she was close enough he could see them better. Then he noticed the flush creeping across her cheeks.

Turn the page for a sneak peak at
the next book by KC Riley-Gyer...

## Changes in Life
### Sarah's Story Part 2
### Now available

# Chapter 1

It had been four hours since he had walked out of her life for the second time since she'd met him. Two days ago, when she woke up, she had thought the New Year was off to a good start. Today she didn't want to know about it. There were still almost eleven months left. She hoped it would improve as time went by, but doubted it would. Not now.

Having had next to no sleep during the past two days, since he had told her the hit was a go, she sat at his kitchen table, in his house and she was stuck there. He had all her stuff packed and moved to his house, and the apartment she used to rent was now occupied by someone else.

Deciding life must go on, she had dragged herself out of bed since she couldn't sleep. Sitting in her usual spot at the table she stared out the window looking at the bushland and the rain, which was a constant drizzle with everything looking grey. The weather suited her mood; miserable and bleak. With her hands wrapped around her cup of tea, she was building up the courage to pick up the phone to call Antonio. She had to do it. She had no choice.

There was less than two weeks to go till the next full moon and that didn't leave much time to learn things before the first change. She sighed, knowing she couldn't put it off any longer, stood up and headed into the kitchen. Rinsing her cup out, she then grabbed the phone and called Antonio.

"Hello, Antonio here." A chirpy Italian male voice answered.

"Hi Antonio. It's Sarah." She greeted hesitantly.

"SARAH! Shit Luv where the hell have you been...?"

"I..." She didn't get the chance to say anything more.

"...No one has heard from you in almost three months. We thought you died in that fire at Danny's place..."

"An..."

"...You are an inconsiderate cow. You know that don't you?" He interrupted with a comment only a friend could get away with.

"ANTONIO!" She shouted in exasperation.

"WHAT?!"

"I'm a therian and need your help." She responded quietly.

"Oh Luv, I'm sorry, but you had us worried you know." Antonio suddenly sounded upset instead of angry.

"I'm sorry. The past three and a half months haven't been the best for me either and it's a very, very long story. This is my address in Gumdale... Are you able to come over?"

"You sound horrid Luv. Sure, I can come over. What flavour are you?"

She sighed softly. "I'm okay, and jaguar."

"Well, shit. They're rare out of the Americas. I didn't even know there were any here at all. I'll do a bit of research and see what info within Australia I can find out for you Luv. Despite the fact that he's the head of the leopards, I'm going to bring Jonathon with me since he's also the chairman of the league. He might have some ideas as to how to help you since jaguars are similar to leopards. See you soon okay?"

"Okay, till then."

They hung up.

Turn the page for a sneak peak at
the next book by KC Riley-Gyer...

***Changes in Choices***
***Conclusion to Sarah's Story***
***Coming soon***
***August 2015***

# Chapter 1

A week later, Sarah finally showed up back home for the first time since that night at the paintball range, and she was sure she looked like crap! She knew she felt like it. Her dress was dirty with the hem shredded in various spots, her hair unwashed and she smelled. She hadn't really cared at the time because she had stayed away from people so no one saw her. If anyone asked her how she got home she wouldn't be able to answer because she didn't know how she had managed it.

However, she didn't even get the chance to get off the scooter before a set of hands grabbed at her arms roughly, savagely pulling her off the scooter.

"Where the fuck have you been Sarah?! We've been so worried, we thought you were dead." Toby yelled at her, his face red with anger.

She just stood there as his grip bruised her arms, letting him stare at her helmeted head as it wobbled on her neck as he shook her. Mick gently placed a hand on Toby's arm. Toby frowned at him. Mick shook his head then Toby let her go with a slight shove so she staggered back a step then rocked on the spot.

Standing there for just a moment she then reached up to take off her helmet. She didn't look at them and didn't make any move towards the house.

"Geez Sarah! What have you been doing?" Mick exclaimed softly. While he knew her dress was a mess, he wasn't expecting the sight of her face and hair. Her hair was matted and her farce dirty with dark circles under her eyes like someone had used her as a punching bag. Suddenly he scooped her up into his arms and headed towards the house. The helmet dropped from her hand as he lifted her. "Toby, grab her walking stick and helmet please."

After a few moments, "Sarah, where's your stick?" Toby demanded.

"Gone." She answered softly and tonelessly as her head rested on Mick's shoulder.

"What do you mean 'gone'?!" Toby demanded angrily as Mick took her upstairs, but she didn't respond.

Mick sat Sarah at the kitchen table, made her a cup of tea and set it in front of her. She just stared at the table with her hands in my lap. "Drink your tea Sarah." Mick encouraged.

She just sat there not moving, staring at nothing.

Mick was becoming worried. 'Sure she had withdrawn before a number of times but never like this.'

"What's wrong with you Sarah?" Toby asked. Even in her current state she could hear the frown in his voice.

"Nothing." She responded in the same tone of voice as before.

Toby threw up his hands in frustration. "I give up. Fine, be that way. We don't hear from you for a week after Antonio told us about the hit Jonathon took out against you and that you said you had organised such a situation with a friend to complete the hit if it should happen. Was it Kaelan...?" He paused after snarling the other man's name, shook his head and made a sound of frustration before continuing, "Fuck Sarah! With no thought about us being worried about you, you then just rock up like nothing is wrong and you think we don't deserve an explanation of any kind. There are times when you are a selfish bitch and this is one of them, Sarah."

"I'm sorry." While the response was automatic she did mean it but still toneless. She couldn't do what he wanted. Tears weren't even welling up.